Battle For Pisgah

# Battle For Pisgah

L G Rice

To my dear family and loved ones,
Your unwavering support, patience, and encouragement mean the world to me. Thank you for enduring my countless hours of writing, editing, and researching, and for inspiring me every step of the way.
This journey is for you, and every word I write carries a piece of my love and gratitude.

The early morning sun had just begun to rise, casting a soft golden glow over the misty grounds of Sage Manor. Lincoln Beaumont walked alongside his daughter Waverly, their steps crunching lightly on the gravel path as they made their way toward the gazebo. The cool air carried the faint scent of dew-covered grass and blooming gardenias, but an undercurrent of tension seemed to ripple through the atmosphere.

"Do you think Mistara and Ambreela will respond?" Waverly asked, her voice quiet but tinged with hope.

Lincoln sighed, his hands tucked into the pockets of his jacket. "I hope so. If anyone can help us figure out how to deal with this portal, it's them. They understand the daggers better than we ever could."

The daggers. The very mention of them brought a chill that had nothing to do with the morning air. The ancient artifacts infused with cosmic energy had been instrumental in defeating the Umbralox on Tanzlora. But now, Earth faced its own crisis, and the stakes felt even higher. The evil force's influence had already taken root, and its presence was spreading like an unseen infection, threatening to destabilize the balance of nature in the Pisgah National Forest.

As they approached the gazebo, its outline emerged through the fog, a delicate structure of white-painted wood adorned with climbing ivy with a massive stone fireplace on one side of it. Waverly squinted into the haze, trying to make out the figures standing inside.

"Do you see that?" she whispered, her steps slowing.

Lincoln nodded, his eyes narrowing. Two silhouettes were barely visible, their features obscured by the dense mist. "Someone's there. But who?"

They exchanged a wary glance, their pace quickening. As they drew closer, one of the figures turned, the motion sharp and deliberate. Waverly's breath caught in her throat.

"Elara," she murmured, a smile breaking across her face.

The slender figure stepped forward, her pale hair glinting in the faint sunlight as she reached out to the other person beside her. When the second figure turned, Lincoln's eyes widened.

"Rykas," he said, his voice a mix of surprise and relief.

Rykas, the Arcmyrian warrior leader, stood tall and imposing, his dark cloak billowing slightly in the breeze. His sharp eyes scanning the Earthlings before a warm smile softened his stern expression. "Lincoln. Waverly. It is good to see you again."

The Beaumonts stepped into the gazebo, where they were greeted warmly by Elara and Rykas. Elara's serene presence was a balm to Waverly, who immediately clasped her hands. Rykas extended a firm handshake to Lincoln, his grip as unyielding as the steel blade strapped to his side.

"The council sent you?" Lincoln asked, his curiosity piqued.

Elara nodded. "Yes. The Arcmyrian council believes the situation on Earth poses a grave threat not only to your planet but potentially to the balance across the cosmos. They've entrusted us to assist you in any way we can."

"We're grateful you're here," Waverly said earnestly. "With the Tanzlorans help, we've managed to eradicate the Umbralox there, but before we could, their influence had already breached Earth. It seems to be growing fast."

Rykas frowned, his expression darkening. "Then we must act quickly. What is the current status of the portal behind the falls?"

"Unstable," Lincoln replied. "Lynx discovered it shortly after the disturbances began around the area, specifically the Looking Glass Falls. We suspect the Umbralox has been using it to establish a foothold here."

"And the daggers?" Elara asked, her gaze intense.

"We have them," Waverly said. "But using them to shut down the portal here might not be as straightforward as it was on Tanzlora. The portal's energy is different—it feels...wild, like it's feeding on Earth's life force."

Before Elara or Rykas could respond, a sudden wave of energy pulsed through the air, vibrating the wooden planks beneath their feet. The mist thickened, swirling as if caught in an invisible current.

"The portal," Elara said sharply, her eyes narrowing.

Lincoln stepped to the edge of the gazebo, his body tense. "Something's coming through."

"We should go," Rykas said, already moving. "We need to see who or what is emerging."

The four of them descended from the gazebo and hurried back toward the main grounds of Sage Manor. Two Tanzloran warriors, clad in their distinctive armor emerged from the tree line where they had been guarding the perimeter of the manor. Their expressions were alert and their weapons drawn. They fell in step with the group, their eyes scanning the foggy morning landscape.

The group halted in front of the large porch of Sage Manor, its expansive structure encompassing the entire front of the house that stood as a silent sentinel against the growing tension in the air. All eyes turned toward the dense mist near the edge of the gazebo, where the energy of the portal was now palpable, a low hum resonating in the air.

"Be ready," Rykas said, his hand resting on the hilt of his laser knife. "We don't know what's coming through."

The energy around the portal intensified, the hum growing louder until it resonated through the air. Lincoln, Waverly, Elara, and Rykas stood ready, their collective focus on the shimmering vortex of light. The Tanzloran warriors at the perimeter tightened their grips on their weapons, their eyes sharp and unwavering.

When the portal finally stabilized, several figures emerged from the misty glow, their silhouettes gradually solidifying into familiar forms. Keelee led the group, his regal stance commanding immediate respect. Beside him, Sanodia moved with practiced grace, her eyes scanning the gathered group on the front porch of Sage Manor. Behind them, a small contingent of Tanzloran warriors followed, their armor gleaming faintly in the morning light.

Waverly's breath caught as she recognized them. "Keelee!" she exclaimed, stepping forward with a mix of relief and joy.

Keelee smiled warmly, extending his arms as he embraced Waverly. "It is good to see you again, Waverly," he said.

Lincoln's face broke into a rare grin as he clasped arms with Keelee in greeting. "Your timing couldn't be better."

Sanodia approached next, her serious expression softening slightly as she acknowledged the Beaumonts. "I've heard of the disturbances here," she said. "It seems the Umbralox is more cunning than anticipated."

As the group gathered on the front porch of Sage Manor, the sense of camaraderie was palpable. The arrival of the Tanzlorans, joining forces with the Arcmyrians and the Beaumont family, filled the air with hope and determination.

Elara stepped forward, her serene presence commanding attention. "With allies from both Tanzlora and Arcmyrin here, we have the means to fight this threat," she said. "But we must plan carefully. The Umbralox thrives on chaos, and its influence is already spreading in your Pisgah National Forest."

Rykas nodded, his sharp eyes meeting those of each warrior present. "We've faced enemies like this before, but the stakes here are different. This is Earth's life force we're protecting, and the unstable portal poses a significant risk."

"Agreed," Keelee said. "We need a strategy that utilizes all our strengths, including the elemental spirits."

The mention of the elemental spirits brought a solemn look to Waverly's face. "We were trying to connect with them this morning, to seek their help with today's mission."

Sanodia crossed her arms, her tone thoughtful. "Then we must act quickly to summon them for help."

At that moment, the sound of the manor's front door opening drew everyone's attention. Gran Celia emerged, her expression lighting up as she took in the assembled group. Her eyes misted with emotion as she stepped forward, embracing Elara and Keelee first before turning to greet the others.

"You're all here," she said, her voice filled with warmth and gratitude. "I cannot express how much it means to see you all gathered from our sister planets to help protect Earth."

Lynx followed close behind, his demeanor brisk and focused. "This is a strong team," he said, scanning the group. "But we've got a serious logistical problem. The portal's location is incredibly tight, and there's no way all of us can get in there to activate the daggers."

Lincoln frowned, his earlier optimism dimming slightly. "Yes, the tight space behind the falls poses a major problem."

"Exactly," Lynx replied. "The area is barely big enough for one person, let alone a group of us trying to position the daggers correctly."

Keelee's brow furrowed in thought. "Then we'll need to figure out a way to get the dagger's energy directly into the portal from outside the cavern it has been constructed in. Is that going to be an option?"

Rykas crossed his arms, his gaze steady. "We need to see the area where this portal has been placed by the Umbralox."

Lincoln nodded, brushing a hand through his hair. "Ridge and I can take you there," he replied. "It's not far from here. The falls are about a fifteen-minute drive." He paused, glancing toward the woods. "We've got two Tanzloran warriors holding vigil at the site. They're keeping an eye on the portal's instability and reporting back anything unusual."

Keelee's expression darkened as he paced along the edge of the porch, his concern evident in every step. "Tanzloran warriors holding vigil near an unstable portal on Earth..." He stopped abruptly, turning to face Lincoln. "Do you understand the risk this poses? If Earthlings see them—"

"They won't," Lincoln interjected firmly, raising a hand to calm Keelee. "The local sheriff has cordoned off that area. Officially, it's 'off-limits' due to recent disturbances, and the stories about strange occurrences at the falls have been enough to scare off any curious hikers. No one's going near it."

Keelee crossed his arms, his brows furrowing as his gaze flickered toward the direction of the falls. "Even so, Earthlings are unpredictable. All it takes is one stubborn soul to ignore the warnings."

Lincoln's lips twitched into a faint smile. "Callum has thought of that too. He's made provisions for cloaking the warriors stationed there. Unless someone gets uncomfortably close—and I mean really close—they won't see a thing."

Keelee exhaled slowly, his shoulders relaxing as the tension eased from his frame. "That's... reassuring," he admitted, though the worry in his voice hadn't entirely disappeared. "The last thing we need is for humans to discover them. It created great panic during the first galactic war and we are trying to avoid a repeat."

Lincoln nodded in agreement, his expression serious now. "We're taking every precaution, Keelee. The warriors are well-trained, and their presence is vital if anything changes with the portal."

Keelee replied. "I'm relieved to hear that," he said softly. "But I'll still rest easier when this portal is closed and we're certain the Umbralox can't use it to reach either of our worlds."

Rykas's expression didn't waver. "Yes, if the Umbralox are meddling with dimensional rifts, this portal could be a key component in their plans. The sooner we assess it and destroy it, the better."

Waverly, who had been listening intently, stepped forward. "I'll go inside and get Ridge," she offered. "He was in the library last I saw him. He'll want to come along for this."

Lincoln shot her a quick smile. "Thanks, Waverly."

As Waverly turned toward the house, Rykas shifted his focus back to Lincoln. "These warriors," he began, "do they have any insights on the portal's origin?"

Lincoln shook his head. "Not much beyond what we already suspect. The portal's energy signature matches what we've encountered before with the Umbralox, but its instability is new. It's like they're experimenting with it, pushing its limits. The warriors have seen flickers of... something... trying to come through, but nothing has fully manifested yet."

Rykas frowned, his sharp features tightening. "If something breaches the portal, it could destabilize the entire area. We need to be prepared for the worst."

Before Lincoln could respond, the front door creaked open, and Waverly emerged with Ridge in tow. Ridge's broad frame and confident stride gave him an air of readiness. He adjusted the strap of the satchel slung over his shoulder, which carried an assortment of tools and his dagger—just in case.

"Ready when you are," Ridge said, his tone brisk but friendly. He glanced at Rykas. "You'll want to see this with your own eyes. It's like nothing we've encountered before."

Rykas inclined his head. "Then let's not waste any more time."

The group set off toward the garage, the crunch of gravel underfoot. They piled into Ridge's Jeep and headed for Looking Glass Falls.

2

As they reached the falls, the two Tanzloran warriors stood at attention near the portal, their sleek armor glinting faintly in the dappled sunlight. The falls shimmered with an eerie, shifting energy.

"This is Looking Glass Falls," Lincoln said, his voice low. "The portal is behind the water down near the base of the falls, we will have to walk down there for you to be able to see the hidden entrance."

Rykas stepped forward, his eyes narrowing as he studied the trail. "Let's go."

The Tanzloran warriors saluted Rykas as he approached them, recognizing the commander of the Arcmyrian warriors. Their movements were precise and disciplined. "No activity yet, Commander," one of them reported. "But the portal's energy is growing stronger."

Rykas turned to Lincoln, his expression grim. "We're going to need a plan. If the Umbralox are behind this, they won't leave it idle for long, more will come through and soon this entire area will be infested."

Lincoln nodded, his gaze never leaving the falls. "Then we'd better come up with one fast."

Rykas and Lincoln descended the steep trail from the viewing deck, the sound of Looking Glass Falls growing louder with every step. The spray from the cascading water filled the air, clinging to their skin and clothing as they reached the base. Mist curled around the rocks like ethereal tendrils, and the roar of the falls made conversation nearly impossible until they stepped closer to the jagged cliff behind the cascade.

"This is it," Lincoln said, motioning toward the narrow, shadowy crevice hidden behind the curtain of water. "The entrance to the portal is back there."

Rykas stepped forward, narrowing his eyes as he scrutinized the hidden opening. He crouched, his hand brushing against the slick moss that clung to the rocks. The portal's faint hum of unstable energy buzzed at the edge of his senses, like a whisper of impending danger. Straightening, he turned to Lincoln, his expression grave.

"This will not be easy," Rykas began, his tone heavy with the weight of the task ahead. "The energies of the four daggers must merge at the precise moment the portal begins to shift. If we fail—if the synchronization is even slightly off—" He paused, his jaw tightening. "The energy from the daggers will do the opposite of what we intend. Instead of collapsing the portal inward, it will stabilize it, amplifying its power. That's exactly what the Umbralox need to unleash themselves fully onto this world."

Lincoln felt the blood drain from his face. He stared at Rykas, his voice faltering. "You're saying... if we mess this up, we don't just lose. We make it worse. We give them a wide open door?"

Rykas nodded grimly. "Exactly. The collapse inward is our only hope. It will trap the Umbralox shadows within their own chaos, cutting them off from Arcmyrin, Tanzlora and Earth. But it requires absolute precision. The daggers were forged for this purpose, but the energies are volatile, especially with a portal this unstable."

Lincoln took a step back, running a hand through his hair as he tried to process the enormity of what they were up against. "This... this is bigger than I thought. If we're even a fraction of a second off—"

"We won't be," Rykas said firmly, interrupting Lincoln's spiraling thoughts. "We can't be. That's why every moment leading up to this must be deliberate. The placement, the timing, your family wielding the daggers—all of it must align perfectly. There is no room for error."

Lincoln nodded slowly, his initial horror giving way to a grim determination. "Then we'd better make sure we get it right. No mistakes. Not this time."

Rykas didn't reply immediately. Instead, he turned back to the falls, his gaze fixed on the hidden entrance behind the crashing water. "The fate of the Triad depends on it."

The Jeep's tires hummed on the newly paved road as Ridge guided it carefully away from the falls. The rhythmic rumble of the engine was the only sound for a moment, the four men deep in their own thoughts. The urgency of the task ahead loomed heavy in the air. Lincoln sat in the passenger seat, staring out at the dense forest as it blurred past, while Rykas and Callum occupied the backseat, speaking in low, measured tones.

Finally, Lincoln broke the silence. "Alright, let's think this through," he said, turning slightly to glance back at Rykas. "The space behind the falls is tight—barely enough for one person, let alone to position ourselves properly with the daggers. How are we supposed to manage this without completely ruining the alignment?"

Rykas leaned forward, his golden eyes sharp and calculating. "It's not just about positioning," he said. "The daggers must be angled perfectly, and the energy flows synchronized to the portal's instability. If any of you are even a fraction of a second late or misaligned, the energy will backfire. The result..." He hesitated, his expression grim. "It would explode the portal and still destroy it but it also allows the Umbralox to have all the power they need to invade Earth."

Callum, seated behind Lincoln, rested a hand on the seatback. "We've trained for situations like this, but I won't sugarcoat it. That space is going to make it nearly impossible to maneuver effectively. The water, the mist, the noise—it'll all add to the chaos. This is almost impossible. The enemy has strategized a close to perfect scenario for themselves, there is no doubt."

Ridge, his hands tight on the steering wheel, let out a low whistle. "So what you're saying is, we need a miracle. Great. Just another day at Sage Manor."

Lincoln shot his brother a wry look but didn't argue. Instead, he leaned his head back against the seat and rubbed his temples. "What if..." he began slowly, his voice thoughtful, "what if we could stop the flow of the waterfall, even temporarily? Would that give us enough time to get into position without the water blinding us or throwing off the energy transfer?"

The Jeep went silent as the suggestion hung in the air. Ridge glanced at him, his brows raised. "Stop the waterfall? You're kidding, right? It's not like we can just turn off a tap."

"It's not as crazy as it sounds," Rykas interjected, his voice cutting through the tension. "Natural waterfalls like Looking Glass Falls are fed by upstream rivers. If we could find a way to temporarily block or divert the flow, even for a few minutes, it could give us the window we need."

Lincoln felt a flicker of hope. "Exactly. We don't need to stop it for long—just long enough to get everyone in position and start the sequence."

Callum frowned, his fingers drumming against the seatback. "You'd be messing with natural forces. There's a risk that tampering with the river could destabilize the area further. The portal's already feeding off the waterfall's energy, and any disruption might accelerate its instability."

"Or," Lincoln countered, "it could weaken the portal's link to the falls, giving us an advantage. If the portal isn't anchored as strongly, it might be easier to collapse."

Ridge let out a low chuckle, shaking his head. "So what's the plan? Build a dam overnight? I don't know if you've noticed, but we're a little short on heavy equipment."

"I'm not suggesting we block the entire river," Lincoln said, exasperation creeping into his voice. "But there might be a natural choke point upstream. If we could temporarily obstruct the flow there, it might slow the water enough to make a difference."

Rykas nodded thoughtfully. "It's a calculated risk, but it could work. We'd need to scout the area upstream, find a point where the river narrows and where a temporary blockage wouldn't cause flooding downstream."

Callum tilted his head, considering. "We'd also need to ensure the blockage is reversible. The last thing we want is to create a permanent disruption. Earth's ecosystems are fragile enough without us adding to the chaos."

Ridge snorted. "I'm still wrapping my head around the fact that we're talking about redirecting a river like it's a weekend DIY project."

"It's not impossible," Rykas said firmly. "On Arcmyrin, we've used similar tactics to weaken enemy positions. The key is precision and timing."

Lincoln glanced at him. "You've done this before?"

"Not exactly like this," Rykas admitted. "But the principles are the same. Manipulate the environment to gain the upper hand. In this case, the waterfall is both our enemy and our ally. Controlling it, even briefly, could tip the scales in our favor."

The Jeep hit a bump in the road, and Ridge muttered a curse under his breath as he adjusted the steering. "Alright, say we figure out how to do this. What about the daggers? Who's handling them? There's not enough room for all of us. Lynx barely fit in that crevice. It took both Lincoln and myself to pull him out of it."

Rykas exchanged a look with Callum. "The daggers must be wielded by your family," he said, glancing at Lincoln and Ridge, "I believe the two of you, Waverly and Lynx are our only chance."

"Great," Ridge muttered. "No pressure."

"It's more than that," Rykas continued. "You'll need to synchronize perfectly. The energy flows from the daggers must merge into the portal at the exact same moment. Even the smallest delay will cause a feedback loop, destabilizing the entire sequence."

Lincoln frowned. "And if that happens, the portal explodes instead of collapsing."

"Exactly," Rykas said, his tone heavy. "And that would give the Umbralox the anchor they need to fully breach into this world."

Ridge let out a low whistle. "So, no pressure at all. Just saving three worlds from complete annihilation."

Callum's lips quirked into a faint smile. "You'll do it. Tanzlorans believe in the strength of allies. And from what I've seen, you and your family are more than capable."

Lincoln exhaled sharply, his mind racing with the weight of the task ahead. "So, first steps—scout the river, figure out how to slow the flow, and make sure we don't cause a disaster in the process. Then we focus on the daggers."

Rykas nodded. "And prepare for the portal to react. If the Umbralox sense what we're doing, they'll fight back. The warriors stationed at the falls will need to be ready."

As Sage Manor came into view through the trees, Ridge slowed the Jeep, pulling into the driveway. The house stood like a sentinel against the encroaching darkness, its lights glowing faintly in the gathering twilight. Lincoln stared at it, a mix of determination and dread settling in his chest.

"We've got a lot to figure out," he said, turning to the others. "But if we're going to win this, we can't leave anything to chance."

Rykas met his gaze, his voice steady. "Then let's get to work."

3

Lincoln climbed out of the Jeep first, his boots crunching on the gravel, while Ridge cut the engine and joined him. Rykas and Callum followed suit, their expressions unreadable as they headed toward the front door.

Inside, the faint murmur of voices drew them toward the library, the heart of Sage Manor during moments of crisis. The door was ajar, and Lincoln pushed it open to find Waverly, Elara, Gran Celia, Lorinda, and Francis gathered around the massive oak table. A collection of ancient texts, maps, and scattered notes lay spread across its surface.

Waverly looked up first, her eyes lighting with a mix of relief and curiosity. "You're back. What did you find?"

Lincoln held up a hand, his eyes scanning the room. "Where are Lynx and Keelee?"

"They're in the chamber under the gazebo," Waverly replied, setting down the leather-bound book she'd been leafing through. "Keelee's consulting with the Tanzloran Council. Lynx went to hear the council's instructions too. He said it might take a while."

Ridge, who had been leaning against the doorframe, straightened and looked at Rykas. "Good. Then we've got time. You need to tell everyone here what you told us on the way back. They need to hear it all."

Rykas nodded solemnly, stepping forward to take his place at the head of the table. His golden eyes swept over the group, pausing briefly on Elara, who watched him intently. "What we discovered at Looking Glass Falls confirms our worst fears," he began, his voice steady but weighted. "The portal behind the falls is extremely unstable, fed by the energy of the waterfall itself. This instability is a double-edged sword—it makes the portal vulnerable, but it also means that any attempt to collapse it must be done with absolute precision."

He glanced at Lincoln, who gave him a small nod of encouragement before continuing. "The only way to destroy the portal is to merge the energies of the four daggers at the exact moment the portal's energy peaks. This will force the portal to collapse inward, trapping the Umbralox shadows within their own chaos. But there is no margin for error. If the synchronization is off, even by a fraction, the energies will explode the portal instead, amplifying its power and giving the Umbralox the foothold they need to fully invade Earth."

Gran Celia's brow furrowed deeply, and she leaned forward, her hands clasped tightly in front of her. "And you're certain this is the only way?"

"It's the only way," Rykas confirmed. "But there are complications. The space behind the falls is incredibly narrow—barely enough room for one person to maneuver. Add the force of the waterfall, the mist, and the portal's destabilizing energy, and it becomes almost impossible to execute the alignment with precision."

Francis, who had been sitting quietly near the fireplace, adjusted her glasses and frowned. "And the daggers themselves—are they stable enough to handle this kind of energy transfer without... catastrophic consequences?"

"They were forged for this purpose," Rykas said. "But their power is volatile, especially when combined. The wielders must have a strong connection to the daggers and to one another which I believe Waverly, Lynx, Lincoln, and Ridge do. Their bond to the elemental spirits and as family gives them a unique advantage."

Ridge let out a low whistle, crossing his arms. "No pressure, right?"

Rykas gave him a faint smile before continuing. "There's one more thing. Lincoln suggested a potential way to make the task more manageable—slowing the flow of the waterfall to give us the time and space we need. It's a risk, but it could work."

"Slowing the waterfall?" Gran Celia echoed, her voice sharp with concern. "You'd be tampering with natural forces. Do you even know what kind of repercussions that might have?"

"It's not a decision we'd make lightly," Lincoln said, stepping forward. "But if we can find a way to safely divert or block the river upstream, even temporarily, it might give us the window we need to get into position and execute the alignment properly."

The room fell silent as everyone absorbed the enormity of what they were discussing. Finally, Elara broke the silence, her voice calm but resolute. "Rykas, you and I need to confer with the Arcmyrin Council. They may have insights or resources we can draw on to improve our chances of success." She looked around the room, her piercing gaze landing on each of them in turn. "And once Keelee and I have spoken with both councils, we'll need to reconvene here to finalize our plan."

Gran Celia nodded in agreement. "The councils must be involved. This is bigger than all of us."

Waverly leaned forward, her elbows on the table. "If this is going to work, we need everyone on the same page. No assumptions, no second-guessing. We have one shot at this, and we can't afford to miss."

Rykas inclined his head. "Agreed. Elara and I will contact the Arcmyrin Council immediately. Once we've gathered their input, we'll regroup here."

"Good," Lincoln said, his voice firm. "We don't have much time, but we're going to use every second we've got to make sure we get this right."

As the group began to break into smaller discussions, the weight of the mission settled heavily over the room. The task ahead was monumental, but the determination in each of their faces made one thing clear—they would not back down. The fate of the Triad depended on their success, and failure was not an option.

The stone stairs descending into the chamber under the gazebo were cool and slightly damp, illuminated by faint light from glowing crystal symbols embedded in the walls. Elara led the way, her robes brushing the stones as she moved gracefully, while Rykas followed closely behind, his sharp gaze scanning the surroundings for any sign of trouble. Ridge and Lincoln brought up the rear, their steps echoing softly.

Halfway down, Ridge froze, tilting his head toward the faint hum of an approaching vehicle. He reached out, gripping Lincoln's arm. "We have company, big brother," he said, his voice low but edged with curiosity. "We need to go head this one off. It's the sheriff."

Lincoln sighed, turning on the step. "Good. We actually need to talk to him. If we're going to pull this off, we'll need his help—and the district park ranger's too, if we can get him involved."

Ridge smirked faintly. "You might be in luck. I think he's here with him."

Lincoln glanced back toward Rykas and Elara, who had paused further down the stairs. "You two go ahead. We'll handle this and join you later."

Without waiting for a reply, Lincoln and Ridge retraced their steps, emerging from the gazebo just as the sheriff's car came into view, rolling up the gravel driveway. Ridge shoved his hands in his pockets, glancing at his brother. "Guess they've decided we're not moving fast enough."

The car came to a stop, and the sheriff stepped out, a burly man with a no-nonsense demeanor. Beside him emerged the district park ranger, a wiry man with an air of calm authority and a clipboard tucked under one arm. Both men exchanged brief nods with Ridge and Lincoln as they approached.

"Sheriff," Lincoln greeted, his tone cordial but guarded. "Ranger. What brings you both by?"

The sheriff crossed his arms, leaning casually against the car. "What do you think? The mess at the falls. We've been keeping people out, but this is becoming a bigger problem than we can contain with some yellow tape and ghost stories. The locals are spooked, and the military's been sniffing around. You don't have much time to sort this out before they come in and take over."

Ridge stiffened slightly, his jaw tightening. "That would be a disaster. They don't understand what they're dealing with."

The ranger adjusted his clipboard, glancing between the two brothers. "Exactly why we're here. The question is, what are you and your 'specialist friends' planning to do about it?"

Lincoln sighed heavily, raking a hand through his hair. "It's not as simple as calling in reinforcements. This situation doesn't respond to brute force. If the military gets involved, they'll do what they always do—bring in heavy firepower. Missiles, explosives, whatever they think will work. But this isn't that kind of problem."

The sheriff raised an eyebrow. "What kind of problem is it, then?"

Lincoln exchanged a glance with Ridge before answering. "The portal at the falls is unstable. If it's not dealt with correctly, it won't just open wider—it'll feed on the energy from anything destructive they throw at it. This isn't something you can blow up. It has to be collapsed inward, controlled and precise, or the whole situation goes from bad to catastrophic."

The ranger frowned, shifting his stance. "So you're saying the usual methods aren't an option."

"Exactly," Ridge chimed in. "If we mess this up, we don't just fail—we hand the enemy exactly what they need to make things worse."

The ranger tapped his clipboard thoughtfully. "Sounds like you need precision, not power. Have you thought about consulting with someone who specializes in controlled demolitions? People who bring down skyscrapers?"

Lincoln froze, his mind racing. "That's... not a bad idea," he said slowly. "Controlled demolitions are all about timing and precision. If we could consult with someone who understands those mechanics, they might help us figure out how to apply the daggers' energy correctly to ensure the portal collapses inward."

The sheriff frowned. "And where are you planning to find someone like that? It's not like they're listed in the phone book under 'portal problem solvers.'"

Lincoln chuckled wryly. "True. But I bet we can find someone who knows how to control energy flows and structure collapse. Rykas and Elara can help translate their expertise into what we need for the portal. It's worth a shot."

The ranger nodded. "If you're serious about this, you'll need to move fast. I'll keep the park service in the loop and stall any military involvement as long as I can. But they won't wait forever."

The sheriff grunted his agreement. "Same here. I'll keep the area locked down on my end, but the higher-ups are getting restless. Whatever you're planning, make it quick."

Lincoln extended his hand to the sheriff, who clasped it firmly. "Thank you. We'll keep you updated."

As the two men got back into the car and drove away, Ridge turned to Lincoln with a grin. "Controlled demolitions, huh? Never thought we'd be calling in experts to blow something up without actually blowing it up."

Lincoln laughed, though the sound was tinged with tension. "Hey, when you're saving three worlds, you've got to think outside the box.

Come on. Let's get back to the gazebo. The others need to hear about this."

4

The chamber beneath the gazebo was bathed in an ethereal glow, the light emanating from the four screens embedded in the stone walls. Each screen shimmered with the visage of an elemental spirit. Mistara, the water spirit, swirled in shades of blue and silver, her form fluid and calming. Ambreela, the air spirit, was a vortex of pale yellows and whites, her presence light and wispy. Ignissa, the fire spirit, flickered in deep reds and oranges, her eyes smoldering with intensity. Terraveta, the earth spirit, stood solid and steadfast, her form etched in shades of green and brown with a grounding presence.

Keelee leaned over the oval stone table, his expression thoughtful as he addressed the group. "The Tanzloran Council agrees that collapsing the portal inward is the only viable solution, but they stress that the daggers must align with the portal's energy flow perfectly. Even a minor miscalculation could destabilize everything."

Elara nodded, her gaze fixed on the image of Terraveta. "The Arcmyrin Council echoes that sentiment. They've emphasized the importance of timing. The moment the portal reaches its peak instability is the only time the daggers' energy can be directed to collapse it inward. If we miss that window, the portal will stabilize and grow stronger."

Rykas, standing by the screen displaying Ignissa, crossed his arms. "And yet, none of this addresses the physical challenges. The space behind the waterfall is a natural hazard. Limited room, rushing water, and an unstable portal feeding off its energy—it's a logistical nightmare."

Lynx, who had been pacing near the screen of Ambreela, turned toward the group. "That's where we come in. We've trained with the daggers, and we know how to channel their energy. If we can position ourselves correctly and focus, we can do this."

Keelee shook his head. "It's not just about focus, Lynx. It's about precision. The council warned that even a slight deviation in the energy's angle could cause a feedback loop. If that happens..." His voice trailed off, the implications clear.

Before anyone could respond, the stone door creaked open, and Lincoln and Ridge stepped into the chamber. The glow from the screens reflected off their faces, making their expressions appear both determined and tense.

"Glad you're all here," Lincoln said, stepping forward. "We've got an update, and it's a big one."

Ridge nodded, leaning against the edge of the table. "The sheriff and the district park ranger just dropped by. They reminded us that the military is watching this situation closely. If we don't take care of the portal soon, they're going to step in—and let's just say their solution won't be helpful."

Lynx frowned. "What do you mean?"

"They're preparing to treat this like any other threat," Ridge replied. "Missiles, explosives, heavy artillery. But as we've discussed, that would be the worst thing they could do. They don't understand that this portal can't be destroyed like that. If anything, it would amplify the problem."

Lincoln nodded grimly. "Exactly. But the ranger suggested something interesting—a controlled demolition expert. Someone who specializes in bringing down skyscrapers with precision."

Keelee's eyes narrowed thoughtfully. "A demolition expert? How would that help us?"

Ridge smirked. "It actually makes a lot of sense. Think about it—those experts know how to use energy, timing, and positioning to collapse something inward. That's exactly what we're trying to do with the portal."

Elara's gaze flickered to the screen showing Ignissa, whose fiery eyes seemed to burn brighter as if in approval. "It's not a bad idea," she said slowly. "If we could consult with someone who understands the physics of controlled collapses, it might give us the insight we need to ensure the daggers' energies are channeled correctly."

Rykas crossed his arms, his expression skeptical but intrigued. "It's unconventional, but it could work. We'd need to find someone willing to help—and quickly. Time isn't on our side."

Mistara's voice echoed softly from her screen, her tone serene but urgent. "Water flows where it is guided. Use the expertise of those who understand control and redirection to ensure success."

Ambreela's image swirled, her airy voice chiming in. "Timing is everything. As the wind aligns with the currents, so must your energies align with the portal."

Ignissa's fiery presence seemed to flare with excitement. "Action is necessary. Do not hesitate. Fire burns brightest when fed by resolve."

Finally, Terraveta's deep, grounding voice rumbled through the chamber. "Strength lies in foundation. Build your plan solidly, and your execution will not falter."

Keelee straightened, the weight of their combined guidance settling over him. "The elemental spirits seem to agree. If this demolition expert can help us refine our approach, we should act on it."

Lincoln nodded. "Then that's our next step. We'll reach out to someone with the skills we need. In the meantime, we continue preparing for the collapse sequence. Everyone needs to be ready."

Ridge glanced at Lincoln, his expression resolute. "I'll assist in finding the expert. Once we have their input, we'll reconvene here to finalize the plan."

The group exchanged nods, the tension in the room thick but laced with determination. The stakes had never been higher.

The small office off the kitchen at Sage Manor was cramped but cozy, its walls lined with old books and maps that had belonged to generations of Beaumonts. Ridge leaned back in the worn leather chair, his phone pressed to his ear as he swiveled slightly, glancing out the window at the dense forest beyond. The house was quiet for the moment, a rare lull amidst the chaos.

The phone clicked, and the familiar voice of Dr. Marshall Stern came through, warm and curious. "Ridge Beaumont! Long time no talk. What's got you calling out of the blue?"

Ridge chuckled, but his tone carried the weight of urgency. "Marshall, I wish this was just a catch-up call. We've got a situation here at Sage Manor—one that goes beyond the usual strange stuff we deal with. I need your help. Or, more specifically, I need someone with a very particular set of skills."

There was a pause, then Marshall's voice turned serious. "Alright, you've got my attention. What's going on?"

Ridge quickly explained the dire circumstances—the unstable portal behind Looking Glass Falls, the looming threat of the Umbralox, and the impossibly delicate task of collapsing the portal inward without unleashing destruction. By the time he finished, there was silence on the other end of the line.

Finally, Marshall spoke. "That's... a lot. And when the Beaumonts say something's serious, I know it's not just a tall tale. Let me think." Another pause, then a spark of recognition entered his voice. "You know, there's a guy. Bronte Sutton. He's the best there is when it comes to controlled demolitions—skyscrapers, massive structures, you name it. If anyone could figure out how to help you collapse that portal, it'd be him."

"Bronte Sutton," Ridge repeated, jotting the name down on a scrap of paper. "And he's good, you're sure?"

"Good? The man's a legend," Marshall said. "But, uh... how do I put this? He's also... eccentric. Different."

Ridge laughed, leaning back in the chair. "Marshall, you do remember who you're talking to, right? Different is kind of the Beaumont brand."

Marshall chuckled in return. "Fair point. Alright, you'll fit right in with Bronte. But here's the thing—he's off-grid. Lives in the Catskill Mountains, completely unplugged from society. Only two people I know can get in touch with him, and one of them happens to be my wife, Madre."

Ridge raised an eyebrow. "Your wife knows the guy? How's that work?"

"Well," Marshall began, sounding slightly sheepish, "they've got this thing they're into—they call themselves Starseeds. I'll admit, I don't fully get it, but it's some kind of spiritual connection thing. They stay in touch, sharing whatever it is Starseeds talk about."

Ridge rubbed his temple, shaking his head with a bemused grin. "Starseeds, huh? Never heard of it. But who am I to judge, considering who I am and what I can do? Okay, Marshall, if Madre can get word to this Bronte Sutton, let him know what's going on here. Give him my contact info and ask him to reach out to me here at Sage Manor."

"You got it," Marshall said. "I'll let Madre know right away. If anyone can get in touch with him, she can."

"Thanks, Marshall. I owe you one. Again."

Marshall laughed. "You owe me more than one, Ridge. But don't worry—I'll add it to your tab. Good luck, and keep me posted."

Ridge hung up, staring at the name scrawled on the paper in front of him. Bronte Sutton. An eccentric demolition expert with a penchant for living off-grid and talking about Starseeds. It wasn't the most conventional lead, but in the Beaumont world, conventional had never been the answer.

"Guess it's time to see if this Bronte guy is as good as they say," Ridge muttered, standing and tucking the paper into his pocket. He stepped out of the office, his thoughts already racing with what might come next.

Ridge strode through the hallway of Sage Manor, his boots clicking against the polished wood floors. The sunlight streaming through the tall windows felt almost mocking in its warmth and brightness. *The world is on the brink of disaster, and it has the nerve to look this perfect,* he thought wryly.

As he passed the open door to the parlor, Gran Celia's voice called out. "Ridge Beaumont, where are you off to in such a hurry?"

Ridge paused, turning to find Gran Celia and Francis sitting comfortably in the parlor. Gran Celia held a delicate china teacup in one hand, a half-eaten scone in the other. Francis leaned back in her chair, a plate balanced on her lap, her expression content.

Ridge blinked at the scene, incredulous. "Tea and scones? Really? The world's about to implode, and you two are just sitting here having a mid-morning break like everything's fine?"

Gran Celia raised an eyebrow, taking a slow sip of her tea before responding. "Well, excuse us for enjoying a little bit of peace amidst all the chaos, Mister Sunshine." She gestured toward the window with her scone. "Look outside. No Umbralox, no portals breaking apart reality, just a beautiful sunny day with birds singing and squirrels scampering. So why don't you enlighten me—how, exactly, is the world on the brink of disaster?"

Ridge opened his mouth to retort but stopped himself, exhaling sharply. He rubbed the back of his neck, feeling a twinge of guilt. "Sorry, Mom. That was... rude. I didn't mean to snap. I know you're just trying to take a break. We probably all need one."

Gran Celia gave him a satisfied smile. "That's better. Now, why don't you sit down and catch us up on what's going on? We've been out of the loop while you've been running around saving the Triad."

Ridge pulled up a chair, glancing at Francis, who was still calmly munching on her scone, seemingly unbothered by anything. "Alright," Ridge began, leaning forward. "Here's the latest. Lincoln and I had a chat with the sheriff and the district park ranger. They reminded us that we're on borrowed time. The military's getting itchy to step in, which would be catastrophic because their idea of fixing this involves missiles and explosions—not exactly what you want near an unstable portal."

Gran Celia nodded, her expression turning serious. "That would make a mess of things, no doubt."

"So, the park ranger suggested something interesting," Ridge continued. "He said we should consult a controlled demolitions expert—someone who specializes in bringing down skyscrapers. Turns out, Lincoln and I think he's onto something. Collapsing that portal inward is like controlled demolition on a cosmic scale."

"And?" Gran Celia prompted.

"And I made a call to Dr. Marshall Stern. He's got connections, and he mentioned this guy named Bronte Sutton—supposedly the best in the business. But there's a catch." Ridge paused, looking bemused. "Bronte Sutton lives completely off-grid in the Catskill Mountains. Apparently, only two people on Earth know how to contact him, and one of them is Marshall's wife, Madre."

Francis raised an eyebrow, finally looking intrigued. "That's quite the setup. Why her?"

"Here's where it gets weird," Ridge said, shaking his head. "Apparently, Bronte and Madre consider themselves... Starseeds." He held up a hand to stop the inevitable question. "Don't ask me what that means because Marshall and I don't have a clue. All I know is that they talk about it, and somehow that's why she can reach him."

Gran Celia tilted her head, a small smile tugging at her lips. "Starseeds, hmm? Sounds suitably strange for this family's orbit."

Ridge snorted. "Right? I figured if anyone would get a laugh out of that, it'd be you."

Francis, who had been silently munching and sipping throughout the conversation, suddenly set down her teacup with a deliberate clink. "I know what a Starseed is," she said matter-of-factly, brushing crumbs off her lap.

Both Gran Celia and Ridge turned to her, startled. "You do?" Ridge asked, his tone half-skeptical, half-curious.

Francis nodded, leaning back with an air of quiet authority. "Oh, yes. Starseeds are people who believe they have a spiritual connection to the stars—other dimensions, higher planes of existence. They think they're here on Earth to bring wisdom and harmony, often feeling like they don't quite belong in the material world. They're... let's call them unique individuals."

Gran Celia chuckled. "Unique is one way to put it."

Ridge blinked at Francis, then let out a low laugh. "Well, that tracks. Sounds like the kind of guy we'd be comfortable dealing with. Still, if he's as good as they say, we'll take whatever help we can get—even if it comes with a side of cosmic wisdom."

Gran Celia raised her teacup in a mock toast. "To eccentric experts and saving the Triad. Sounds like we're in good hands."

Ridge rose from his chair, shaking his head but smiling. "Thanks for the intel, Francis. You always manage to surprise me. Now, I'd better go find Lincoln and the others to let them know what I've found out. Enjoy your tea and scones while you can—something tells me it's about to get a lot more chaotic around here."

Gran Celia winked. "We'll be ready. Go on, Ridge. Save the worlds."

With that, Ridge left the parlor, the weight of the situation still heavy on his shoulders but buoyed by the unexpected normalcy of the moment—and the invaluable insight from Francis, who, as always, seemed to know just a little more than anyone expected.

5

The gazebo stood as a serene contrast to the tension that gripped its occupants and the surrounding area. Lincoln leaned against one of the wooden beams, arms crossed, while Waverly and Lynx sat on the steps, their expressions troubled. Keelee paced the outer edge, occasionally glancing toward the forest as though expecting something—or someone—to appear. Elara and Rykas stood a few steps away, quietly exchanging observations, while Callum stood sentinel at the perimeter, his sharp eyes scanning the horizon.

The conversation was grim. Reports had been coming in steadily from the Tanzloran and Arcmyrin warriors stationed throughout the Pisgah National Forest.

"They've seen more signs," Keelee said, pausing mid-step. "Strangeness in the woods—shadows moving where no shadows should be, faint whispers that vanish when approached. The Umbralox is gathering strength, building in both power and number."

Elara nodded, her tone measured but urgent. "And it's not just the forest. The warriors have spotted strange birds in the skies—except when they described them, the Earthlings identified them as helicopters. Military surveillance, most likely."

That revelation landed like a bomb among the group. Waverly sat up straighter, alarm flickering in her eyes. "Helicopters? If the military's already snooping around, we're running out of time faster than we thought."

"They'll do more than snoop," Lynx muttered, his voice low. "Once they decide there's a threat, they'll move in—and we all know how that'll end."

Waverly frowned, frustration bubbling to the surface. "Then maybe we should stop waiting and take the bull by the horns. Reach out to the general who visited before. Explain what's happening and—"

"No." Lincoln's voice was sharp and final, cutting off Waverly mid-sentence. She turned to look at her father, startled by the force in his tone.

"You don't give the governments of this planet even an inch," Lincoln said, pushing off the beam and stepping into the circle. "Because they'll take a thousand miles and ruin everything we're trying to do. Power and greed don't make people receptive to hearing the truth or accepting successful ways of solving problems. They'll only care about how this situation can make them more powerful in the end. Collateral damage—losing lives—means nothing to them as long as they win."

Keelee and Elara exchanged a glance, subtle but enough for Waverly to notice. There was something in their expressions—pity, perhaps, or a quiet resignation—that made her stomach twist. She filed it away for later, resolving to ask Elara how the people of Tanzlora and Arcmyrin viewed humanity on Earth. It felt different, somehow, from the way the Beaumonts did.

Before Waverly could dwell on it further, she noticed Ridge striding toward them, his dark hair catching the sunlight as he moved purposefully down the hill. The sight of him sent a ripple of hope through the group.

"He better have good news," Lynx muttered, standing and brushing off his jeans. "Because we're running out of time."

As Ridge reached the gazebo, he glanced around at the tense faces surrounding him. "Well," he began, his voice lighter than the mood demanded, "it's not a cavalry charging in, but I might have a lead."

Lincoln straightened, his eyes narrowing. "What kind of lead?"

Ridge stepped up into the gazebo, resting a hand on the wooden railing. "Dr. Marshall Stern. He's got connections, and he mentioned someone who might be able to help us—a guy named Bronte Sutton. This guy's supposed to be a legend when it comes to controlled demolitions. If anyone can help us figure out how to collapse that portal inward, it's him."

"That's a start," Callum said, his voice thoughtful. "But what's the catch?"

Ridge chuckled dryly. "The catch is that Bronte Sutton lives off-grid in the Catskill Mountains, and apparently only two people on Earth know how to contact him. Lucky for us, one of them happens to be Marshall's wife, Madre."

"Elara and Keelee's worlds are full of mysteries," Waverly said, "but we Earthlings sure do like to make things complicated too."

"So how long before this Bronte guy gets back to us?" Lynx asked.

"I'm not sure," Ridge admitted. "Madre's working on reaching out to him now. It could be hours, maybe a day. But we don't have much choice."

"Let's hope he's worth the wait," Lincoln said, the tension in his voice mirroring the urgency they all felt.

Ridge nodded, then glanced toward the forest again. "In the meantime, we need to stay sharp. If the Umbralox is gaining strength and the military's circling like vultures, we might not have the luxury of waiting too long for Bronte."

Waverly crossed her arms, glancing toward Elara and Keelee. The weight of their earlier exchange lingered in her mind, and she couldn't shake the feeling that there was more to their view of Earth than they were letting on.

"Well," Waverly said, breaking the silence, "I guess we keep preparing. And hope this Bronte Sutton is everything we need him to be."

The group gathered near the gazebo had fallen into a tense silence, each member lost in their own thoughts about the challenges ahead. The warm sun filtered through the trees, casting dappled patterns on the grass. It was Waverly who broke the quiet, glancing around with a small, hesitant smile.

"Not to downplay the seriousness of everything," she said, "but it's getting close to lunchtime, and I don't know about the rest of you, but I think better on a full stomach."

Lincoln smirked. "Leave it to Waverly to bring up food while the galaxy's falling apart."

Elara's expression softened, a rare smile gracing her lips. "It's not an unreasonable suggestion, Lincoln. In fact, it's also time for my warriors and the rest of my group to take their herbal mixtures. The environment here is different from Arcmyrin, and the herbs help them stay energized and attuned."

Keelee nodded in agreement. "The same applies to the Tanzlorans. Earth's atmosphere is heavier and its energy unbalanced for us. The mixtures Sanodia prepared this morning are vital for keeping everyone sharp and in sync."

Lincoln raised an eyebrow. "Herbal mixtures, huh? You two really come prepared."

Waverly clapped her hands together. "Alright then, let's all go our separate ways for a bit. Grab some food, take your herbs, or whatever you need to do to recharge. But stay in touch. If anything happens, we reach out immediately."

The group murmured their agreement, and soon Keelee and Elara were gathering Callum and Rykas to discuss the distribution of the herbal mixtures. Elara gestured toward the entrance to the chamber beneath the gazebo. "Sanodia has been working tirelessly to prepare enough vials for everyone. Let's head down and collect them to distribute to the warriors—both here on the property and in the national forest."

The group descended into the cool, dimly lit chamber where Sanodia awaited them in the seed vault. She stood near a workbench laden with glass vials of varying sizes, their contents glowing faintly in hues of green and gold. Her hands moved deftly as she corked another vial, placing it in a wooden crate.

"Ah, there you are," Sanodia said, looking up with a smile. "I've been busy all morning mixing these. These vials should keep everyone energized and attuned, but I've also prepared some medicinal tinctures for any injuries we might encounter."

Keelee picked up a vial, inspecting it closely. "You've outdone yourself, Sanodia. But I noticed you've been focusing on something specific. Lead poisoning, am I right?"

Sanodia nodded, her expression darkening. "Yes. It's our greatest fear when battling on Earth. You remember the first galactic battles—several of our people were shot with Earthling bullets. While the wounds didn't kill them, the lead poisoned their systems. It took weeks of suffering and the efforts of many healers to find a cure."

Elara frowned, crossing her arms. "And the cure—does it rely on the Tanzloran herb? The rare one from the hard-hit regions?"

Sanodia sighed. "It does. I brought as much as I could from our supplies, but the Umbralox's recent attack destroyed a significant portion of it on Tanzlora. I'm hopeful that what I've brought, combined with what Sage Manor has stored, will be enough."

Keelee exchanged a look with Elara, concern flickering in his eyes. "If we run out, we could be in trouble. That herb is critical."

Elara's expression turned thoughtful. "Sanodia, you should speak with Celia. She oversees the greenhouses here and may know if there are any seedlings of the herb growing. If not, we should plant some immediately. Even a few seedlings could make a difference."

Sanodia's face brightened. "That's an excellent idea. I'll find her as soon as we're done here."

Elara placed a hand on Sanodia's shoulder. "Thank you for your tireless work. We can't afford to leave anything to chance."

Sanodia handed extra vials to Keelee, Elara, Callum, and Rykas. "These are for you. Don't forget to take them. I'll distribute the rest to the warriors here and in the forest."

Keelee smiled as he accepted the vial. "We'll make sure everyone has what they need."

The group shared a moment of quiet resolve, knowing that every small effort—from taking herbal mixtures to planting seedlings—was a step toward survival and victory. As they left the chamber, the sun outside seemed a little brighter, and the path ahead, though perilous, felt just a bit more manageable.

The dining room at Sage Manor buzzed with the rare sound of laughter and relaxed conversation. The long oak table was laden with a bountiful spread that Lorinda and Bethany had lovingly prepared: platters of roasted chicken, fresh garden salads, baskets of warm rolls, bowls of mashed potatoes and gravy, and an array of homemade pies and tarts for dessert. The tantalizing aroma filled the room, mingling with the golden afternoon sunlight streaming through the tall windows.

Gran Celia sat at the head of the table, her smile soft and warm as she watched her family and their guests savor the meal. Francis, at her right, was animatedly discussing the history of Sage Manor's kitchen garden with Maya and Maddox, who were trying not to laugh at her detailed enthusiasm.

Waverly and Lynx sat side by side, their plates piled high as they teased each other about who could eat more. Ridge and Lincoln were at the other end of the table, arguing playfully over whether Ridge's third helping of mashed potatoes counted as an "unfair share."

Bethany beamed from her seat near Lorinda, pleased that the food had brought some much-needed levity to the group. Even Monica, usually reserved, joined in with a soft laugh when Lynx tried—and failed—to balance a roll on his nose, earning him a scolding look from Waverly.

The rare moment of joy and normalcy was interrupted by the sharp, insistent ring of the office phone. The sound cut through the cheerful chatter, causing everyone to pause mid-bite.

Gran Celia waved a hand dismissively. "Let it ring. Whatever it is can wait until after lunch."

Ridge glanced toward the hallway, his expression thoughtful. "We are waiting on a call, remember?"

"From the Starseed, you mean?" Waverly quipped with a grin.

"Call it what you want," Ridge muttered, standing up and brushing crumbs off his shirt. "I just hope it's the call we've been waiting for."

As he made his way out of the room, he added under his breath, "Here's hoping the Starseed actually knows how to use a phone."

Francis and Celia exchanged a knowing grin, their amusement barely concealed.

"He has such faith in the unconventional," Francis remarked dryly.

Celia chuckled softly. "Well, considering our family, can you blame him?"

The conversation at the table resumed as Ridge disappeared into the hallway. The sound of his boots echoed faintly as he walked toward the office. The laughter and chatter in the dining room continued, though a subtle undercurrent of anticipation lingered, each person silently hoping Ridge's phone call would bring good news.

6

The dining room at Sage Manor was still alive with conversation and laughter when Ridge returned, his boots clicking against the hardwood floor as he entered. His expression was a mixture of amusement and exasperation, which immediately caught the attention of everyone at the table.

"Well," Ridge began, taking his seat and leaning back casually, "I've got news. Bronte Sutton is officially on board and plans to leave ASAP to help us out."

A wave of relieved murmurs swept through the room. Lincoln, sitting a few chairs down, leaned forward. "That's great. What'd you say to convince him?"

Ridge smirked. "Not much. I offered to pay for his flight, told him not to worry about lodging or meals because we'd house him here at Sage Manor."

"And?" Waverly prompted, her fork paused mid-air.

"He said—and I quote—'No worries, got my own plane.'" Ridge paused for effect, glancing around at the astonished faces. "So, I said, 'In that case, we'll cover your fuel.' Then he just grunted and hung up on me."

The room erupted in laughter, a rare lighthearted moment in the midst of their dire situation.

"So... I'm assuming that grunt means he's packing up and getting ready to fly down soon," Ridge finished, grabbing a roll from the basket near him.

Lincoln frowned, his practical side kicking in. "Did he mention where he's flying into? We'll need to pick him up at the airport."

Ridge shrugged, tearing the roll in half. "Nope. Didn't say. He hung up before we could get that far."

Bethany looked aghast. "Why didn't you call him back?"

Ridge raised an eyebrow, clearly enjoying the reaction. "Bethany, I don't have his number. Madre made the connection, and the old rotary phone in the office doesn't exactly come with caller ID."

Gran Celia chuckled, setting her teacup down with a soft clink. "Oh well. I suppose we'll wait to hear from him again—or he'll just show up. Sage Manor isn't exactly hard to find, and anyone living off-grid has to be good with directions."

Francis nodded, her expression amused. "I have a feeling Mr. Sutton is resourceful enough to make his way here without much trouble."

Lynx leaned back in his chair, grinning. "I like this guy already. Sounds like he's our kind of eccentric."

Waverly rolled her eyes but couldn't hide her smile. "Let's just hope he's as good at demolitions as he is at abrupt phone calls."

"Agreed," Lincoln said, standing and grabbing his plate. "We'd better get ready. If Bronte Sutton is as unpredictable as he sounds, he could show up at any time."

As the group resumed their meal, the sense of urgency hadn't diminished, but the laughter and shared camaraderie had given them a brief reprieve. They all knew the stakes, but for now, they allowed themselves the comfort of knowing help was on its way.

The dining room had grown quiet as the meal ended, leaving only the faint sounds of clinking plates and muted footsteps as the family began clearing the table. Gran Celia carried a stack of plates with ease, her sharp eyes catching Lorinda's hesitant expression. Lorinda, balancing a tray of glasses, lingered near the table, glancing at Celia before finally speaking.

"Celia," Lorinda began softly, "do you think we could talk in the parlor after we finish up in the kitchen?"

Celia paused mid-step, tilting her head. "Of course. Is something wrong?"

Lorinda hesitated, then shook her head. "Not exactly. I just need to bounce something off you—get your opinion. No rush, though. Let's finish up here first."

Celia nodded, giving Lorinda a reassuring smile. "Alright. Let's get these dishes settled, and then we'll have some time to talk."

The two women moved through the butler's pantry into the kitchen, where Bethany had opened the French doors onto the patio.

The warm breeze carried the sound of children laughing as Maya, Maddox and Monica played in the side yard, just within sight of the adults. The cheerful atmosphere contrasted with the weight of the conversations inside.

Bethany and Francis were at the kitchen sink washing and rinsing the dishes, deep in discussion.

"So, Starseeds," Francis said, her eyes bright with excitement. "They're essentially beings with advanced spiritual awareness, often feeling out of place in their current environment because they come from other realms or star systems. They're said to bring wisdom and higher knowledge, though most people think it's just a myth."

Bethany nodded, her expression thoughtful. "It's not just a myth. I've read about Starseeds in the Tanzloran archives. The texts agree with your explanation. Origin, in His infinite wisdom, created many different entities and scattered them across the galaxy. Some are far more advanced than even the Triad's peoples. These beings can travel without portal systems—some can even teleport using only their minds."

Francis's jaw dropped. "You're serious? The Tanzloran archives say this?"

"They do," Bethany confirmed, smiling at Francis's astonishment. "It's rare knowledge, but it's there. I remember reading it and wondering if we'd ever encounter one of these beings."

Francis clapped her hands together, unable to hide her excitement. "I cannot wait to meet Bronte Sutton. If he's truly a Starseed, he might be willing to talk about it. Imagine what we could learn!"

Bethany laughed lightly. "Let's hope he's as fascinating as he sounds. And willing to share."

Celia and Lorinda, busy drying dishes and wiping down counters, listened quietly to the exchange. Though neither had anything to contribute, they absorbed the information with mild curiosity. Neither had ever heard the term "Starseed" before, and the idea of such advanced beings stirred a sense of wonder—and a bit of skepticism—in Celia's pragmatic mind.

Eventually, the four women finished their work in the kitchen. Francis and Bethany wiped their hands on dish towels and headed out to join the children in the yard, still chatting animatedly about Starseeds and their possible encounter with Bronte Sutton.

Celia turned to Lorinda, her tone light but curious. "Well, my dear, shall we head to the parlor now?"

Lorinda nodded, a faint shadow of concern still flickering in her expression. "Yes. I think it's time."

Leading the way, Celia exited the kitchen, her thoughts swirling as she wondered what was on Lorinda's mind. Whatever it was, it seemed to weigh heavily on her friend. Celia resolved to offer whatever help or advice she could, even as she braced herself for whatever revelation awaited in the parlor.

The parlor was quiet, the sunlight filtering softly through the lace curtains. Celia and Lorinda sat across from each other on the floral-upholstered chairs near the hearth, the scent of fresh flowers from a vase on the table between them filling the room. Lorinda fidgeted with the edge of her sleeve, her face etched with worry.

Celia tilted her head, studying her friend. "Alright, Lorinda. We're here. What's troubling you?"

Lorinda hesitated, her voice barely above a whisper when she spoke. "I've been thinking, Celia... with all the people here—your family, the visitors from Tanzlora, Arcmyrin, and even across Earth—I can't help but feel like Monica and I are just taking up space. Maybe it's time for us to return to our home."

Celia sat up straighter, her expression firm. "Absolutely not. With the dangers of the Umbralox, no one should be leaving Sage Manor, let alone going back to live alone. Have you forgotten why you came here in the first place? What happened in your home that made you run for shelter?"

Lorinda's eyes dropped to her lap, her hands clasping tightly. "I haven't forgotten. How could I? But it's different now. That was a temporary escape. Now... now it feels like we're intruding. You and your family are focused on fighting and destroying the Umbralox. I just don't want Monica and me to be a burden."

Celia reached across the table and placed a gentle hand over Lorinda's. "A burden? Lorinda, don't be ridiculous. You are not taking up space that anyone else needs. Do you know what the family would do if you went back to that house? They'd worry endlessly about you and Monica. They'd be distracted, unable to focus fully on the battle at hand. You're not helping anyone by being isolated and vulnerable."

Lorinda blinked back tears, her voice trembling. "I just... I felt different during the battles on Tanzlora. I wasn't in the way there. But here, with so many people involved, I feel like Monica and I are just an imposition."

Celia squeezed her hand. "Your worries are unfounded, my dear. You're exactly where you need to be. And you are helping. That lunch you helped prepare today? It was incredible, Lorinda. Exactly what everyone needed to stay strong and energized. Never underestimate the power of simple things like a warm meal in times like these."

Lorinda's tears finally spilled over, and she leaned forward, pulling Celia into a heartfelt hug. When she pulled back, her eyes glistened with gratitude. "Thank you, Celia. For everything. For making Monica and me feel so welcomed, for making us feel like part of this family. I don't know what we'd do without you."

Celia smiled warmly, her voice soft and steady. "You are part of this family, Lorinda. And we're stronger with you here. Now, enough of this nonsense. Dry those tears, and let's go join the others outside. It's a beautiful afternoon, and the gardens are calling."

Lorinda laughed softly, wiping her eyes. "You're right. Let's go."

With a sense of renewed purpose, the two women rose and made their way out of the parlor, their steps lighter as they walked toward the sound of laughter and play coming from the gardens. For the moment, the weight of the battle ahead seemed just a little easier to bear.

Celia and Lorinda joined Francis and Bethany in the garden, settling into the patio furniture arranged in a semi-circle under the shade of a large oak tree. The children, Maya, Maddox and Monica, darted around the yard, laughing as they chased each other with sticks they had turned into makeshift swords. The air was filled with the sweet scent of blooming flowers, and the scene was momentarily peaceful despite the turmoil that loomed over them.

Bethany glanced at Lorinda, her brow creased slightly. "Are you alright? You seemed a bit quiet during lunch."

Lorinda offered a faint smile. "I'm fine now, Bethany. I was just feeling like a burden and needed to talk it out with Celia. I thought maybe Monica and I should go back home to give everyone here more space during this time."

Bethany's face softened, and she shook her head. "Everyone would worry themselves sick about you and Monica living alone with the Umbralox danger out there—especially after they already attacked your home."

Francis chimed in, leaning back in her chair. "Not to mention, it's not just about the space. It's about safety. You're far safer here, surrounded by people who can protect you."

As they spoke, Bethany's expression grew thoughtful. "You know, Lorinda, it just hit me—when you came to Sage Manor, you left everything behind, didn't you? I mean, you and Monica have been wearing clothing that Celia, Waverly, and I could spare."

Lorinda nodded. "Yes. We didn't have time to gather much of anything. Celia managed to find some of Waverly's old clothes for Monica, but they're still too big for her."

Bethany smiled. "Would you like to take a ride to your house and gather some of your things? Clothes, personal items—anything that would make you and Monica feel more at home here?"

Lorinda's face lit up. "Oh, I'd love that! It would mean so much to have some of our own things. Monica's been asking about her pillow and her favorite bedtime books, and I know she'd be thrilled to have them."

Bethany turned to Celia and Francis. "Would you two mind watching the kids for a bit while I take Lorinda over there?"

Celia waved a hand dismissively. "Of course. Maddox, Maya and Monica are keeping us plenty entertained. But I don't think the two of you should go alone."

Francis nodded in agreement. "With everything going on, it'd be safer if one of the others went with you—Waverly or Lincoln, perhaps."

Lorinda looked hesitant for a moment but quickly agreed. "That makes sense. I'd feel better knowing we weren't taking any chances."

Bethany stood, brushing off her jeans. "Alright, let's go see who we can find."

Lorinda smiled and stood as well, walking over to where Monica was playing. She knelt down, placing a gentle hand on her daughter's shoulder. "Monica, will you stay here at the manor and help Celia and Francis with Maddox and Maya while I go with Bethany to pick up some things from our house."

Monica's eyes lit up. "Will you bring back my pillow and my nighttime books?"

Lorinda pulled her daughter into a hug. "I promise I'll bring them back. Anything else you want me to grab?"

Monica thought for a moment, then shook her head. "Just those."

"Alright, sweetheart," Lorinda said, giving her a kiss on the forehead. "Be good for Celia and Francis, okay?"

Monica nodded eagerly and ran off to rejoin the other children.

Bethany and Lorinda exchanged a glance and then turned back to Celia. "We'll check inside to see if Waverly or Lincoln can come with us," Bethany said.

"Good idea," Celia replied. "Be careful, both of you."

With that, the two women headed back into the manor, their steps purposeful as they sought out someone to accompany them on their brief but important errand.

7

The library was alive with debate as Ridge, Lincoln, Lynx, and Waverly sat around the table, papers spread out in front of them. The topic? How long it would take Bronte Sutton to fly from the Catskill Mountains to Sage Manor, depending on his exact location. Lincoln had a map of the Northeast laid out, and Ridge was pointing at various counties.

"If he's somewhere in Greene County, it'll take about three hours," Ridge speculated, tracing a route with his finger.

"Unless he's in Delaware County," Lynx countered, leaning over the map. "Then it's more like four hours. The terrain there is rougher, so it might take longer to get off the ground."

"Oh, come on," Lincoln said, shaking his head. "He's flying a private plane, not hiking through the woods. It won't make that big of a difference."

Waverly, sitting off to the side with her arms crossed, let out an exaggerated sigh. "Does it even matter? None of you know his exact location, so you're just guessing. Men." She threw her hands in the air and rolled her eyes.

At that moment, Lorinda and Bethany entered the library, catching the tail end of Waverly's exasperation. Lorinda hesitated, then asked, "Is this a bad time? We need someone to go with us to my house to pick up some of Monica's and my personal items."

Ridge looked up from the map, his brow furrowed. "Why now? You've been here for a while and haven't needed anything. What's changed?"

Lorinda started to explain, but Ridge waved her off dismissively. "Women," he muttered, shaking his head. He glanced at Waverly with a teasing smirk. "Isn't this what you were just doing to us?"

Waverly stuck her tongue out at him in response. "For your information, Ridge, I'll gladly go with Lorinda. Men just don't understand that there are certain things a lady needs."

"Like what?" Ridge challenged, leaning back in his chair. "She has clothes, Monica has clothes, they've got food, a bed. What else do you need?"

Waverly glared at him, about to launch into a tirade, but Bethany quickly stepped between them. "Okay, you two, enough! We don't have time for this nonsense. Now, who's coming with us? Celia made a good point—there's strength in numbers. We should go now, while it's quiet, before our demolition expert gets here."

"I'll go," Lynx offered, standing.

"And I'm going too," Waverly said, glaring at Ridge.

"Bye-bye," Ridge mouthed at her, waving dramatically.

Waverly stomped her foot and stormed out of the room, muttering under her breath.

Bethany turned to Lorinda with a wry smile. "No wonder you want to stay at your house. If I had to deal with Ridge and Waverly acting like this all the time, I'd move in with you too."

"Wait a minute!" Ridge said, suddenly alarmed. "You said she's picking stuff up to bring back here, right? You're not planning on staying at your house, are you? That's not safe for you and Monica to be alone over there."

"Of course not, Ridge," Bethany replied, exasperated. "Were you even listening earlier? Lorinda and I are going to her house to gather some of her and Monica's personal items to bring back here so it feels more like home."

"Ohhh... gotcha," Ridge said, relaxing. "Okay, well, I'll go with you two while we wait on Bronte Sutton to get here. Can you hold down the fort, big brother?"

Lincoln smirked. "I've got it covered. I'm heading down to the gazebo to check in with Elara and Keelee while you're gone. Shouldn't take you long."

"Great," Ridge said, clapping his hands together. "We're out of here. And I'm driving!"

As Ridge led the way out of the library, Lynx followed with an amused grin, and Bethany and Lorinda exchanged knowing looks. Waverly reappeared in the hallway, still fuming but ready to go. Together, the group headed for the Jeep, leaving Lincoln behind to manage things at Sage Manor.

Lincoln strolled down the gravel path toward the gazebo, the afternoon sunlight glinting off the metal roof. As he approached, the faint hum of the chamber beneath the gazebo reached his ears. He paused for a moment to glance over his shoulder, catching sight of Ridge's Jeep disappearing down the driveway in a cloud of dust. Shaking his head with a wry grin, he turned back and descended the steps into the cool, dimly lit chamber.

Inside, Keelee and Elara stood at the oval table, their postures tense but composed. On the walls, the four screens glowed softly, each depicting one of the elemental spirits. Mistara, Ambreela, Ignissa, and Terraveta observed silently, their forms shifting slightly as if attuned to the mood of the room. The conversation between the Tanzloran and Arcmyrin envoys had just concluded, their echoes of formal deliberation still lingering in the air.

Keelee looked up as Lincoln entered, his expression brightening. "Ah, good. I was just about to summon you to the chamber."

Lincoln raised an eyebrow, stepping closer. " What's the latest?"

Keelee gestured to the table, where a holographic map of the area shimmered faintly. "We just finished speaking with the councils. They're concerned about the situation escalating. Both councils believe we need to bring more warriors here as a precaution."

Lincoln leaned over the map, his brows furrowing. "More warriors? I thought we already had enough stationed here and in the national forest near the falls."

Elara, standing opposite Keelee, folded her arms across her chest. Her tone was calm but firm. "We do, for now. But if the situation worsens, we'll need reinforcements. The councils feel that the portal's instability and the growing presence of the Umbralox demand a stronger contingency."

Mistara's soft voice echoed from her screen, her watery form shimmering. "The currents of danger flow ever stronger. Preparation is not a luxury but a necessity."

Ambreela's airy voice followed. "The winds bring whispers of battle. Delay could cost dearly."

Lincoln exhaled sharply, straightening. "I get it. And honestly, they're not wrong. If this portal doesn't collapse as planned, or if the Umbralox breach it before we're ready, we'll need every hand we can get."

Ignissa's fiery eyes flared as her voice rang out. "The blaze of conflict grows brighter. Strength must be met with strength."

Terraveta's deep, grounding tone was the last to speak. "A strong foundation withstands the greatest storms. Reinforce your position."

Keelee nodded solemnly, glancing at Lincoln. "Their wisdom is clear. What are your thoughts? Should we request reinforcements now?"

Lincoln rubbed his chin, considering. "If we wait too long, we might not have enough time to get the help here when we need it. On the other hand, bringing in more warriors could attract unwanted attention—especially if the military is already sniffing around."

Elara stepped forward, her gaze steady and unwavering. "If the demolition expert—this Bronte Sutton—cannot do what we need him to do, then the worst-case scenario will unfold. The portal will explode, the Umbralox will spill onto Earth, and we will have no choice but to fight. If that happens, every warrior we can muster will be needed. We must be prepared for the possibility that this battle will not end with a simple collapse of energy."

Lincoln sighed heavily, the weight of the situation pressing down on him. "You're right. If it comes to that, we'll need all the help we can get. Go ahead and make the request for reinforcements. Let's just hope they're here as backup and not as our last line of defense."

Keelee inclined his head, his expression resolute. "I'll inform the councils immediately."

Elara placed a hand on Lincoln's arm, her tone softer now. "The situation is grim, but we're not without hope. The strength of our people, your family, and even your demolition expert—it all matters. Together, we'll fight whatever comes."

Lincoln nodded, his jaw set. "Let's just make sure we're ready for anything."

As Keelee moved to the communication orb, the elemental spirits flickered slightly, their presence a silent testament to the enormity of the task ahead. Lincoln felt the weight of the moment but also the faint stirrings of determination.

As Keelee finished contacting the councils to request reinforcements, the atmosphere in the chamber shifted to one of focused strategy. The elemental spirits remained on their screens, their watchful eyes lending a sense of urgency to the conversation.

Elara turned back to Lincoln, her expression thoughtful. "The warriors stationed in the forest are doing their best to stay out of sight, but the risk of being seen is always there. Humans are curious, and if they stumble upon them, it could create chaos."

Lincoln nodded, crossing his arms as he leaned against the edge of the table. "You're right. The warriors are already blending into the terrain as best as they can, but we'll need to be extra careful. Thankfully, with everything happening, the forest isn't exactly crawling with people right now."

Keelee raised an eyebrow. "How do you know?"

"Because I've been keeping tabs," Lincoln said. "The locals are spooked. Word's been spreading fast—through social media, local gossip, even a few news outlets. It's harming tourism in the area. Most people don't want to go anywhere near the forest after hearing stories about strange sightings, shadows and eerie sounds."

Elara tilted her head. "The news outlets are reporting on this?"

Lincoln nodded. "Yeah, but here's the thing—they're only reporting from the entrance to the Pisgah National Forest. They're not going in. Liability concerns, mostly. Their staff is refusing to go past the signs, which makes things a little easier for us. Right now, I'm more concerned about keeping the military out than dealing with a few spooked tourists."

Ignissa's voice broke in, fiery and commanding. "Fear is a tool, but it can also turn against you. Humans who are afraid are unpredictable."

Lincoln sighed. "Tell me about it. Fear spreads fast, and that's why I'm keeping an eye on the situation. As of now, the locals and reporters are too scared to venture far. The warriors should be safe as long as they stick to the deeper parts of the forest."

Keelee frowned. "But what about the military? You've mentioned this general before. How much of a threat is he, really?"

Lincoln's face darkened. "Big. The military doesn't think like we do. If they sense a threat, they respond with firepower—guns, missiles, bombs. And that's the worst-case scenario for us. If they get involved, they'll do more harm than good. They won't understand the delicacy of the situation. If they try to destroy the portal outright, they'll only stabilize it and give the Umbralox the opening they need."

Terraveta's deep voice rumbled from her screen. "Strength must be tempered with wisdom. The blade that strikes without understanding cuts both ways."

Elara nodded, her expression grim. "So, what's the plan? How do we keep the warriors hidden and the military at bay?"

Lincoln pushed off the table, pacing the room. "I'll reach out to the sheriff and the district park ranger. They've been good about keeping people out of the forest, and I'll let them know we need that vigilance to continue. As far as the military goes..." He paused, his jaw tightening. "We need to stay off their radar. The second they think we're handling things, they'll back off. But if they sense weakness—or if someone reports something they don't like—we'll have a real problem on our hands."

Ambreela's airy voice filled the chamber. "The winds of danger shift quickly. Steady yourselves, and prepare for the unexpected."

Keelee exchanged a glance with Elara. "The warriors will need to re-double their efforts to stay hidden, especially with reinforcements coming. The last thing we need is for someone to stumble across a group of Tanzloran or Arcmyrin soldiers patrolling the forest."

Lincoln nodded. "Exactly. Let's keep them out of sight and let the fear of the unknown keep people away. It's working so far. But we've got to move quickly—because the longer this drags on, the more likely someone's going to push too far."

Elara's gaze was sharp as she addressed the group. "Then we have no time to waste. Let's secure the forest, prepare for reinforcements, and focus on Bronte Sutton. If he succeeds, none of this will matter. But if he doesn't..."

Keelee finished her thought, his voice low and firm. "Then we'll need every warrior, every ounce of strength, and every bit of courage to fight what's coming."

The elemental spirits flickered, their presence steady and watchful as the group steeled themselves for the days ahead.

8

The Jeep hummed along the quiet backroads, filled with the sound of chatter and laughter as Ridge, Lorinda, Bethany, Lynx, and Waverly made their way toward Lorinda's house. Ridge was in the middle of a teasing remark about Lynx's idea of "fire safety" when he suddenly trailed off, his grip on the wheel tightening.

As they turned onto Lorinda's long driveway, Ridge's eyes narrowed. The trees and underbrush lining the path bore signs of devastation—wilting leaves, blackened branches, and gnarled roots clawing out of the dirt as if scorched and poisoned simultaneously. The eerie sight was all too familiar to Ridge.

"Do you see that?" he murmured, his voice tense.

Everyone in the Jeep fell silent, their eyes scanning the grotesque scene unfolding outside. The vibrant greens of the forest were gone, replaced with the withered remnants of life.

"What... what is that?" Lorinda finally asked, her voice trembling. "Why does everything look like this?"

Before anyone could respond, Ridge rounded a curve in the driveway, and a collective gasp filled the vehicle as the Jeep came to a jolting stop.

Lorinda's two-story home stood before them—or rather, what was left of it. The house was engulfed in a mass of writhing, black, oozing tentacles that lashed out erratically from its walls and roof. The structure itself appeared to be breathing—its exterior pulsating in and out like a grotesque, living organism. The scene radiated malevolence, and the air seemed to thrum with an otherworldly energy.

"Oh no... oh no... oh no," Lorinda repeated, clutching Bethany's arm. "What is that? What's on my house?"

Bethany placed a comforting hand on Lorinda's shoulder, her voice calm but firm. "It's going to be okay, Lorinda." Turning to Ridge, she said, "Get us out of here, Ridge. Now."

Before Ridge could throw the Jeep into reverse, a sickening sound—like wet fabric tearing—echoed from the house. The black tentacles began slithering toward them, several of them latching onto the Jeep's hood.

Lorinda screamed, her terror piercing the tense silence.

"Get ready!" Ridge barked as Lynx and Waverly flung open the back doors of the Jeep.

Lynx leapt out first, summoning a burst of flame from his hands and directing it toward the advancing tentacles. The fire licked across the Umbralox's grotesque forms, forcing them to recoil momentarily.

Waverly spun in a circle, her arms outstretched as she summoned a vortex of air. The winds whipped around the Jeep, forming a protective barrier against the encroaching darkness.

"Bethany, shut the doors!" Ridge ordered, throwing his own door open. "You and Lorinda stay inside, get down in the seats, and don't move."

Bethany nodded, pulling Lorinda down with her as she shut the doors. "Stay calm," she whispered to Lorinda, who was shivering uncontrollably. Inside the Jeep, Bethany clasped her hands together and prayed aloud. "Origin, send them the help they're calling for. Protect us all."

Outside, Ridge dropped to one knee and slammed his hands into the ground, calling upon his power. The earth trembled in response, a barrier of stone and dirt erupting between the Jeep and the monstrous house. The barrier slowed the Umbralox's advance, but it didn't stop them.

"Terraveta!" Ridge shouted, his voice echoing through the chaos. "We need you!"

Beside him, Lynx unleashed a wave of flame, driving the tendrils back. "Ignissa! I need your strength!" he roared.

Behind them, Waverly pushed her vortex forward, encircling the Jeep entirely and moving toward Ridge and Lynx's positions. "Ambreela! Protect us!" she cried, her voice carrying on the winds.

The Umbralox, enraged, lashed out more aggressively. The house's pulsations grew faster, and the air grew heavier with malice.

Inside the Jeep, Bethany's whispered prayers grew louder. "Please, Origin. They need you. We need you. Send them the strength to fight this evil."

In the dimly lit chamber beneath the gazebo, Lincoln, Keelee, and Elara stood in tense conversation. The elemental screens glowed faintly, their presence a comforting reminder of the guidance they offered. But then, as if a switch had been flipped, three of the screens—Ignissa, Terraveta, and Ambreela—suddenly went dark, leaving only Mistara's watery form flickering on the remaining screen.

"Mistara!" Elara exclaimed, her sharp voice cutting through the silence. "What's happening?"

Mistara's voice was urgent, her watery form trembling. "The family is in trouble. Danger surrounds them, and the shadows grow stronger. Go to them now!"

Lincoln's heart leapt into his throat, and he wasted no time. "Let's go!" he barked, bolting up the stone stairs. Keelee and Elara were right behind him, their footsteps echoing in the narrow passage.

Bursting out of the gazebo into the daylight, Lincoln spotted Callum and Rykas standing off to the side, their heads bent in discussion over battle strategies.

"Callum! Rykas!" Lincoln shouted, his voice carrying urgency.

The two warriors looked up, alarmed at the sight of Lincoln, Keelee, and Elara running toward them. They exchanged a brief glance before rushing to meet them.

"What's happening?" Rykas demanded, his sharp eyes scanning for immediate threats.

"No time to explain," Lincoln said, his voice clipped as he sprinted toward his truck parked nearby. "The family's in trouble. We need to move. Now!"

Elara jumped into the front seat beside Lincoln while Keelee, Callum, and Rykas piled into the bed of the truck without hesitation. Gripping the sides of the truck bed, they braced themselves as Lincoln started the engine and peeled out of the driveway, gravel spraying in his wake.

The truck roared down the winding road, its tires squealing as Lincoln took the corners with barely controlled speed. In the cab, Elara clutched the dashboard, her face pale but resolute. "Mistara's warning was clear. The shadows are growing stronger."

Lincoln's jaw tightened, his focus razor-sharp on the road ahead. "If they're at Lorinda's house, they're isolated. We can't let them face this alone."

In the bed of the truck, Keelee leaned over to Callum and Rykas, his voice low but firm. "Be ready for anything. If the Umbralox have manifested enough to attack, we'll need to move fast. We don't know what we're walking into."

Callum nodded, gripping the edge of the truck bed tighter. "If the family's in danger, we'll protect them. No matter what."

Rykas, his golden eyes narrowed, added, "And if the Umbralox think they'll take another inch of this world, they're about to learn otherwise."

The truck careened down the road, its engine growling as Lincoln pushed it to its limits. In the cab, he glanced at Elara, his voice tight with determination. "We get them out of there, no matter what it takes."

Elara nodded, her gaze steely. "We will. They're counting on us."

The forest blurred past as the truck sped toward Lorinda's house, each second stretching into eternity as they rounded the final curve toward Lorinda's house. The sight that greeted them was both awe-inspiring and terrifying.

Waverly stood just in front of the Jeep, her arms outstretched, her vortex spinning furiously around the back and one side of the vehicle. Her face was set in fierce concentration as she yelled, her voice carrying over the chaos. "Ambreela! Help me!"

The vortex suddenly surged, glowing brighter, and Lincoln could feel the shift in the air even from the truck. Ambreela's presence was undeniable as the winds howled in response to Waverly's plea, expanding the vortex to completely surround the Jeep.

But just beyond the Jeep, Ridge and Lynx were still exposed, fighting relentlessly. Ridge knelt with his hands on the ground, an earthen barrier rising in a semi-circle to hold back the advancing tentacles of the Umbralox. Beside him, Lynx stood tall, fire erupting from his hands and blasting the black, writhing mass that had consumed the house.

Suddenly, a brilliant red-orange glow surrounded Lynx. Ignissa had arrived. Her fiery energy radiated outward, amplifying Lynx's power. His flames grew hotter, brighter, and extended further, reaching the walls of the house. The Umbralox let out a guttural, otherworldly shriek as the flames licked across its grotesque surface, setting the tentacles alight.

"Keep pushing!" Lynx shouted, his voice fierce as he channeled the intense fire at the house.

On Ridge's side, the ground rumbled, and Terraveta's deep, grounding energy flowed through him. The earthen barrier surged higher, its curved wall now stretching across the road and forming an impenetrable barricade in front of the Jeep. The tentacles, desperate to advance, slammed against the barrier but were unable to break through.

In the truck, Elara gasped, her hand gripping the dashboard. "The elemental spirits are with them. They're fighting with everything they've got."

Lincoln didn't hesitate, slamming on the brakes and jumping out of the truck. Keelee, Callum, and Rykas leapt from the bed, landing with practiced precision.

"Go!" Lincoln barked. "Help them!"

Elara didn't wait for an invitation, sprinting toward the Jeep and raising her hands. A shimmering shield of energy enveloped Waverly, reinforcing her as she continued to direct the vortex. Keelee joined Ridge, his hands glowing with Tanzloran energy as he strengthened the earthen barrier further. Callum and Rykas took position near Lynx, their weapons drawn, striking at any Umbralox tendrils that escaped the flames.

Ridge looked up briefly, sweat streaming down his face. "Good timing, Lincoln!" he shouted.

Lincoln stood back, watching as the combined power of his family and their allies turned the tide. Waverly's vortex swirled with unrelenting force, keeping the Jeep protected. Lynx's fire, enhanced by Ignissa, burned brighter and hotter, causing the Umbralox to writhe in agony.

Ridge, with Terraveta's aid, maintained the impenetrable barrier that kept the mass from advancing further.

The house itself began to shudder, its grotesque breathing slowing as the flames consumed the black mass clinging to it. The screeches of the Umbralox grew weaker, fainter.

"We're driving them back!" Lynx shouted triumphantly, unleashing another wave of fire.

Lincoln's voice rang out over the chaos. "Finish it! Don't let up until it's gone!"

The combined power of the family and the elemental spirits surged one last time, a brilliant display of earth, fire, wind, and energy enveloping the house. The Umbralox shrieked one final time before the writhing mass burst into flames, collapsing in on itself and through the roof of the house causing the entire structure to burst into flames.

The vortex faded, and Waverly staggered, catching herself against the Jeep. Ridge dropped his hands, the earthen barrier holding firm but no longer needed. Lynx's flames flickered out as Ignissa's glow subsided, leaving him breathing hard but victorious.

For a moment, the group stood in stunned silence, the only sound the crackling of the flames consuming the house.

Lincoln stepped forward, his voice steady. "Is everyone okay?"

Ridge nodded, wiping sweat from his brow. "We're good. Thanks to the elementals—and the timing of reinforcements."

Waverly gave Lincoln a shaky smile. "I'd say we just leveled up in family bonding, wouldn't you?"

Elara placed a hand on Waverly's shoulder, her expression solemn as she watched the house burn. "This isn't over. The Umbralox won't stop here. But for now, we've won this battle."

Lincoln's jaw tightened as he surveyed the burning house. "Then we regroup and get ready for whatever's next. This was just the beginning."

As the last echoes of the Umbralox's screeches faded into the air, the scene settled into a tense quiet. The smoldering remnants of Lorinda's house hissed and crackled, sending thin wisps of black smoke into the sky. Waverly leaned heavily against the Jeep, catching her breath, while Lynx wiped soot from his face, his hands still trembling from the intensity of the battle.

Bethany climbed out of the Jeep first, helping Lorinda out after her. Lorinda's legs buckled as soon as her feet hit the ground, the weight of the experience crashing down on her. She staggered forward, sobbing uncontrollably, and fell into Ridge's waiting arms.

Ridge caught her effortlessly, wrapping his arms tightly around her trembling frame. "I've got you," he murmured, his voice soft and soothing. He kissed the top of her head, his chin resting on her hair. "It's going to be okay. I promise. You're safe now."

Lorinda clung to him, her tears soaking into his shirt as her body shook. "My home... it was alive... it was..." She couldn't finish, her sobs cutting her off.

"Shh," Ridge whispered, gently rocking her. "It's gone now. We won't let anything else happen to you or Monica. I swear."

The rest of the group stood in silence, the gravity of the moment heavy in the air. Waverly brushed tears from her own eyes, her heart aching for Lorinda. Lynx ran a hand through his hair, his jaw tight as he stared at the smoldering ruin.

Finally, Lincoln broke the silence, his voice steady but tinged with urgency. "We have to put this fire out before it draws attention we don't need."

He stepped forward, glancing at the glowing embers and then up at the sky. "Mistara," he called, his tone respectful yet commanding. "Can you help us extinguish this before anyone notices?"

The air around them grew cool and damp as Mistara's watery form shimmered into being beside Lincoln. Her voice was calm but firm. "I will aid you, but your strength will also be needed to contain what remains of the destruction."

Lincoln nodded, moving toward the scorched ground and raising his hands. Mistara's presence intensified, and a soft mist began to form, growing denser until it became a steady drizzle that blanketed the area.

"Everyone, help if you can," Lincoln said, his voice carrying over the hiss of steam rising from the wet ground.

Waverly stepped forward, summoning a gentle breeze to carry the mist across the ruins, helping it settle over every glowing ember. Ridge, still holding Lorinda, glanced down at her tear-streaked face. "Stay here," he said softly, brushing a strand of hair from her cheek. "I'll be right back."

She nodded weakly, letting him go. Ridge moved to Lincoln's side, pressing his hands to the ground to reinforce the earth around the scorched areas, ensuring the fire had no place to reignite.

Together, with Mistara's aid, the flames were slowly extinguished, leaving behind only smoke and charred remnants. The group stood back, surveying the scene, the acrid smell of ash lingering in the air.

Lincoln turned to Mistara, his expression grateful. "Thank you."

Mistara's watery form shimmered and faded, her voice lingering like a gentle ripple. "Protect your own, Lincoln. The battle is far from over."

Lincoln nodded, his gaze shifting to the others. "Let's regroup at the Manor. We need to figure out our next move."

Ridge returned to Lorinda, who was now leaning against Bethany for support. Without a word, he scooped her up into his arms, holding her close as she buried her face in his shoulder.

The group silently made their way back to the vehicles, the weight of the encounter pressing down on them. The fight was over, but the scars it left were fresh, and the war was far from won.

9

The Jeep rolled to a stop in front of Sage Manor, its occupants exhausted and emotionally frayed. The soft glow of lanterns on the porch cast a welcoming light, but the group inside the vehicle carried a darkness that couldn't be left behind.

Gran Celia appeared at the top of the porch steps, alerted by one of the warriors who had been keeping watch. Her keen eyes scanned the group as they began climbing out of the Jeep. Lynx stumbled slightly, his face and clothes streaked with soot, the acrid smell of fire and ash clinging to him.

"Oh my heavens," Celia whispered, her hand flying to her chest. "What on Earth happened?"

Her gaze shifted to Ridge, who stepped out of the driver's seat, cradling Lorinda in his arms. Her limp body was motionless, her face pale and streaked with dried tears.

Celia's voice sharpened, laced with alarm. "Ridge, is she injured?"

"No, Mama," Ridge said, his voice strained but steady. "She's in shock. We need to get her inside, lay her down, and have Sanodia take a look at her." Without waiting for a response, Ridge started up the stairs, carefully carrying Lorinda.

As he reached the porch, the sound of small feet pounding on the wooden floor echoed through the entryway. Monica, followed by Francis, Maya, and Maddox, appeared in the doorway. Monica froze, her wide eyes fixed on her mother.

"Mom!" Monica screamed, bursting into tears. "Mom! What's wrong with her?"

Francis knelt beside Monica, her voice calm and steady as she tried to console her. "She's going to be okay, sweetheart. She's just tired and needs rest."

Monica threw herself into Francis's arms, sobbing uncontrollably. Celia knelt beside them, smoothing Monica's hair and whispering soothing words. Meanwhile, Bethany and Lincoln gently ushered Maya and Maddox back outside, their firm but kind words keeping the twins from asking questions that might upset Monica further.

Waverly, her expression tight with determination, turned on her heel and strode toward the gazebo. She had barely made it halfway when she saw Elara and Sanodia rushing up the path, their faces set with purpose. Elara had already alerted Sanodia of Lorinda's condition.

"Thank goodness," Waverly said, stopping to let them catch up. "Lorinda's in shock. She needs help."

Sanodia nodded, her healer's instincts kicking in. "Where is she?"

Waverly pointed back toward the house. "Upstairs in her room. Ridge and Celia are with her."

The three women hurried into the manor and up the stairs. As they reached the landing outside Lorinda and Monica's suite, they could hear Celia's calm, steady voice coming from inside.

"Ridge," Celia was saying, "take her shoes and socks off and cover her. She needs to feel comfortable and safe."

Inside the room, Ridge knelt beside the bed, his hand resting gently on Lorinda's head. He leaned in, his voice soft and pleading. "Lorinda. It's me. Please wake up. You're safe now. We've got you."

When she didn't respond, Ridge dropped his head, his shoulders sagging. When he finally looked up at his mother, there were tears in his eyes.

"She'll be okay, son," Celia said firmly, her hand gently stroking Lorinda's arm. "She'll snap out of this. We just have to be patient."

Ridge nodded, though the worry in his eyes didn't fade. He kept his hand on Lorinda's head, his connection to her unwavering.

Sanodia approached quietly, her presence calming. She knelt beside Ridge and Celia, her voice soft but resolute. "Let me take a look. I'll do what I can to bring her back to us."

Celia and Ridge exchanged a glance, then both nodded and stepped back, giving Sanodia the space she needed.

Sanodia placed her hands gently on Lorinda's temples, her eyes closing as she began to work. A soft glow emanated from her fingertips, the energy soothing and warm. The room fell into a hush, the only sound the faint hum of Sanodia's power as she called on her knowledge and the energy of Tanzloran healing.

Celia placed a reassuring hand on Ridge's shoulder. "She's in good hands now. Sanodia will bring her through this."

Ridge nodded again, though his eyes never left Lorinda's face. His silent vigil was unbroken, his quiet hope echoing the sentiment of everyone in the room.

The early evening sky glowed faintly as the first stars began to peek through the darkening blue. Maddox and Maya were running around the yard, their laughter echoing as they chased the lightning bugs blinking softly in the growing dusk. Bethany sat on the porch steps, watching the children with a small smile, while Lincoln and Keelee stood nearby, their postures tense as they talked quietly.

Lincoln glanced at Keelee, his voice low. "What now? The fact that the Umbralox was able to take over that entire house without any of us feeling it is... unsettling."

Keelee nodded, his brows furrowed in thought. "I agree. The enemy is becoming unpredictable, and that's dangerous. If they're evolving, finding new ways to gain footholds, it's going to make them harder to track and contain. We need to spread out, survey the region, and see if they've taken hold like that anywhere else."

Bethany stood, brushing her hands on her jeans as she joined them. "Don't forget, Lorinda's house was the first place where the shadows and whispers were seen and heard. That's also where the mirror was shattered. Maybe that broke something open—like a portal—on that property."

Keelee looked thoughtful. "You might be right. The family left Earth immediately after that, focused on the battles on Tanzlora. No one went back to check on the house after the mirror was destroyed. That gave the Umbralox time to grow stronger, to fester unchecked. It was my responsibility to anticipate this. I should have sent warriors to ensure the enemy wasn't lingering there."

Lincoln shook his head, his tone firm. "Keelee, don't start blaming yourself. None of us could have predicted this. We thought the mirror was their anchor and that by destroying it, we destroyed their hold. It made sense at the time."

Keelee crossed his arms, his jaw tight. "But we were wrong. The enemy doesn't need an anchor—they adapt, they evolve. And now we're facing a portal at the falls, potentially an even bigger threat. What if no matter what we do, it opens a way for them to come in and take over, just like they did at Lorinda's house?"

Lincoln exhaled sharply, glancing out at the yard where Maddox and Maya continued their game. Their carefree laughter felt like a distant reminder of what was at stake. "That's the risk we're taking. But what's the alternative? If we don't collapse the portal, the Umbralox come through anyway, and we lose everything. We have to trust that we can stop them, no matter how unpredictable they get."

Bethany placed a hand on Keelee's arm, her voice steady but warm. "We're all doing the best we can, Keelee. No one could have predicted how the Umbralox would twist and adapt. The important thing now is that we've seen what they're capable of, and we won't let it happen again."

Keelee sighed, his shoulders relaxing slightly. "You're right. The fight's not over. It's not even close. But knowing the enemy is this unpredictable... it means we have to be more vigilant than ever."

Lincoln nodded. "We'll spread out tomorrow, check the region. If there are other places like Lorinda's house, we need to find them before it's too late. But for now, let's keep an eye on the kids and make sure they have at least one night of normalcy."

The three of them fell silent, watching Maddox and Maya dart through the yard, their hands cupped, trying to catch lightning bugs. The innocence of the moment stood in sharp contrast to the weight of the conversation, but it was a reminder of why they fought—to protect that innocence, to ensure the darkness couldn't consume everything.

Keelee finally spoke, his voice softer now. "We'll stop them. No matter what it takes."

Lincoln's expression hardened, his determination unwavering. "We have to."

The soft glow of the lamps in Lorinda's room cast long shadows as Sanodia worked, her hands glowing faintly with Tanzloran energy as she performed her healing treatment. The room was quiet save for the hum of her power and Celia's gentle voice as she spoke soothingly to Lorinda, trying to coax her out of the shock that gripped her.

Just then, the sound of soft sniffling came from the doorway. Celia turned, her keen eyes softening as she saw Francis and Waverly standing just inside, each holding one of Monica's small hands. Monica's tear-streaked face was a picture of worry, her wide eyes darting to her mother lying motionless on the bed.

Celia extended her arms, her voice warm and inviting. "Come here, dear."

Monica let go of Francis and Waverly's hands and darted across the room, her little feet pattering against the floor. She ran into Celia's waiting arms, and Celia pulled her into a comforting hug, whispering in her ear. "See, sweetheart? Your mommy is right here. She's very tired and needs rest, but Sanodia is helping her have good, healing sleep. She'll be just fine."

Monica nodded, her sniffling subsiding a little as her gaze locked onto her mother. Her wide, curious eyes took in the scene—Sanodia's glowing hands moving methodically, the faint shimmering energy enveloping Lorinda, and the calm, focused expression on the healer's face.

The room seemed to hold its breath, everyone moved by the quiet moment. Finally, Monica stood on her tiptoes and tugged gently at Celia's arm to bring her ear closer. In a small, hopeful voice, she whispered, "Gran Celia, can I give Mommy a kiss on her cheek?"

Sanodia, hearing the soft plea, turned and smiled at Monica. She motioned toward the bed, patting the side closest to Lorinda's head. "Come here, little one. It's okay."

Ridge stepped forward, his movements careful and deliberate. He knelt down and extended his arms toward Monica. "Come on, sweetheart. Let me help you."

Monica nodded, allowing Ridge to lift her gently. He carried her to the bed and held her close so she could lean in toward Lorinda. Monica placed a soft kiss on her mother's cheek and whispered, "Get better, Mommy."

The quiet sincerity of her words brought tears to everyone's eyes. Celia dabbed at her face with a handkerchief, and even Waverly had to blink rapidly to hold back her emotions.

Monica turned and hugged Sanodia tightly around the leg, surprising the healer. Sanodia smiled, placing one hand on Monica's head and gently rubbing it. "Your mommy will be okay," Sanodia said softly. "She'll wake up soon. I promise."

Monica nodded solemnly, as if trusting Sanodia's words completely. Ridge carefully pulled Monica away and cradled her against his shoulder. "Let's give Sanodia some space to finish helping your mommy," he murmured, his voice steady but warm.

He began walking toward the door, Monica resting her head on his shoulder. The rest of the group followed quietly, leaving Sanodia to finish her healing treatment. The soft glow of her power bathed the room as the door closed behind them, carrying with them the hope that Lorinda would soon awaken, her strength restored.

10

The soft glow of lanterns on the porch cast warm light over Sage Manor's yard, where the sound of children's laughter mingled with the chirping of crickets. Ridge stepped onto the porch, carrying Monica in his arms. Her little hands clutched his shirt as she looked around with wide, curious eyes.

"Where are Maddox and Maya?" Monica asked, her voice still tinged with the lingering emotions of the evening.

Bethany, sitting on the porch steps, pointed to the yard where the twins were darting around, their laughter ringing out as they chased tiny dots of glowing light. "They're catching lightning bugs, sweetheart. Why don't you go join them?"

Monica's face lit up with a smile as Ridge set her down. She hopped off the steps and ran toward the twins, her giggles blending with theirs as they ran through the grass, their arms reaching for the flickering insects.

Ridge leaned on the porch railing, watching them with a wistful expression. "Oh, to be young again and have that kind of carefree innocence," he murmured.

Bethany stood and joined him, her gaze also on the children. "Yes, I second that sentiment," she replied, her voice soft. After a moment, she turned to Ridge, her expression more serious. "How's Lorinda? Has she woken up yet?"

Ridge shook his head, his jaw tightening briefly. "Not yet, but with Sanodia's healing, I'm hopeful it'll be soon. She just... needs time."

They stood in silence for a moment, the quiet punctuated only by the sound of the children's laughter and the occasional hum of a lightning bug. Finally, Bethany spoke again, her tone thoughtful. "She's been through a lot. I can't imagine how hard it must be for her to process everything that happened. This time of rest will probably be the best thing for her. But when she wakes up, Ridge, and those memories come flooding back—that's when she's really going to need us. All of us."

Ridge's gaze remained fixed on the yard, his eyes reflecting the flickering lights of the fireflies. "You're right," he said quietly. "And I'll be there for her. No matter what. This evil... it's taken so much already. Not just from us, but from our friends, from Tanzlora, from the very land we're trying to protect. After all the loss we've seen, there's no way I'm letting it take any more."

Bethany watched him closely, hearing the steel in his voice. Ridge's normally easygoing demeanor was replaced with a fiery determination. "I want to take out that portal right now," he continued, his hands gripping the railing. "And whatever comes out of it? It better be stronger than me, because I'm ready to see the Umbralox eradicated into oblivion for what it did—to Lorinda, to all of us."

Bethany hesitated for a moment, choosing her words carefully. She'd noticed the subtle changes in Ridge lately—the way he glanced at Lorinda, the way he softened when she was near. There was something there, something budding and fragile, and she didn't want to tread on it. After a brief pause, she smiled and said, "I've never seen this side of you before, Ridge. But I have to say… I like it."

Ridge turned to her, his expression softening into a wide grin. "Yeah?" he said with a playful lilt. Then, with a nod toward the others gathered further down the porch, he added, "Well, I'll take that as a compliment."

Without another word, he strode off toward where Lincoln, Keelee, Waverly, Francis, and Gran Celia were huddled in conversation, leaving Bethany to watch him go. She smiled faintly to herself, then turned her gaze back to the yard, where Monica and the twins laughed and played, blissfully unaware of the weight of the world on the shoulders of the adults who loved them.

The soft glow of lamplight in Lorinda's bedroom suite cast long, warm shadows across the walls. Sanodia knelt beside the bed, her hands glowing faintly as she performed her healing treatment. Her gentle humming filled the room, a low, soothing melody that seemed to harmonize with the energy radiating from her hands. The air was thick with the scent of herbs, and the atmosphere had a serene, almost otherworldly quality.

The door opened quietly, and Elara entered, her arms full of carefully prepared supplies. She paused for a moment, her sharp eyes taking in the scene. Lorinda lay still, her breathing steady but shallow, her face pale against the soft pillows. The light from Sanodia's hands and the sound of her humming gave the room an ethereal quality, and Elara felt a sense of calm wash over her despite the urgency of the situation.

Sanodia glanced up, her lips curving into a small smile when she saw Elara. "You've come to help," she said softly, her voice barely breaking the rhythm of her humming.

Elara nodded, setting down the items she carried on the small bedside table. "I gathered what I could from the seed vault and the garden," she replied, her voice low and steady. "I've prepared a healing essence that may help ease her transition back when she wakes. It should soothe her body and her spirit."

Sanodia didn't stop her treatment, her hands continuing their gentle, glowing movements over Lorinda's form. "Perfect. Together, we'll give her the strength she needs to return to us."

Elara pulled up a chair and unwrapped a cloth compress she had soaked in the healing essence, the aroma of the herbs filling the room even more intensely. The scent was a blend of earthy and floral notes, with a hint of citrus and mint, designed to calm and energize simultaneously.

Dipping the cloth into the warm essence, Elara wrung it out gently before leaning over Lorinda. She began to rub the compress lightly across Lorinda's face, her touch delicate. As she worked, she joined Sanodia's humming, her voice weaving into the melody like a second thread in a tapestry. The combined hums created a resonance that seemed to vibrate through the air itself, filling the room with a palpable energy.

Starting with Lorinda's temples, Elara worked the essence into her skin, moving down to her neck and shoulders. She took her time, her movements deliberate and precise. "This essence contains calming and grounding herbs," Elara explained softly, though she knew Sanodia already understood its purpose. "It should help release the tension her body is holding and smooth the pathway for her spirit to reconnect fully with her mind."

Sanodia nodded, her hands still glowing as they hovered over Lorinda's chest, sending waves of healing energy into her heart and lungs. "She's holding onto the shock deeply," Sanodia murmured. "The Umbralox's influence is strong, even in its absence. But with this, we're guiding her back."

Elara moved to Lorinda's arms, gently massaging the essence into her skin from her shoulders down to her fingertips. The glow from Sanodia's hands seemed to ripple outward, merging with the soft light that began to emanate from the healing essence. The vibrations from their combined humming grew stronger, filling the room with a comforting, almost tangible warmth.

As Elara worked on Lorinda's legs, her humming grew softer, almost like a lullaby. She glanced at Sanodia, who met her gaze with a small, knowing smile. "It's working," Sanodia whispered. "Her energy is stabilizing."

The room seemed to respond to their efforts. The combination of the aromatic herbs, the light from their treatments, and the harmony of their voices created an otherworldly glow that bathed everything in a gentle, soothing radiance. The air felt lighter, as if the weight of Lorinda's trauma was slowly lifting.

Elara finished applying the essence to Lorinda's legs and gently covered her with the soft blanket that Ridge had laid over her earlier. She sat back for a moment, taking in the change in the atmosphere. Lorinda's face had lost some of its pallor, and her breathing was deeper, more even.

Sanodia sat back slightly, lowering her hands but keeping them close to Lorinda, her energy still flowing. She tilted her head toward Elara. "We've done what we can for now. The rest is up to her spirit. But she's surrounded by strength and love—she'll find her way back to us."

The evening air was thick with the tension of unresolved questions as Elara and Sanodia stepped onto the porch of Sage Manor. The soft hum of conversation greeted them, blending with the sounds of katydids and distant owls. The family had gathered in a loose circle, their faces illuminated by the warm glow of the porch lanterns.

Ridge leaned against the railing, his arms crossed, while Waverly sat on the steps, absently twisting a strand of her hair. Lincoln stood with his hands on his hips, his eyes focused on the horizon, while Gran Celia and Francis shared the swing, speaking in low tones. Bethany had taken Maddox, Maya and Monica inside to start preparing for bedtime, leaving the adults to their discussion.

"We're running out of time," Lincoln said, his voice low but steady. "The fire at Lorinda's house could've shortened our timeline. If anyone was watching—and we know the General's always watching—it's going to draw attention."

"That's the understatement of the year," Waverly muttered. "We didn't just draw attention. We practically sent up a signal flare."

Ridge nodded grimly. "And that's assuming we don't already have a bigger problem. The portal under the falls isn't going to wait for us to get our act together. If Bronte Sutton doesn't show up soon..."

Gran Celia cut in, her voice calm but firm. "He'll show. Madre wouldn't have sent us to him if she didn't believe he could help. And Ridge, you said yourself—he's a Starseed. They don't operate on normal timelines according to Bethany and Francis."

Francis rubbed her chin thoughtfully. "Still, we've no idea when he'll actually get here. He could be pulling into the driveway any second, or he could be flying over the Appalachians right now."

Lincoln sighed. "And every minute we spend waiting is a minute we can't afford. The General's not going to sit around twiddling his thumbs. If he's got even the smallest excuse to turn the forest into a combat zone, he'll take it."

As if in answer to his words, the faint glow of headlights appeared in the distance, weaving through the trees as a vehicle made its way up the long drive to the Manor.

"Is that him?" Waverly asked, springing to her feet.

"Could be," Ridge said, squinting at the approaching lights. "But I wouldn't hold your breath. My money's on the sheriff—or worse, the General himself."

"I'm hoping for the sheriff," Francis said, folding her arms. "At least he'll talk to us without trying to blow something up."

11

The vehicle pulled closer, revealing itself as a park ranger truck with the official seal of the U.S. Forest Service emblazoned on the side. When it came to a stop, the driver's door opened, and Seth Dixon, the district park ranger, stepped out, followed by two deputies.

The family exchanged wary glances as Ranger Dixon approached the porch, his hat in hand. His face was grim, lined with the weight of unwelcome news.

Lincoln stepped forward to meet him. "Ranger Dixon. This is a surprise. What brings you out here so late?"

Dixon glanced at the others, nodding respectfully before speaking. "I apologize for intruding at this hour, but I'm here on behalf of Sheriff Bowen. He's tied up in a meeting with General Adamson at the moment."

At the mention of the General, the atmosphere on the porch shifted, the tension becoming almost palpable.

Dixon continued. "The General's people picked up some footage earlier—video from one of their birds in the air. They caught the fire at the Rooney house. They also saw... something else." His voice dropped, and his eyes flicked briefly toward Ridge and Waverly.

"What did they see?" Ridge asked, his tone hard.

"They saw the fight," Dixon admitted. "The flames, the shadows, the... energy. The General's very disturbed by what he saw. He's convinced it's a national security threat, and he's in talks with a Congressional representative and the White House to get approval for taking military action against the threat in the Pisgah National Forest."

A stunned silence followed his words, broken only by the faint rustling of leaves in the trees.

"Military action?" Waverly echoed, her voice sharp. "What does that even mean?"

"It means military jurisdiction," Lincoln said grimly. "It means troops, weapons, and no more room for negotiation."

Dixon nodded. "The forest is federal land. The sheriff has no authority to stop the General, though he's doing what he can to plead for more time. But Adamson... he seems eager to act. Too eager. He's ready to move his troops in immediately."

"Of course, he is," Ridge muttered. "Because that's what we need right now—a bunch of trigger-happy soldiers making everything worse."

Elara and Sanodia, standing just inside the doorway, exchanged concerned glances but remained silent. They knew their presence would only complicate matters, their otherworldly nature still too jarring for most humans to accept.

Keelee, standing with them, whispered, "This is what happens when fear drives decisions. Earth isn't ready to understand us or the threats we face."

Elara nodded, her gaze thoughtful. "One day, perhaps. But not today."

Back on the porch, Francis spoke up, her voice calm but tinged with urgency. "Ranger Dixon, do you have any sense of how much time we have before the General moves in?"

Dixon shook his head. "Not much. Hours, maybe a day at most. He's already mobilizing his forces. If you've got a plan, now's the time to act."

"We have a plan," Lincoln said firmly. "But it depends on Bronte Sutton getting here in time."

"And if he doesn't?" Dixon asked.

Lincoln's jaw tightened. "Then we'll figure something else out. But one thing's for sure—we can't let the General turn this into a war zone. He doesn't understand what he's dealing with. Missiles and gunfire won't stop the Umbralox. They'll only make things worse."

Gran Celia stepped forward, her voice steady. "Seth, is there any way you can delay him? Distract him, stall him, anything?"

"I'll do what I can," Dixon said. "But I can't promise much. He's got his sights set on this, and he's not the kind of man who takes no for an answer."

The group fell silent, the weight of the situation settling heavily over them. In the background, the sound of children's laughter drifted through the open windows, a poignant reminder of what they were fighting to protect.

Finally, Waverly broke the silence, her voice low but determined. "We've got to be ready for whatever happens. If Bronte shows up, great. If not, we do what we always do—we fight. Together."

Heads nodded around the porch, the resolve in the air unmistakable.

Inside the house, Elara and Sanodia exchanged a glance. Keelee whispered, "They're ready to fight for their world, just as we fought for ours."

Sanodia's voice was soft but sure. "And we'll stand with them, as allies and as friends. No matter what comes."

As Ranger Dixon turned to leave, he hesitated, glancing back at Lincoln and the group gathered on the porch. His expression was serious, and his voice carried a weight that drew everyone's attention.

"One more thing before we go," he said, his gaze steady on Lincoln. "One of my deputies has been keeping a close eye on the perimeters of the forest. He's noticed... strange things happening in certain areas. Justin, show them the pictures."

Deputy Ranger Justin Foster stepped up onto the porch, his boots creaking against the wooden planks. He held out his phone, swiping through a series of images as Lincoln, Ridge, Waverly, and Gran Celia moved closer to see. They formed a tight semi-circle, the porch light casting their shadows long across the floorboards.

The first photo showed a section of the Pink Beds, the once-lush greenery now blackened and twisted, with gnarled roots clawing out of the earth as if they had been scorched and poisoned. Another image revealed Sliding Rock, its smooth surface marred by dark streaks and strange, creeping tendrils. Sycamore Flats picnic area looked abandoned and desolate, the trees stripped of their leaves and the ground covered in a sickly black sludge. The Davidson River Campground was barely recognizable, the devastation almost complete, with the ground appearing as though it had been burned and eaten away simultaneously.

The only exceptions were the Cradle of Forestry buildings and the area around Looking Glass Falls, where the portal was located. Those places seemed untouched by the creeping corruption.

Lincoln muttered a curse under his breath, his jaw tightening as he flipped through the photos. Ridge let out a low whistle, his brow furrowing deeply. Waverly's fists clenched at her sides, and Gran Celia, ever composed, crossed her arms, her sharp eyes narrowing at the images.

"This..." Lincoln began, his voice tight, "this is bad. Really bad."

Ridge turned to the rangers, his expression grim. "What you're looking at isn't natural. It's the work of the Umbralox, the same evil that took over Lorinda's house. And it's not going to stop. This—" he gestured to the photos "—this is only the beginning. It will spread. It will consume everything unless we stop it."

The weight of Ridge's words settled heavily over the porch. Deputy Foster shifted uncomfortably, his eyes darting between the family members. "What... what can we do?"

Ridge's gaze was hard, unflinching. "The only thing we can do is eradicate the Umbralox. But to do that, we need time. And we need the General to stand down, not bulldoze in here with his tanks and missiles and make things worse."

Ranger Dixon nodded solemnly. "We'll do what we can to hold him off. But this..." He glanced back at the photos on Foster's phone. "This is beyond anything we've ever dealt with. You say this is going to get worse—how much worse are we talking?"

"Total devastation," Waverly said bluntly, her voice tight with barely contained anger. "It won't just take the land. It'll spread to everything—wildlife, water, air. The Umbralox doesn't stop until it consumes everything in its path."

Inside the house, just behind the doorway, Elara, Keelee, and Sanodia listened intently. They exchanged grim looks as they processed the dire news.

Elara leaned closer to Keelee, her voice a whisper but filled with urgency. "We need more warriors. Now. We can't wait any longer. We have to report this to the councils immediately."

Keelee nodded, his expression set. "Agreed. Every second we wait, the Umbralox gains more ground. We have to act."

Sanodia, her healer's instincts always at the forefront, added softly, "And we must prepare for the toll this will take—on the land and on the people."

As the rangers turned to leave, Dixon paused on the steps, addressing Lincoln one last time. "We'll do everything we can on our end. But if there's anything else you need from us, don't hesitate to call."

Lincoln nodded, his face hard with determination. "Thank you. And stay safe out there. The Umbralox... it's not something you can fight with conventional means."

Dixon tipped his hat and climbed back into the truck with his deputies. The sound of the engine roared to life, and the truck disappeared down the long drive, its taillights fading into the darkness.

Elara, Keelee, and Sanodia stepped out onto the porch, their expressions resolute. Elara's voice was steady but firm as she addressed the family. "We're heading to the gazebo to confer with the councils. This can't wait any longer. Reinforcements are coming—now."

Lincoln nodded. "Do what you need to do. We'll hold the line here until you're ready."

Without another word, Elara, Keelee, and Sanodia made their way toward the gazebo, their figures silhouetted against the faint glow of lantern light. The family remained on the porch, the weight of the situation pressing heavily on them.

"We're running out of time," Waverly said quietly.

Lincoln nodded, his gaze fixed on the horizon. "Then we make every second count."

The porch had grown quiet, the earlier tension settling into a somber stillness as everyone processed the grim news. Gran Celia stood at the edge of the group, her hands folded in front of her, her expression thoughtful but resolute. She broke the silence with her steady voice.

"I'm going back in to check on Lorinda," she said.

Francis nodded immediately. "I'll go with you. I want to check on Monica and make sure she's holding up."

Gran Celia gave her a small, appreciative smile. "Good. She needs the reassurance right now."

Lynx, leaning against the porch railing, pushed himself upright. "I'm heading to the gazebo," he announced. "I want to hear what the councils have to say. This situation's escalating too quickly—we need to know what reinforcements are coming and when."

Ridge clapped him on the back as Lynx started down the steps. "Good idea. We're going to need all hands on deck for what's coming."

Lincoln nodded in agreement. "We'll join you. The more of us there to hear the councils' decisions, the better."

Waverly followed, her expression determined. "Count me in. I want to know what we're doing next too."

As the group headed toward the gazebo, Ridge called out to Gran Celia, who was making her way toward the front door. "Mama, come get me if Lorinda wakes up. No matter what I'm doing."

Gran Celia paused at the door, turning back to him with a reassuring smile. "I will, son. Don't worry."

Ridge nodded and jogged down the steps to catch up with Lynx, Lincoln, and Waverly, their footsteps crunching on the gravel path as they made their way toward the gazebo. The lanterns lining the porch cast long shadows behind them, the light dimming as they moved further away.

Gran Celia and Francis exchanged a look before stepping inside the manor, the warmth of the house greeting them like a comforting embrace. The hallway was quiet, the distant sound of the children's laughter faint but reassuring.

"I'll check on Monica first," Francis said, her voice low. "She was so upset earlier. I want to make sure she's settled down."

Gran Celia nodded. "Good. I'll head upstairs to Lorinda's room. If she stirs, I'll come let you know."

They parted ways in the hall, each heading to fulfill their responsibilities. Outside, the group heading toward the gazebo disappeared into the night, their determination driving them forward as the clock continued to tick down on the battle they knew was coming.

12

The dim glow of the seed vault illuminated the rows of shelves filled with carefully stored herbs and plants, their earthy aroma filling the cool air. Elara and Sanodia stood just inside the doorway, their voices low as they discussed what would be needed to prepare for the battles to come.

"We'll need a variety of mixtures," Elara said, her tone calm but urgent. "Something to treat burns, lacerations, and lead poisoning, as well as general energy restoratives. The Tanzloran and Arcmyrin warriors will require strong healing salves, and we can't overlook the Earthlings. They'll need treatments tailored to their physiology."

Sanodia nodded, her hands running over the jars and bundles of dried herbs. "I've already begun preparing for lead poisoning. The Tanzloran archives have detailed instructions from the last time Earthling weapons injured our people. We'll need a substantial supply of the rare root from Tanzlora, mixed with what Earth can provide."

Elara glanced at her, her expression thoughtful. "It's unfortunate that Lorinda can't assist us right now. With her training as an Earthling nurse, she'd be an invaluable ally in this effort."

Keelee, standing just outside the vault with his arms crossed, raised an eyebrow. "Lorinda is trained in Earthling healing?"

Elara turned toward him. "Yes. Here on Earth, she worked in their Haven or I believe they call it a hospital and she is what they call a nurse. This is before everything happened when she had to leave her house. Her earthling healing training could be crucial once she recovers."

Keelee nodded, his expression contemplative. "I wasn't aware. That's good to know. When she's ready, she'll be a significant help to the cause. For now, we'll manage."

He stepped back into the main chamber, where the communicator orb sat on its pedestal. The orb glowed faintly, its surface shimmering with potential. Keelee placed a hand on it, his voice firm. "Draven and Sylvaris, we request your presence. The council needs to hear what has transpired."

The orb pulsed brighter, its light filling the chamber. Moments later, two holographic figures materialized, their forms clear and lifelike. Draven, the elder that was overseer of the Tanzloran warriors, stood tall, commanding and regal, while Sylvaris, the council's visionary elder, exuded an aura of quiet strength and determination.

Draven's voice was calm but inquisitive. "Keelee, Elara. How are things progressing on Earth?"

Elara stepped forward, her tone even. "We have much to report. The Umbralox's influence is spreading beyond the portal. It has taken over areas of the forest, including Lorinda's home, and the devastation is growing. The Earthlings are understandably alarmed, and their military is poised to act. We are running out of time."

Sylvaris's hologram flickered slightly as he leaned forward, his expression grim. "The portal must be dealt with swiftly. If it stabilizes, Earth is lost. What reinforcements are needed?"

Keelee began listing the current situation, including the positioning of Tanzloran and Arcmyrin warriors, the state of the portal under the falls, and the urgency of preventing Earth's military from interfering. As he spoke, the sound of footsteps echoed from the stairway leading into the chamber.

Elara turned and saw Waverly, Lincoln, Ridge, and Lynx entering. She silently motioned for them to join her, and the group filed into the oval room at the heart of the chamber, their faces tense but resolute.

The room was dominated by the large oval table, its surface smooth and gleaming, with the four screens on the wall glowing faintly. Each screen displayed the elemental spirits—Mistara, Ambreela, Ignissa, and Terraveta—who observed the proceedings silently, their presence a constant reminder of the power and wisdom they offered.

Lincoln nodded at Elara and Keelee before taking a seat. "What's the status?" he asked quietly.

"We're briefing the council now," Keelee replied, gesturing toward the holograms of Draven and Sylvaris.

Draven's gaze shifted to the newcomers. "Lincoln Beaumont. Your family's resolve is impressive. The situation on Earth is dire, but with your determination, we believe this battle can be won."

Sylvaris added, his tone sharp but encouraging, "But you must act swiftly. The Umbralox thrives on hesitation and fear. What is your plan for the portal?"

Before Lincoln could respond, the elemental spirits began to glow more brightly, their voices resonating in turn.

Mistara's soothing tones flowed like water. "The currents of time grow perilously short. The portal must be sealed, or it will consume all."

Ambreela's airy voice followed. "The winds of fate are restless. Trust in your strength, but do not delay."

Ignissa's fiery voice burned with passion. "You carry the power to fight this evil. Wield it without hesitation."

Terraveta's deep, grounding voice concluded. "Stand firm. Your unity is your greatest weapon."

The room fell silent for a moment as the weight of their words settled over the group. Lincoln exchanged a glance with Ridge, then spoke, his voice steady. "We'll do whatever it takes. The portal under the falls is our priority. But we need to contain the Umbralox's spread in the forest. If it reaches the Cradle of Forestry or beyond, we'll lose any chance of stopping it."

Draven nodded. "Then you must act decisively. We will send reinforcements immediately. Expect their arrival within the hour."

Keelee inclined his head. "Thank you, Draven. Sylvaris. Your support will make all the difference."

The holograms flickered and faded, leaving the group alone in the chamber with the glowing presence of the elemental spirits.

As the holograms of the Tanzloran council faded, the chamber grew quiet for a moment, the weight of their words still lingering in the air. Elara stepped forward to the communicator orb, her steps purposeful and measured. Placing her hands on its shimmering surface, she closed her eyes briefly, sending a silent request for connection to her own council on Arcmyrin.

The orb pulsed faintly at first, then began to glow brighter as it established the connection. The wait stretched into a few tense minutes before the light flared, and the holographic forms of all six Arcmyrin council members materialized. They stood tall and regal, their forms shimmering with a faint, otherworldly golden hue. Each member radiated a calm but commanding presence, their gazes focused and steady.

"Elara," one of the council members, Councilor Aduralina, spoke first, her voice resonant and serene. "We have received your request. What news do you bring from Earth?"

Elara straightened, her tone both respectful and urgent. "Councilors, the situation is escalating rapidly. The Umbralox influence is spreading far beyond the portal under the falls. It has taken hold in multiple areas of the Pisgah National Forest, and its devastation is growing. We are working with the Earthlings to contain it, but we need reinforcements—and wisdom."

Keelee, who had remained near the communicator orb, gestured for the Beaumont family to join them. Waverly, Ridge, Lincoln, and Lynx followed Keelee into the central chamber, gathering in a semi-circle around Elara and the glowing orb. Behind them, the crystal gate shimmered faintly, its presence a reminder of the interstellar connections they were leveraging.

Councilor Milestree, a figure with sharp eyes and an air of authority, spoke next. "The spread of the Umbralox is deeply troubling. It thrives on fear and chaos, exploiting every vulnerability. What measures have been taken so far to contain it?"

Lincoln stepped forward, his voice steady. "We've been tracking its spread and working to limit its reach. We've identified areas already affected—Lorinda Rooney's house, Sliding Rock, the Pink Beds, Sycamore Flats, and the Davidson River Campground. The Cradle of Forestry and the falls are currently untouched, but we don't know for how long."

Ridge added, "We've reinforced patrols, but our numbers are limited. The military presence in the area complicates matters. If they step in, they'll only make things worse. We're racing against time to collapse the portal before the Umbralox spreads further."

Councilor Aduralina's expression softened with understanding. "Your plight is grave, but not insurmountable. Reinforcements from Arcmyrin are on their way as we speak. Warriors trained in combating shadow forces will join your efforts. Once this meeting concludes, we will send them through the portal to your location."

Waverly nodded gratefully. "Thank you. We need all the help we can get. The areas already infected need to be guarded and protected. We can't afford to let the Umbralox gain more ground."

Elara spoke again, her tone resolute. "We must also keep a close watch on Lorinda's house location. The Umbralox influence there was strong, but we believe it has been eradicated. However, we cannot assume it won't try to regain a foothold. That site must remain under constant surveillance."

Councilor Lunarcher nodded. "Agreed. It would be best to assign specific units to monitor and secure the location. The same applies to all areas affected by the Umbralox. The warriors arriving will be briefed and prepared for this task."

Councilor Releesia's gaze swept over the group. "The portal under the falls is the key. Its implosion must be precise. Any failure will not only stabilize the portal but strengthen the Umbralox's hold on this world. Do you have the means to ensure its success?"

Lincoln exchanged a glance with Ridge and Waverly before answering. "We've brought in an Earth expert—a demolition specialist named Bronte Sutton. If anyone can help us with the technical side of collapsing the portal, it's him. But we'll need your warriors to hold the line while we do it."

Councilor Silastoria inclined his head. "Then we will trust in your expertise and commitment. You have our warriors and our guidance. Together, we will face this threat."

The holograms began to flicker as the meeting neared its conclusion. Elara stepped forward, her expression one of gratitude. "Thank you, Councilors, for your wisdom and your aid. Your reinforcements will make all the difference."

The council members nodded in unison. "May the light of Origin guide you," Aduralina said. "Prepare yourselves. The warriors will arrive shortly."

As the holograms faded, the orb's light dimmed, and silence settled over the group. Keelee turned to Sanodia, who had remained nearby, and motioned toward the door. "It's time. Let's give them the space they need to come through."

The group began filing out of the chamber, their steps purposeful. As they ascended to the front porch of the manor, the cool night air greeted them, filled with the distant hum of crickets and the rustling of leaves.

The family and envoys gathered together, their faces a mix of determination and anticipation. Lincoln spoke first, his voice calm but resolute. "This is it. The reinforcements will be here soon. We regroup, we prepare, and we fight."

Gran Celia, who had just returned from checking on Lorinda, nodded her approval. "The battle ahead will be difficult, but with unity and resolve, we will prevail."

The group fell into a contemplative silence, their eyes on the path leading to the gazebo, waiting for the Arcmyrian warriors to arrive and bring with them the strength needed to turn the tide of the battle ahead.

13

The air around Sage Manor crackled with anticipation as the crystal gate shimmered to life in the gazebo. The energy radiating from the portal created an ethereal glow that spilled onto the lawn, illuminating the night in an otherworldly light. The Beaumont family stood together on the porch—Gran Celia, Lincoln, Ridge, Lynx, and Waverly—watching silently as the Arcmyrin warriors began to emerge.

Elara stood at the edge of the lawn, her regal presence commanding respect. Rykas was beside her, his posture straight and his golden eyes sharp as he greeted the first of their warriors stepping through. The Arcmyrin warriors were tall and strong, their armor gleaming with a faint iridescence. Each bore the calm but resolute expression of someone who had trained for centuries for moments like this.

"Welcome," Elara said warmly to the first warrior, bowing her head slightly. "Your service to Arcmyrin and our ally, Earth, will not be forgotten."

Rykas extended a hand to each warrior as they stepped onto Earth soil, directing them to move to the side and make room for those who followed. One by one, the Arcmyrins arrived, each standing taller than the last, their ranks assembling in a disciplined formation under the clear night sky.

The Beaumonts watched from the porch, their expressions a mix of awe and gratitude. "It's hard to believe this is real," Waverly murmured, her eyes fixed on the procession. "They're incredible."

Gran Celia nodded. "This is the kind of unity that changes the course of history."

The last of the Arcmyrin warriors stepped through, the portal shimmering brightly as Elara and Rykas exchanged a glance. Keelee approached them, his violet-blue hued Tanzloran presence a contrast to the golden iridescent elegance of the Arcmyrins.

"The Tanzloran warriors are ready to cross," Keelee informed them. "As soon as the portal to Arcmyrin closes, the elders will open the gate between Tanzlora and Earth. They're prepared."

Elara inclined her head. "Good. Rykas and I will make sure the transition is smooth."

The crystal gate pulsed one final time as the Arcmyrin portal connection closed. For a moment, the gazebo was quiet, the energy dissipating briefly before the Tanzloran portal began to shimmer into existence. The atmosphere shifted, the energy taking on a deeper, earthen tone as the Tanzloran elders activated the connection.

As the first Tanzloran warriors stepped through, Keelee and Callum took their places beside Elara and Rykas to welcome their comrades. The Tanzlorans emerged in their battle-ready attire, their movements precise and deliberate. Each warrior carried an air of grounded strength, their connection to their home planet evident in their every step.

"Welcome," Keelee said, his voice steady as he clasped the forearm of the first warrior. "Your dedication honors Tanzlora and strengthens our bond with Earth."

Callum mirrored Keelee's actions, his presence as the Tanzloran warrior leader commanding immediate respect. The warriors moved to stand alongside the Arcmyrins on the lawn, forming an impressive and unified force.

The Beaumonts watched in silence, the gravity of the moment sinking in. Lincoln crossed his arms, his face solemn. "This is it," he said quietly. "We have the reinforcements. Now we have to make it count."

"It's going to count," Ridge said firmly, his eyes fixed on the warriors. "There's no way the Umbralox stands a chance against this."

One by one, the Tanzloran warriors filed through the portal, until the final soldier stepped onto Earth. The gate shimmered brightly one last time before closing, leaving the lawn bathed in starlight and the glow of the lanterns from Sage Manor.

With all warriors assembled, Elara and Keelee stepped forward to address their respective forces. Elara's voice was calm but commanding, carrying easily across the lawn.

"Arcmyrin warriors," she began, her gaze sweeping over the ranks, "you have been called here to stand against a force that threatens not only our allies but the balance of the universe itself. Your dedication and strength will help turn the tide. You are here not just as soldiers but as protectors of life, defenders of hope."

She turned to Rykas, her tone softening slightly. "Rykas, I entrust these warriors to you. Lead them with the wisdom and courage of the Arcmyrians. The Earthlings stand with us, and together, we will prevail."

Rykas bowed deeply. "It will be done."

Keelee stepped forward next, his voice resonating with quiet authority. "Tanzloran warriors, your mission is clear. The Umbralox's corruption spreads through this land, but we will not let it prevail. You fight not only for Earth but for Tanzlora and the unity of our sister planets. Your bravery will be the light that guides us through the darkness."

He turned to Callum, meeting his gaze with respect. "Callum, I give you command of our forces. Lead with honor and strength. Stand firm, and we will not falter."

Callum nodded, his expression resolute. "Tanzlora will not fail Earth."

Rykas stepped forward, his authoritative presence immediately commanding attention. His iridescent armor caught the light, and his golden eyes swept over the Arcmyrian warriors, who stood tall and ready for orders.

Rykas's voice rang out, firm but calm. "Arcmyrian warriors, the Umbralox has already begun to spread its corruption across this land. Our duty is clear: to protect these vulnerable areas and ensure the enemy gains no further foothold."

He gestured toward a small group of warriors. "You, five, will post at the location of the Rooney home. The structure has been destroyed, but we must ensure no remnants of the Umbralox remain. Search the ashes thoroughly. If you find any active tendrils, eradicate them immediately. Under no circumstances should the enemy regain a foothold there."

The selected warriors nodded sharply, their expressions resolute.

Rykas continued, his gaze shifting to another group. "The Sycamore Flats picnic area has already shown signs of corruption. You will set up a perimeter of protection there. Keep your senses sharp. The Umbralox thrives in stealth, but we cannot allow it to spread unchecked."

Turning to the largest contingent, he said, "The Davidson River Campground is vast and critical to this mission. Arcmyrins and Tanzlorans will work together to guard this area. Your combined strength will ensure its protection. Be vigilant and report any anomalies immediately."

When Rykas finished, he stepped back, his eyes meeting Callum's. The Tanzloran warrior leader stepped forward, his towering figure and grounded demeanor radiating calm strength.

"Tanzloran warriors," Callum began, his deep voice steady, "your posts are just as critical. A few of you will remain here at Sage Manor, joining the current guardians of these grounds. Your presence will strengthen the manor's defenses against any potential attacks."

He gestured toward another group. "The rest of you will be split among the key locations already identified. Some of you will join the Arcmyrians at the Davidson River Campground, forming a united front to protect that area."

Callum turned to another set of warriors. "A group of you will join the guardians already stationed at the portal area at Looking Glass Falls.

This is the focal point of the Umbralox's power. Protecting this site is critical to our mission's success."

Finally, Callum addressed the remaining warriors. "The rest of you will split into teams to cover Sliding Rock, the Pink Beds, and the Cradle of Forestry. These areas are vulnerable and must be guarded against further corruption. Be sharp and observant. Report anything you see immediately."

He stepped forward, his piercing gaze sweeping over all the warriors. "No warrior is to go out alone. Always move in pairs or threes. There is strength in numbers, and the Umbralox seeks to isolate and exploit its prey. Do not give it the chance."

Both Arcmyrian and Tanzloran warriors nodded in unison, their faces a blend of determination and discipline. The two leaders, Rykas and Callum, exchanged a brief look of mutual respect.

Rykas turned back to the assembled warriors. "This is not just a fight for Earth. It is a fight for balance, for the unity of all our worlds. Stay vigilant, stay strong, and remember the purpose of your mission."

Callum nodded in agreement. "Your service will be remembered and honored. Let's ensure that the enemy knows we will not falter. Protect each other, protect this land, and trust in your training."

With that, the warriors from both planets dispersed, moving in pairs and small groups toward their assigned locations. The quiet murmur of strategizing replaced the earlier stillness as they prepared to carry out their duties.

As the ceremonies of duty concluded, Keelee and Elara made their way back to the porch. The glow of the lanterns highlighted their determined expressions as they stepped onto the wooden planks where the Beaumont family stood.

Gran Celia watched the warriors go, her hands clasped tightly in front of her. "It's a remarkable thing," she said softly. "To see our allies stand together like this. It gives me hope."

Lincoln nodded. "They're impressive, no doubt. But the real fight's ahead of us. This is just the beginning."

Waverly leaned against the railing, her gaze following the warriors as they disappeared into the trees. "We're ready," she said, her voice steady. "Whatever comes next, we're ready."

Ridge rested a hand on her shoulder. "We have to be. There's no room for error now."

The night air felt heavier now, filled with the weight of the task ahead. Lincoln, Ridge, Lynx, Waverly, and Gran Celia watched the two envoys approach, their postures reflecting both readiness and exhaustion.

Keelee was the first to speak, his voice calm but carrying an unmistakable gravity. "The warriors from Tanzlora and Arcmyrin are here, and their presence will be invaluable. They will hold the lines, guard the corrupted areas, and buy us time."

Elara stepped forward, her piercing gaze sweeping over the family. "But make no mistake—the true warriors in this fight are you. The Beaumont family. The daggers are the key to imploding the portal and trapping the Umbralox once and for all. Without you wielding them at the precise moment, everything else will be in vain."

Waverly nodded slowly, her jaw tightening. "We understand. We'll do whatever it takes."

Gran Celia's voice was steady but tinged with concern. "You're right, Elara. But wielding those daggers is no small thing. It will require precision, timing, and courage. We'll rise to the challenge, but it's a heavy burden."

Keelee inclined his head. "We would not entrust this task to you if we did not believe you were capable. Origin and the elemental spirits chose your family for a reason. And now, with the demolition expert's help, we can ensure that the portal collapses inward—if the timing is exact."

Ridge, who had been leaning against the railing, straightened at the mention of the demolition expert. "Speaking of which," he said, his tone edged with frustration, "where is Bronte Sutton? He should've been here by now."

Lincoln frowned, his arms crossed. "Good question. We're cutting it close. If he doesn't show up soon, we're going to have to figure out the implosion on our own—and that's not a risk I want to take."

Elara exchanged a glance with Keelee, then looked back at Ridge. "We understand your urgency. If he's as skilled as you say, his expertise will make all the difference. But if he doesn't arrive in time, the fallback plan is clear: the daggers, wielded at the right moment, will have to be enough."

Ridge muttered under his breath, running a hand through his hair. "He better show up. This isn't something we can wing."

Lynx, leaning against the porch post, added, "I get that he's this eccentric off-the-grid genius or whatever, but time's running out. If he's coming, he needs to get here now."

Gran Celia placed a calming hand on Ridge's arm. "Let's not panic yet. Bronte Sutton knows the urgency of the situation. If he's as capable as we've been told, he'll find a way to get here. Until then, we focus on what we can control."

Elara's gaze softened, her voice steady. "Celia's right. You've already come so far. Trust in yourselves, your allies, and your instincts. The daggers are powerful because of the ones who wield them. That's you."

Keelee stepped closer, his expression firm. "Your family has faced insurmountable odds before. This is no different. You will rise to the occasion, as you always have."

The family exchanged determined glances, the weight of the envoys' words settling over them. Ridge finally sighed, nodding. "Alright. But if Bronte doesn't show up soon, someone's going to have to figure out how to demolish that portal—and fast."

Lincoln clapped him on the back, his voice calm but resolute. "We'll figure it out, brother. One way or another, we're not letting the Umbralox win."

The group fell into a moment of silence, the gravity of their mission sinking in. The warriors in the forest were a reassuring presence, but the Beaumonts knew the final battle would rest on their shoulders—and the daggers in their hands.

The fight for Earth had truly begun.

14

The Beaumont family stepped back into the warm glow of Sage Manor, their shoulders heavy with the weight of the evening's events. Elara and Keelee followed closely behind, their faces calm but serious. The tension lingered in the air, though the house provided a brief sense of sanctuary from the mounting threat outside.

Sanodia, ever focused, paused at the doorway. "I need to check on the delivery I requested," she said, addressing the group. "I asked for all the Thymazincus the elders could spare. It's crucial we have enough in case any of the warriors are struck by Earthling bullets."

Gran Celia nodded. "You're doing incredible work, Sanodia. And I've confirmed the seedlings in the greenhouse are strong and healthy. You should take a look when you're able."

Sanodia's face softened in gratitude. "Thank you. I'll check the greenhouses as soon as I've inspected the delivery in the chamber. The elders promised it would be left to the side of the crystal gate. It's critical to ensure we're prepared."

Elara placed a hand on Sanodia's shoulder. "Your dedication is unmatched. Thank you for everything you're doing to keep all of us safe."

Keelee added with a solemn nod, "Your efforts are invaluable. We are fortunate to have you."

Sanodia offered them a small smile before excusing herself. She moved swiftly down the hall, her focus already on the tasks ahead.

As Sanodia disappeared into the hallway, Ridge turned to Gran Celia and gently pulled her aside. "Mama, how's Lorinda?" he asked quietly, his voice tinged with concern.

Celia placed a comforting hand on his arm. "Before I joined you all on the porch, I peeked in on her. She's still fast asleep, but her breathing is normal. That's a good sign. Her body and spirit are resting, Ridge. Give it time."

Ridge exhaled deeply, a weight visibly lifting off his chest. "That's a relief. I was worried."

Celia tilted her head, her perceptive gaze softening. "You care for her, son. More than you're willing to admit. And that's good. Origin always sends us who and what we need. The challenge is recognizing it, holding onto it, and treasuring it."

Ridge nodded, her words sinking in. "I understand, Mama."

Celia smiled and pulled him into a hug. "Good. Time and patience will heal her. She'll come back to us, Ridge. You just have to believe."

Before Ridge could respond, the sound of hurried footsteps echoed from the hall. Francis appeared, her face pale and her eyes wide with alarm. "You all need to come with me," she urged. "Now."

Francis led them into the media room, where Bethany stood frozen in front of the television. The glow from the screen illuminated her shocked expression as she stared at the broadcast.

"What is it?" Lincoln asked, his tone sharp.

Bethany didn't turn around. "The local news," she said, her voice tight. "They're airing footage from the fight at Lorinda's house this afternoon."

Everyone's eyes snapped to the screen. The video showed flames consuming the Rooney home, tendrils of shadow writhing in the firelight. The footage was shaky, likely captured from the military's surveillance drones. It panned to glimpses of the family fighting—Lynx's fire, Waverly's vortex, Ridge's earthen barriers. The energy and chaos of the battle were unmistakable.

"Unbelievable," Celia murmured, her voice laced with disbelief.

Ridge and Lincoln exchanged furious glances, both muttering curses under their breaths.

"What were they thinking?" Ridge growled. "Whoever made this decision has no idea what kind of panic this is going to cause."

"Or they do, and they just don't care," Lincoln said darkly. "This isn't just going to terrify the locals. Once this goes viral, it'll spread globally. Everyone's going to see it—people who don't understand what they're looking at. And that's going to lead to chaos."

The news anchor's voice was solemn as she narrated the footage. "...speculation about the source of these extraordinary phenomena remains unanswered. Military officials have yet to release a formal statement, but the video speaks for itself. Something unusual—and dangerous—is happening in the Pisgah National Forest."

Bethany shook her head, finally tearing her gaze from the screen. "Dangerous isn't the word for it. This will fuel fear, and fear will make everything worse."

Waverly stepped forward, crossing her arms as she stared at the screen. "This isn't just bad decision-making—it's reckless. The last thing we need is for people to start flocking to the forest, looking for answers. Or worse, for the General to use this as an excuse to escalate things even further."

Celia remained quiet, her head shaking slowly as she absorbed the scene. "Unbelievable," she said again, her voice filled with quiet frustration. "Just absolutely unbelievable."

Lynx, standing by the door, spoke up. "We need to get ahead of this somehow. If the General uses this footage to justify turning the forest into a combat zone, we're going to lose control of the situation."

Keelee, who had been watching silently, stepped forward. "I will contact the Tanzloran elders. Perhaps they can offer advice—or an alternative plan."

Elara nodded. "And I'll consult the Arcmyrin council. This isn't just an Earth issue anymore. It's affecting all of us."

Ridge clenched his fists, his jaw tight with anger. "We can't let this derail everything we've been working for. We've got warriors in place, plans in motion. We'll fix this."

Lincoln placed a hand on his brother's shoulder. "We will. But we need to move fast. If this video keeps circulating, it'll be out of our hands by morning."

Gran Celia finally turned from the screen, her expression resolute. "Then we don't wait. We act now. Gather everyone. It's time to figure out our next move."

As the family and their allies filed out of the media room, the weight of the broadcast lingered heavily in the air. The ominous footage on the television was a stark reminder of the escalating stakes. The corridors of Sage Manor, usually a haven of calm, seemed to hum with the urgency of their collective thoughts.

Ridge, walking beside Lincoln, exhaled sharply and muttered, "I guess no one's sleeping tonight."

"Nope," Lynx replied from behind him, his tone dry but resolute. "We're pulling an all-nighter."

Waverly, trailing just behind them, managed a tight smile. "Good thing we're used to long nights. Just another chapter in the saga of our lives."

Gran Celia, ever the steady presence, stopped at the bottom of the staircase and turned to face them. "Then let's make it a productive one. Every minute we waste is a minute the enemy gains ground. If the world wants to see a fight, let's make sure we're ready to give it one—and win."

Keelee and Elara exchanged approving glances. "She's right," Keelee said. "The council will be standing by for further updates, and we need to ensure we're prepared to respond to any new developments. Rest can wait."

Bethany, standing beside Francis, placed a hand on her hip. "We'll keep the coffee coming. No one's dozing off on my watch."

Francis nodded, her expression firm. "We've got this. Together."

Lincoln looked around at his family and their allies, his chest swelling with pride despite the chaos. "Alright," he said, his voice steady but commanding. "We regroup in the main hall. Everyone brings something to the table—updates, strategies, ideas. We need to be ten steps ahead of the Umbralox and anyone else who's watching."

As the group dispersed to gather their thoughts and resources, the atmosphere shifted. Determination replaced despair, and the hum of activity began to echo through the house.

The Beaumont family and their allies were ready to face the long night ahead—because if the world thought it was watching a battle, they would ensure it witnessed a victory.

The soft glow of the desk lamp illuminated the office just off the kitchen in Sage Manor, casting long shadows across the walls. Ridge and Lincoln sat side by side at the heavy oak desk, the rotary phone between them. Lincoln dialed the sheriff's number, his fingers methodical as Ridge leaned back in his chair, arms crossed, his expression tense.

"It's late," Ridge muttered. "You think he's even going to pick up?"

"He'll pick up," Lincoln replied without looking at him, the steady hum of the phone ringing in his ear. "He has to."

It took several rings before the line connected. A gruff, familiar voice answered. "Sheriff Marshall Bowen here."

"Sheriff," Lincoln said, exhaling a breath he hadn't realized he was holding. "It's Lincoln Beaumont. Sorry to bother you so late, but we've got a situation brewing, and I need your help."

There was a brief pause on the other end before the sheriff replied. "I figured you'd be calling. Saw the news tonight. I've been on the phone with the General all evening, trying to keep him from moving forward with his plan to militarize the forest."

Ridge leaned forward, his hands gripping the edge of the desk. "Marshall, we need you to do more than keep him at bay. You've got to stop him—and anyone else who thinks they can stroll into the forest and play hero. They have no idea what they're dealing with."

Lincoln nodded, picking up where Ridge left off. "This isn't just a wildfire or a rogue bear, Sheriff. The force we're fighting—the Umbralox—it's not of this world. It's dangerous in ways no one here can understand. And Earth's medical systems? They're not equipped to handle the kind of injuries this thing inflicts."

The sheriff let out a heavy sigh. "I get it, Lincoln. I do. But you've got to understand something: the General isn't the kind of man who takes no for an answer. He's got Congress breathing down his neck, and now with that footage airing, he's got a green light to do whatever he thinks is necessary. You're asking me to hold back a tidal wave with my bare hands."

Ridge slammed his palm on the desk, the sound reverberating through the small room. "Then use both hands! Marshall, you know us. You know we wouldn't ask for this if it wasn't life or death—for everyone. If the General gets his way, he's not just putting his soldiers in danger. He's putting every person in this area at risk."

The sheriff was silent for a moment, the weight of Ridge's words hanging in the air. Finally, he spoke, his tone cautious but sincere. "Alright. I'll do everything I can. But it's going to take more than words to keep people out of that forest. What do you need from me?"

"We need you to meet us," Lincoln said firmly. "Come out to Sage Manor. We can explain everything—what we're up against, what's at stake. You'll see why this can't become a military operation."

"When?" the sheriff asked.

"Now," Lincoln replied without hesitation. "We don't have time to wait, and neither do you."

There was a long pause, then the sheriff exhaled audibly. "Alright. Give me thirty minutes. I'll head over."

"Thank you," Lincoln said, relief softening his tone. "We'll be waiting."

The line went dead, and Lincoln set the receiver back on its cradle. He glanced at Ridge, whose knuckles were still white from gripping the desk.

"He's coming," Lincoln said.

Ridge leaned back, letting out a slow breath. "Good. Let's hope he gets here before the General does something stupid."

Lincoln stood, placing a hand on his brother's shoulder. "He'll listen. He has to."

Ridge nodded, standing as well. "Let's get back to the others. We'll need everyone ready when he arrives."

The two brothers stepped out of the office, the tension in the air thick as they prepared to face yet another challenge in the long night ahead.

15

Waverly followed Gran Celia up the grand staircase of Sage Manor, her curiosity growing with each step. Her grandmother's cryptic request for help had been intriguing, and now, as they entered Celia's sitting room adjacent to her master suite, Waverly's mind was racing with questions.

Celia closed the door softly behind them, turning to Waverly with an air of seriousness. "Take a seat, dear," she said, gesturing to the floral-patterned armchair near the window.

Waverly complied, her curiosity now fully piqued. "Okay, Gran, what's this about?"

Celia moved to stand in front of her, a slight smile playing on her lips. "Can you keep a secret?"

Waverly raised an eyebrow but nodded. "Of course, Gran. What is it?"

Celia held out her pinky, a playful twinkle in her eyes. "Pinky promise?"

Waverly couldn't help but laugh, her nerves easing slightly. "Gran, you're serious?"

"Dead serious," Celia replied, her pinky unwavering.

With a grin, Waverly extended her own pinky and locked it with her grandmother's. "Alright, I pinky promise. Now spill."

Celia's expression grew more somber as she moved to her writing desk in the corner of the room. Waverly watched as her grandmother opened one of the drawers and pulled out something unexpected—a sleek, modern cell phone.

Waverly blinked in disbelief. "Wait... what?"

Celia returned to her, holding the phone out like it was a hot potato. "I need your help to make a call on this thing. I don't know how to use it, but it was given to me for an emergency. And, well, I think we're in one now."

Waverly stared at the device, her mind reeling. Her grandmother had always been proudly low-tech, relying on the rotary phone in the office or simply driving to talk to someone in person. Seeing her with a cell phone was like spotting a fish climbing a tree.

"Gran, where did you get this?" Waverly asked, carefully taking the phone from her.

"It doesn't matter right now," Celia replied, brushing the question aside. "What matters is that we use it. Can you make sure it's working?"

Waverly turned the phone on, relieved to see it had about 40% battery life. "It's got power," she said, swiping to the contacts app.

Her breath caught when she saw the single name listed in the contact list: Charles P. Houston.

Waverly's eyes widened as she looked up at her grandmother. "Gran, this is... Charles P. Houston? As in, the Vice President of the United States?"

Celia nodded calmly, as though this revelation was no big deal. "That's right."

Waverly gaped at her. "Gran, why do you have a direct line to the Vice President? And why haven't I ever heard about this?"

Celia's gaze softened, and she sat down on the edge of the chair across from Waverly. "There are a lot of things about me you don't know, sweetheart. And that's by design. But trust me when I say, I've always had my reasons for keeping this a secret."

Waverly looked back at the phone, her mind racing. "You're telling me you've been sitting on this... this nuclear option and never thought to mention it?"

Celia chuckled softly. "Not everything is meant to be shared, dear. But this phone was given to me years ago by someone I trust implicitly. I was told only to use it in the direst of situations—when no other options remained. And I think we're there now, don't you?"

Waverly nodded slowly, still processing. "So, what do you want me to do? Call him and... what? Tell him about the Umbralox? About the portal?"

Celia leaned forward, her tone steady. "I want you to help me explain what's happening, in a way he'll understand and take seriously. Charles is a pragmatic man, but he's also a good man. If anyone in that administration can stop the General from turning this into a military disaster, it's him."

Waverly swallowed hard, staring at the contact on the screen. "Alright, Gran. Let's do this."

She tapped the name, and the phone began to ring. Celia leaned back, her hands clasped tightly in her lap, her calm demeanor belying the gravity of the moment.

As the ringing continued, Waverly glanced at her grandmother. "You're sure about this?"

"Absolutely," Celia replied firmly.

The line clicked, and a deep, measured voice came through. "This is Charles Houston."

Waverly handed the phone to her grandmother, her heart pounding as she watched Celia take it.

"Charles," Celia said, her tone warm but serious. "It's me—Celia Beaumont. I'm calling in that favor you promised me years ago."

Waverly's jaw dropped as she listened, her grandmother's calm confidence shining through. Whatever was about to happen, she knew one thing for certain: Gran Celia wasn't someone to underestimate.

The parlor of Sage Manor was alive with the soft clinking of coffee cups and the low hum of conversation as the Beaumont family gathered well past midnight. The weight of the evening hung in the air, but Francis and Bethany moved purposefully around the room, ensuring everyone had a cup of strong coffee in hand.

Gran Celia and Waverly settled into the upholstered chairs near the fireplace. The flames danced softly, casting flickering shadows across the walls. Gran Celia took a sip of her coffee, her sharp eyes scanning the room as she adjusted the shawl draped over her shoulders.

A sudden knock on the front door broke the uneasy quiet. Everyone but Ridge and Lincoln froze, their gazes darting toward the hall.

"Relax," Lincoln said, his voice calm. "That's the sheriff. I called him to come meet us. We need to talk about holding off the General and anyone else who thinks they can march into this situation uninvited."

Lincoln stood and made his way to the front door, his heavy boots echoing against the hardwood floor. Ridge leaned back in his chair, arms crossed, his face set in a grim expression. "It's already getting out of control," he muttered, "and it's not even half-past midnight."

Francis placed a steaming cup of coffee in front of him, patting his shoulder lightly. "Stay awake, stay sharp," she said. "We'll get through this."

Lincoln returned a moment later with Sheriff Marshall Bowen in tow. The sheriff's broad shoulders filled the doorway as he entered, his expression weary but resolute. He removed his hat, running a hand through his graying hair as he surveyed the room.

"Evening, folks," he said, nodding to the group as he took a seat near the center of the room.

"Sheriff," Gran Celia greeted, her tone polite but firm. "We appreciate you coming out here at this hour."

Bowen placed his hat on his knee, letting out a long sigh. "It's no trouble. Figured it was better to talk in person, anyway. Phones are practically useless with how much they've been ringing off the hook."

Bethany handed him a cup of coffee, which he accepted gratefully. After taking a sip, he set the cup down on the side table and leaned forward, resting his elbows on his knees. "Alright, here's where we stand," he began, his voice low and steady.

"The General is relentless. He's determined to bring in his troops as soon as possible. They've already started staging at the WNC Agricultural Center across from the airport. Military planes have been flying in all evening, bringing them in by the dozens."

The room grew noticeably tenser as the sheriff continued.

"The news is on top of it, of course. Every station has reporters camped outside the Ag Center. People are driving by, snapping pictures, sharing videos. They're calling it the government's answer to an alien invasion. And let me tell you, it's stirring up trouble. Phones at my department haven't stopped ringing. Folks are scared, curious, or both. And every law enforcement officer in Galen Valley is on duty with no leave until this crisis is over."

Waverly shifted uncomfortably in her seat. "What about other counties? Are they helping at all?"

Bowen nodded. "I've already reached out for reinforcements. Surrounding counties are sending what they can spare, and the state highway patrol is deploying their special teams as backup. We're stretched thin, but we're managing—for now."

"That's not enough," Ridge said, shaking his head. "It's spiraling out of control. You've got reporters and locals stirring up chaos, and the General's breathing down your neck with an army. All this, and it's not even morning yet."

Bowen gave a heavy nod, his face drawn. "I know. That's why I'm here. I need to know exactly what we're dealing with and how to stop this before it blows up—literally."

Lincoln leaned forward, his voice measured. "Sheriff, we're dealing with something far beyond what the General or the public can comprehend. If his troops come marching into that forest, they're going to be fighting something they can't see, can't understand, and definitely can't handle with conventional weapons."

Gran Celia added, her voice steady and commanding, "You've seen what the Umbralox can do, haven't you, Sheriff? The footage on the news showed enough to terrify anyone. But that's only a fraction of its power. If we don't handle this precisely, it won't just take the forest. It'll spread—unchecked."

Bowen's jaw tightened. "What do you need from me?"

Lincoln exchanged a glance with Ridge before answering. "We need you to stall the General. Buy us time. Keep the looky-loos out of the forest. If they get in there, they're not just risking their lives—they're putting the whole operation in jeopardy."

Bowen looked between them, weighing their words carefully. Finally, he nodded. "I'll do what I can. But you have to understand—this General doesn't take kindly to delays. If he gets the green light from Washington, there's not much I can do to stop him."

"Then we make sure he doesn't get that green light," Waverly said firmly.

Bethany, standing by the fireplace, crossed her arms. "And if he does?"

Ridge's eyes darkened. "Then we do what we've always done—we fight. But on our terms."

The room fell into a heavy silence, the only sound the faint crackle of the fire. Finally, Bowen stood, placing his hat back on his head. "I'll do my part," he said. "You just make sure you're ready to do yours."

Lincoln stood as well, shaking the sheriff's hand. "We will. Thank you, Marshall."

As Bowen headed toward the door, Gran Celia's voice stopped him. "Sheriff, remember this: the Beaumonts have never backed down from a fight. And we won't start now."

The sheriff nodded, tipping his hat before stepping out into the night. As the door closed behind him, the family sat in silence for a moment, the weight of the situation pressing down on them.

Finally, Ridge broke the silence, running a hand through his hair. "We've got a long night ahead of us."

Gran Celia lifted her coffee cup, her expression resolute. "Then we'd best make it count."

The atmosphere in the parlor was tense as the Beaumont family discussed their next move. Ridge sat with his elbows on his knees, a deep frown creasing his face. "I should call Madre again," he said, breaking the silence. "If anyone can reach Bronte Sutton, it's her. We need to know where he is and when he's getting here. We're running out of time."

Gran Celia, seated across from him, nodded thoughtfully but didn't respond immediately. Waverly, perched on the arm of Lynx's chair, glanced at her grandmother, noticing an unusual glint in her eye. Before she could ask about it, another knock echoed through the house.

Lincoln stood, his face set in a mix of determination and exhaustion. "I'll get it," he said, striding toward the door.

The family exchanged uneasy glances, each bracing for whatever news or visitor might come next. When Lincoln returned, Sheriff Marshall Bowen was right behind him, his heavy boots thudding against the floor as he strode purposefully back into the room. He dropped his hat onto the same side table as before and sat in his previous chair, his expression a mix of disbelief and amazement.

"Well," Bowen began, leaning forward with his elbows on his knees. "You're not going to believe this."

"What now?" Ridge muttered, sitting up straighter.

The sheriff exhaled sharply. "As I was getting into my car just now, the General called me directly. He told me that the President himself had just called him and ordered him to stand down for the next 72 hours. Not one military boot is to step into the Pisgah National Forest. And if that wasn't enough, the President also declared a no-fly zone over the entire area, so the General's 'birds' are grounded as of now."

The room fell into stunned silence, everyone staring at the sheriff as if he'd just announced that gravity no longer existed.

Gran Celia leaned back in her chair, sipping her coffee with a calm, unreadable expression.

Bethany was the first to speak, her voice tinged with disbelief. "You're serious? The President? A no-fly zone? A full stand-down?"

Bowen nodded. "Dead serious. I have no idea who managed to get into the Oval Office and make this happen, but it's official. You, your family, and your... specialist friends," he said, "have 72 hours to deal with this situation. I've been ordered to use whatever resources I have to keep the public out of the forest and ensure only the people you need get through. Galen Valley is at your disposal."

Lincoln leaned back in his chair, rubbing a hand over his face. "72 hours," he murmured, the words almost incredulous. "This changes everything."

Ridge whistled low, shaking his head in disbelief. "It's like we just hit the biggest lottery in history."

Everyone was buzzing with amazement, talking over each other in stunned excitement. But amid the commotion, Waverly caught Gran Celia's eye and noticed something—a quiet, knowing look and a subtle wink.

Waverly blinked, processing what she'd just heard. No way, she thought, her mind racing. The pieces clicked together, and she suppressed a grin. Don't ever mess with Gran Celia.

Her heart swelled with pride as she looked at her grandmother, who was now calmly sipping her coffee like she hadn't just orchestrated a direct intervention from the highest office in the land. Waverly felt a surge of gratitude and admiration. In that moment, she had never been prouder to be a Beaumont—or to be Gran Celia's granddaughter.

The sheriff stood, adjusting his hat and looking around the room. "I'll head back to the station and start coordinating roadblocks and patrols. If you need anything—or anyone—just let me know."

Lincoln stood to shake his hand. "We will. Thank you, Marshall. For everything."

The sheriff tipped his hat and left, the sound of his boots fading as he exited the house.

As the door closed behind him, the family turned to each other, the stunned silence giving way to a renewed sense of determination.

"This is it," Lincoln said, his voice steady. "We've got 72 hours. Let's get started."

Gran Celia smiled softly, the light of the fire dancing in her eyes. Waverly caught her gaze again, sharing a private moment of understanding. She couldn't help but think, Gran Celia isn't just the heart of this family. She's the force that keeps us standing.

16

Ridge, Lincoln, and Lynx descended the stone stairway into the chamber beneath the gazebo, their hurried footsteps echoing in the dimly lit area. They moved with purpose, their expressions a mix of determination and excitement. They could hardly believe the news themselves, but the urgency of the moment propelled them forward.

Keelee and Elara stood near the communicator orb, their holographic council members Draven and Sylvaris visible and deep in discussion. The tension in the room was palpable, the weight of their deliberations filling the air.

The Beaumonts burst into the chamber, drawing the attention of everyone present. Keelee and Elara turned to face them, their expressions shifting to surprise at the trio's energy.

"Lincoln," Keelee began, his brows furrowed. "What's going on? You look like you've just seen the portal collapse on its own."

"Not quite," Lincoln said, a wide grin breaking across his face. "But we've got news that's just as good."

Ridge stepped forward. "You're not going to believe this. The General's been ordered to stand down for 72 hours."

Elara blinked in disbelief. "What? Ordered by whom?"

"The President of the United States," Lynx chimed in, leaning against the nearest wall to catch his breath. "Sheriff Bowen told us. The President called the General directly. No troops, no military interference, and a no-fly zone over the entire forest."

Keelee and Elara exchanged incredulous glances. "How is that even possible?" Keelee asked.

Ridge shrugged, his grin undiminished. "We don't know, and frankly, we don't care. The important thing is, we've got three days to take down that portal and end this."

The holographic figures of Draven and Sylvaris, who had been silently observing, stepped forward. Draven's calm voice broke the momentary silence. "This is a significant development. A window of opportunity this large is rare in situations of this magnitude."

Sylvaris nodded, his fiery demeanor tempered by the gravity of the news. "The question is, how do you plan to use this time? The Umbralox will not wait idly."

Lincoln crossed his arms, his expression thoughtful. "We need to get to the falls immediately and start planning. We've already got warriors stationed there, and I'm thinking they might be able to help us figure out how to temporarily diminish the flow of the river."

Keelee tilted his head. "Diminish the river? Why?"

"To get access to the crevice behind the falls," Ridge explained. "If we can reduce the water flow, even for a short time, we can get into the small cavity behind the falls where the portal is anchored. That'll give us the space we need to set up for the demolition."

Sylvaris raised a hand, his holographic image flickering slightly. "Damming the river, even temporarily, will require precision. A misstep could cause flooding downstream."

Draven added, his voice steady, "But if done correctly, it could be a key strategic move. The Tanzloran warriors at the falls are well-equipped for such tasks. They can guide you to the optimal location for the dam."

Elara's eyes lit with realization. "Keelee, we should send a message to Callum immediately. Have him coordinate with the warriors at the falls to assist Lincoln and Ridge."

Keelee nodded. "Agreed. They'll need tools and reinforcements. I'll ensure Callum receives the instructions."

Lynx, who had been pacing the room, stopped and turned to Lincoln. "You're going to need me there too. My fire power can help clear debris or melt anything that gets in the way."

Ridge smirked. "You just want an excuse to set something on fire."

Lynx grinned back. "And?"

Elara raised a hand, her voice cutting through their banter. "Focus, gentlemen. The Umbralox will sense any disruption near the portal. You'll need to be prepared for resistance."

Keelee stepped toward the communicator orb, activating its surface with a gentle touch. The orb pulsed, sending a message to Callum at the falls. "I'll alert the warriors now," he said, his tone brisk. "They'll begin scouting the river for potential damming points."

Sylvaris leaned forward, his fiery gaze fixed on Lincoln. "And what of the demolition expert? Has he arrived?"

Lincoln sighed. "Not yet, but we're holding out hope. In the meantime, we're not waiting around. We've got the daggers, and we'll use them if we have to."

Draven's holographic image inclined his head. "Your resourcefulness continues to impress, Lincoln Beaumont. But remember, precision is paramount. If the portal is not collapsed inward, the consequences will be catastrophic."

"We know," Ridge said grimly. "We're not taking any chances."

Keelee's orb pulsed again, signaling that the message had been sent. He turned back to the group, his expression resolute. "Callum and his warriors are on it. They'll have a plan ready by the time you reach the falls."

Elara stepped forward, her gaze steady. "This is your moment. Use these 72 hours wisely. The fate of this planet—and the balance of the sister worlds—depends on it."

Lincoln nodded, his jaw set. "We'll get it done."

As the brothers turned to leave, Draven's voice called out one last time. "May Origin's wisdom guide you. The strength of Tanzlora and Arcmyrin is with you."

"And so are we," Elara added softly.

The Beaumonts left the chamber with renewed determination, the echoes of their footsteps fading as they ascended toward the surface. The countdown had begun, and there was no room for error.

Ridge's Jeep rumbled along the road leading to Looking Glass Falls, the predawn darkness still clinging to the forest. The headlights cut through the fog, illuminating the towering trees and rocky terrain. Inside the Jeep, Ridge drove with a determined focus, Lincoln sat in the passenger seat, and Lynx leaned forward between them from the back seat.

"Callum and the warriors should already be there," Lincoln said, breaking the silence. "Let's hope they've scouted the area upstream and have a spot in mind."

"They will," Ridge replied confidently, his knuckles tightening on the steering wheel. "Tanzlorans don't waste time."

"And neither do we," Lynx added, his tone lighter, though his posture was tense. "Let's just hope the Umbralox hasn't figured out what we're up to yet."

As they pulled up to the falls, the sound of rushing water filled the air, its roar a reminder of the power they needed to harness—or stop. Callum and a group of Tanzloran warriors stood at the base of the trail leading upstream, their forms silhouetted against the faint light of the approaching dawn.

Ridge killed the engine, and they all climbed out, greeted by the quiet but commanding voice of Callum. "Beaumonts," he said with a nod. "We've scouted a location upstream. It's not far, and it should allow for a temporary dam without causing significant downstream flooding."

"Good," Lincoln said, stepping forward. "Lead the way."

The group moved quickly along the riverbank, the sound of the falls growing fainter as they ascended. Callum pointed out a narrowing in the river, where large boulders and a natural curve in the land created the perfect spot to block the water's flow.

"This is it," Callum said. "We can stack stones here and reinforce them with the earth Ridge can bring up. It should hold long enough for you to work in the crevice behind the falls."

Ridge nodded, already envisioning the structure. "Let's mark the spot and get to work."

The group spread out, placing markers and examining the terrain. Ridge knelt by the water's edge, pressing a hand to the ground and focusing on the stability of the bedrock beneath. Lincoln stood a few feet away, studying the flow of the river, while Lynx surveyed the trees for materials they might use to bolster the dam.

Then it began—the faint, eerie whispering that sent chills down their spines.

The sound of tires crunching on the gravel driveway drew Bethany's and Waverly's attention as they sat on the porch, sipping their coffee and discussing the latest updates on the battle plans. A dark sedan came into view, pulling to a stop in front of the manor. The driver's door opened, and a tall, wiry man stepped out, his appearance catching them both off guard.

Bronte Sutton was an imposing figure despite his unkempt look. His long, scruffy hair and beard framed a face that seemed as much a part of the wilderness as the trees surrounding Sage Manor. His clothes were worn but sturdy, and his boots were caked with mud from miles of hard travel. He moved with a slow, deliberate purpose, seemingly unaffected by the grandeur of the estate before him.

Without a word, Sutton opened the trunk of his rental sedan, revealing a collection of duffel bags, backpacks, and various tools. One by one, he unloaded them, piling them haphazardly on the ground. Then he moved to the backseat, pulling out additional gear, which he added to the growing pile.

Bethany leaned forward, curiosity etched on her face. "Is that him?" she whispered to Waverly.

"Has to be," Waverly replied, her voice uncertain but intrigued.

As if unaware of their presence, Bronte walked to the edge of the yard, his gaze sweeping over the landscape. His eyes lingered on the pond, the gazebo, and the woods beyond. He stood still for a moment, hands on his hips, as though assessing the land itself.

Unbeknownst to Sutton, several Tanzloran warriors, stationed on the perimeter of the property, had already noticed his arrival. They stepped back into the shadows of the trees, watching his every move. Though they didn't sense immediate danger, the sight of an unfamiliar human armed with so much gear put them on edge.

One warrior activated a small communicator to relay a message to the other warriors on the backside of the property. "A newcomer has arrived. Appears non-threatening but heavily equipped. Monitoring closely."

Waverly and Bethany exchanged glances before setting their coffee mugs down and heading down the porch steps towards the visitor. Sutton hadn't noticed them yet, still standing at the edge of the yard and taking in the scenery.

"Can we help you?" Bethany called out, her voice carrying across the driveway.

Sutton turned slowly, his gaze locking onto them for a long moment before he started lumbering toward the porch. His gait was unhurried, his expression unreadable, but there was a calm intensity about him that made Waverly a tad wary.

He spoke right as he reached them, his voice low and gravelly. "Bronte Sutton. Heard you needed someone to implode a portal."

Bethany blinked, momentarily taken aback by his directness. "Uh, yes. We have been waiting on you."

Sutton nodded and gestured toward his pile of gear with a thumb. "Got everything I need right there. Now, where can I set up my tent?"

"Your... tent?" Waverly asked, startled.

Bethany frowned. "We've prepared a room for you inside the manor. You don't need to camp out."

Sutton shook his head firmly. "Nope. I don't do houses. Too boxed in. Prefer to sleep outside." He pointed toward the pond, his eyes narrowing as he studied it. "That spot over there looks nice. I'll set up there."

Bethany and Waverly exchanged incredulous looks. "You... want to camp out by the pond?" Waverly asked, still processing his unconventional request.

"That's right," Sutton replied, his tone leaving no room for argument. "Don't worry, I don't need much. Just a flat spot and some quiet."

Bethany sighed, still trying to wrap her head around the man's odd preferences. "Alright, Mr. Sutton, if that's what you want. But if you need anything—anything at all—just let us know. We've got food, supplies, whatever you might need."

Sutton nodded curtly. "Appreciate it. Now, if you'll excuse me, I've got work to do."

Without another word, he turned and strode back to his pile of gear. One by one, he slung the duffel bags and backpacks over his shoulders, carrying them toward the pond. Waverly and Bethany watched as he moved with surprising efficiency, staking out a flat spot and unpacking a compact tent.

"Well," Waverly muttered, still trying to process the encounter, "he's definitely not what I expected."

Bethany shook her head, half amused and half bewildered. "Me neither. But if he's as good at his job as everyone says, I guess he can camp wherever he wants."

As they turned to head back inside, they couldn't help but chuckle at the sight of Sutton meticulously setting up his tent by the serene pond, oblivious to the Tanzloran warriors watching him from the shadows and the sheer absurdity of the situation.

17

Lynx straightened, his eyes scanning the dark forest. "You hear that?"

The whispering grew louder, a haunting, guttural sound that seemed to come from every direction. The Tanzloran warriors tensed, drawing their laser daggers, their movements sharp and deliberate.

"It's them," Ridge muttered, rising to his feet. "The Umbralox knows we're here."

The first tendril lashed out from the shadows, slamming into a tree with enough force to splinter it. More followed, writhing and twisting as they emerged from the darkness, their inky blackness almost tangible.

"Positions!" Callum barked, his voice steady despite the chaos.

The warriors formed a defensive line, their laser daggers glowing faintly in the dim light. Ridge, Lincoln, and Lynx stepped forward, their powers already surging as they prepared for battle.

"Terraveta!" Ridge called, his voice firm and commanding. The ground beneath him rumbled in response, and sharp crystals erupted from the earth, slicing through the nearest tendrils with deadly precision. The Umbralox shrieked, the sound like nails on a chalkboard as the crystals disintegrated their shadowy forms.

Lincoln thrust his hands toward the river. "Mistara, we need you!" The water answered immediately, surging upward in a powerful wave that Mistara amplified into a small tidal force. The wave crashed into the advancing tendrils, pushing them back and scattering their masses.

Lynx grinned, his hands already glowing with fiery energy. "Ignissa, let's turn up the heat!" The fire spirit answered with a brilliant red-orange glow, magnifying Lynx's power. He unleashed a torrent of flames, incinerating the masses of Umbralox that surged toward him and the warriors beside him. The tendrils hissed and writhed as the fire consumed them, leaving only charred remnants in its wake.

The Tanzloran warriors moved in sync, their laser daggers cutting through the shadowy tendrils with precision. Each strike elicited a shriek from the Umbralox, the blades slicing through the darkness like hot knives through butter. The warriors worked in pairs, their movements fluid and disciplined as they held the line.

Despite their efforts, the Umbralox surged forward relentlessly, their numbers seemingly endless. Ridge planted his feet, calling on Terraveta again. Larger crystals erupted from the ground, forming barriers that slowed the tendrils' advance. "They just keep coming!" he shouted, sweat beading on his brow.

Lincoln sent another wave crashing into the enemy, Mistara's power amplifying its force. "We have to hold them here! We can't let them get to the falls!"

Lynx, his flames blazing brighter than ever, burned through another wave of tendrils. "Then let's make sure they regret showing up!"

The battle raged on, the combined efforts of the Beaumonts, the elemental spirits, and the Tanzloran warriors turning the tide. Slowly but surely, the Umbralox began to retreat, their tendrils recoiling into the shadows with each strike and blast. The air was filled with the acrid smell of smoke and the sharp tang of ozone from the laser daggers.

Finally, as the first rays of dawn broke over the horizon, the last of the Umbralox shrieked and disintegrated into the ground. The forest fell silent, the whispering gone, replaced by the gentle sound of the river and the distant roar of the falls.

Ridge lowered his hands, the crystals retracting into the earth. He took a deep breath, his chest heaving from the exertion. "Is it over?"

"For now," Callum said, his voice calm but wary. "They'll be back. The Umbralox doesn't give up easily."

Lincoln nodded, his hands still wet from the river. "But we held them off. That's what matters."

Lynx clapped Ridge on the back, a triumphant grin on his face. "Not bad, huh? Team Beaumont and company, still undefeated."

Ridge managed a tired smile. "Let's hope it stays that way."

The group began to regroup and assess the damage, the sunlight filtering through the trees a welcome sight after the long, dark night. The falls roared on, a reminder of the task still ahead. But for now, they had a moment of victory—and the promise of 72 hours to finish what they had started.

Bethany and Waverly entered the kitchen, their expressions caught somewhere between amusement and bewilderment. Gran Celia was at the counter arranging herbs and plants for Sanodia's herbal mixtures, her calm demeanor a stark contrast to the whirlwind going on around the area.

"Celia," Bethany began, setting her coffee mug down. "You won't believe this."

Celia turned to face them, raising an eyebrow. "What's happened now?"

"Bronte Sutton just arrived," Waverly said, her tone still carrying a note of disbelief. "He popped out of his car, unloaded a mountain of gear, and then asked us where he could set up his tent."

Celia frowned. "His tent? You mean to tell me he doesn't want to stay in the house? We prepared a room for him."

"Exactly!" Bethany said, throwing up her hands. "But he insisted. He wants to camp by the pond."

Celia shook her head firmly, already setting the plants and herbs aside. "Absolutely not. A guest of Sage Manor will not sleep outside in a tent when we have perfectly good beds inside this house."

Celia stepped out onto the porch, smoothing her apron as she walked. She spotted Bronte Sutton carrying several duffel bags and pieces of gear down toward the woods surrounding the pond. His long strides made it clear he had no intention of reconsidering his plans.

"Mr. Sutton!" Celia called out, her voice carrying easily across the yard.

Sutton paused mid-step, a tent pole slung over his shoulder. He turned to see Celia descending the porch steps, her determined expression unmistakable. He waited as she approached, standing among his half-unpacked gear with an air of patience.

"Ma'am," he said with a polite nod. "Something you need?"

"Yes," Celia replied, gesturing toward the house. "I am Celia Beaumont, welcome to Sage Manor. I wish to convince you to take the room we've prepared for you inside. You're a guest of Sage Manor, and we take hospitality seriously. I won't have you sleeping outside when we can offer you a comfortable bed."

Sutton gave her a small, appreciative smile but shook his head. "I mean no disrespect, ma'am, but I prefer to be outdoors. Always have. A roof over my head feels... confining."

"But it's going to get cold tonight," Celia argued gently. "And the ground isn't exactly forgiving."

"I've slept on worse," Sutton replied with a shrug, already kneeling to stake his tent into the ground. "I'll be fine. Besides, I don't plan to stay here long. Once I get my gear settled, I'm heading to the falls."

Celia crossed her arms, still unconvinced. "At least let us bring you a hot meal and some coffee."

Sutton glanced up at her, his hands deftly securing the tent's framework. "I appreciate it, ma'am, truly. But I don't need much. Just directions to the Beaumont boys."

"They're already at Looking Glass Falls," Celia informed him, her tone softening. "Ridge, Lincoln, and Lynx left earlier to scout the river."

Sutton stopped what he was doing, his sharp eyes meeting hers. "Well, then I'll just head that way."

He stood, brushing his hands on his pants and tipping his hat to her. "Thank you for the information. And for the offer of the room. You're a gracious host, ma'am, but I'll stick with my tent."

Celia sighed but couldn't help a small smile at his stubbornness. "Very well, Mr. Sutton. But the offer stands."

"I appreciate that," Sutton said, picking up a smaller duffel bag and slinging it over his shoulder. "Now, if you'll excuse me, I'll be heading to the falls. Got work to do."

Sutton walked briskly up the slope toward his rental sedan, leaving his tent fully set up in the woods by the pond. Celia followed at a slower pace, watching as he loaded a few carefully selected tools into the trunk. As he slid into the driver's seat, he tipped his hat to her one last time.

"Have a good day, ma'am," he said, his gravelly voice carrying a note of respect.

"Be safe," Celia replied. "The falls are no walk in the park right now."

Sutton grunted in acknowledgment, turned the key, and backed the car out of the driveway, heading toward the Looking Glass Falls. Celia watched until the sedan disappeared down the road before turning back toward the house. Her eyes wandered to the tent, and she shook her head with a mix of exasperation and amusement.

"Stubborn as a mule," she muttered as she made her way back to the porch.

The sun had risen fully over the Pisgah National Forest by the time Ridge, Lincoln, and Lynx made their way back to the viewing deck of Looking Glass Falls. The adrenaline from their battle with the Umbralox still coursed through their veins, but fatigue was beginning to creep in. As they emerged from the trail, the sight of Ridge's Jeep brought a sense of familiarity—but it wasn't alone.

Parked beside the Jeep was a dusty rental sedan, its tan paint flecked with dirt and leaves from the forest road. Two large, weathered duffel bags rested on the hood. Standing next to the car was a man who looked as though he'd stepped straight out of the wilderness.

Bronte Sutton was a tall, slim figure, his wiry frame wrapped in a flannel shirt and a worn canvas jacket. His boots were scuffed and caked with mud, jeans frayed at the hems, and his beard looked as though it hadn't seen a trimmer in well over a year. His shaggy hair fell into his face, and his piercing blue eyes squinted in the sunlight as the Beaumonts approached.

"Bronte Sutton, I presume?" Lincoln called, raising a hand in greeting.

The man didn't respond immediately, his sharp gaze sweeping over the three men. After a moment, he gave a single, curt nod.

"Thanks for coming," Ridge said, stepping forward and extending a hand. Sutton looked at it for a second before giving it a firm shake, his grip strong despite his lean build.

"Don't mention it," Sutton said in a low, gravelly voice, his words clipped. He glanced at the Beaumonts, then gestured vaguely toward the falls. "Portal's here?"

"Yes," Lincoln replied. "It's behind the falls, in a small crevice cave. We've been working on a plan to get to it and—"

Sutton held up a hand, silencing him. "Show me," he said simply, his voice devoid of curiosity or doubt.

Ridge raised an eyebrow at Sutton's abruptness but motioned toward the trail. "Alright, follow us."

Before Ridge could take the lead, Sutton grabbed one of his duffel bags, slung it over his shoulder, and picked up the second. Without another word, he strode past the Beaumonts and headed toward the trail leading down to the falls.

"Well, he doesn't waste time," Lynx muttered, exchanging a look with Ridge and Lincoln.

"Apparently not," Ridge replied, stepping aside to let Sutton pass.

Ridge, Lynx and Lincoln quickly fell in behind him, their boots crunching on the gravel as they followed the lanky demolition expert. Sutton moved with surprising ease, his long strides eating up the trail as though he'd walked it a hundred times before.

The roar of the falls grew louder as the group descended, the mist from the water hanging in the air like a fine veil. Sutton remained silent, his focus unwavering as he navigated the uneven terrain. The Beaumonts exchanged occasional glances but said little, unsure how to break the silence surrounding the enigmatic man.

As they reached the base of the falls, Sutton stopped abruptly, setting his bags down on a flat rock. He turned to Ridge, Lincoln and Lynx, his expression unreadable.

"Where's the entrance?" he asked.

Ridge pointed toward the wall of rushing water. "It's behind the falls. There's a narrow crevice that leads to a small cave. That's where the portal is."

Sutton grunted, then crouched down to unzip one of his bags. He pulled out a flashlight, a small tool kit, and a handheld scanner that looked like it had been cobbled together from spare parts.

"Stay here," he said, tucking the scanner into a pocket and slinging the flashlight around his wrist.

"Wait," Lincoln said, stepping forward. "You can't just go in alone. The Umbralox could still be active in there."

Sutton straightened, fixing Lincoln with a piercing stare. "You said you cleared it."

"We pushed them back," Ridge clarified. "But that doesn't mean they're gone. The portal is still active, and they could return at any time."

Sutton studied Ridge for a moment, then gave a slight nod. "Fine. You lead. I'll look."

Ridge sighed but didn't argue. "Alright. Follow me."

The group moved toward the falls, the mist soaking their clothes as they approached the wall of water. Ridge led the way, his movements steady and deliberate as he reached through the narrow crevice. The roar of the falls dampened slightly as they entered behind the falls, the air damp and heavy with the scent of moss and stone.

Looking into the crevice, the portal glowed faintly on the far wall, its dark, swirling energy casting eerie shadows on the tiny cave's walls. Sutton stepped up to peer inside, his flashlight cutting through the dimness as he surveyed the interior of the small cave.

"Stay back," he said, motioning for the others to give him space.

They complied, watching as Sutton moved closer to the opening of the crevice. He knelt down, running his flashlight over the ground and interior walls of the cave, his scanner beeping softly as he took readings. He muttered to himself occasionally, his voice too low to catch.

"What's he doing?" Lynx whispered to Lincoln.

"Figuring out how to implode it," Lincoln replied, keeping his voice low.

After several minutes, Sutton stood, tucking his scanner back into his pocket. He turned to face them, his expression still inscrutable.

"I can do it," he said simply.

Ridge let out a breath he hadn't realized he was holding. "Good. What do you need from us?"

Sutton gestured toward the portal. "Time. And quiet."

"That might be a problem," Lynx said, glancing toward the entrance. "The Umbralox isn't exactly known for staying quiet."

Sutton grunted, his gaze sharp. "Then keep them busy."

Lincoln nodded, his jaw set. "We'll handle the Umbralox. You handle the portal."

Sutton didn't respond, turning back to his work. Ridge, Lincoln, and Lynx exchanged determined looks before stepping back away from the crevice's entrance.

As they turned to climb back up the trail to the viewing deck, Ridge couldn't help but glance back at Sutton, who was already unpacking more tools from his bag. The man might be rough around the edges, but there was no denying his focus—or his skill.

"Think he can do it?" Lynx asked quietly.

Ridge nodded. "He wouldn't be here if he couldn't."

Lincoln placed a hand on Ridge's shoulder. "Then we make sure he gets the time he needs. No matter what."

The Beaumonts moved to stand guard near the falls, their resolve unshaken. They had 72 hours—and they intended to make every second count.

The soft morning light filtered through the curtains of Lorinda's bedroom suite at Sage Manor. Gran Celia quietly pushed open the door, her steps light but purposeful. She had been checking on Lorinda periodically, waiting for signs that her body and spirit were recovering from the trauma of the previous day.

As Celia approached the bed, her heart leaped with joy. Lorinda's eyes were open, and though she looked tired, there was a healthy flush to her cheeks that hadn't been there before.

"Well, good morning," Celia said warmly, her voice filled with relief. "It's so good to see those beautiful eyes of yours open. How are you feeling, dear?"

Lorinda blinked a few times, her lips curling into a faint smile. "Good morning, Celia. I... I think I'm okay." She shifted slightly, testing her strength. "A little sore, but my head feels clearer than it has in days."

"That's wonderful to hear," Celia said, settling into the chair beside the bed. She took Lorinda's hand in hers, giving it a gentle squeeze. "Your color looks so much better. You gave us quite the scare."

Lorinda's brow furrowed slightly, and she asked softly, "Where's Monica? Is she okay?"

Celia smiled reassuringly. "Monica is just fine, sweetheart. She's in the playroom with Bethany, Francis, Maya, and Maddox. They've all just finished breakfast and are having a grand time. That little girl of yours is as bright and lively as ever."

Lorinda exhaled in relief, her shoulders relaxing against the pillows. "Thank goodness. I was so worried about her."

"You don't have to worry about Monica," Celia said firmly. "She's safe here, and she's surrounded by people who love her. Now, the question is—how are you feeling? Do you think you could eat something? I'd be happy to prepare something for you and bring it up."

Lorinda shook her head gently. "Thank you, Celia, but I'd rather go downstairs and eat in the kitchen. It'll be nice to be around everyone again." She paused, her expression turning more determined. "And then I'd like to join them in the playroom."

Celia raised an eyebrow but smiled. "That's a good sign. Do you need help getting up and ready for the day?"

Lorinda shook her head again. "No, I think I can manage. I might need to take it slow, but I've got it handled."

"Well, if you're sure," Celia said, standing and smoothing her skirt. "Just take your time. There's no rush. And if you need anything, you call me, alright?"

Lorinda nodded, her eyes softening with gratitude. "I will, Celia. Thank you—for everything."

Celia leaned in and gave her a light kiss on the forehead before stepping back toward the door. But before she could leave, Lorinda's voice stopped her.

"Celia?"

"Yes, dear?" Celia turned, noticing a shadow of hesitation on Lorinda's face.

"Did I... Did I have a nightmare, or did my house really burn down?"

Celia's expression softened, and she came back to sit on the edge of the bed. She took Lorinda's hands in hers again, her tone gentle but firm. "I wish I could say it was just a nightmare, but no, dear. Your house did burn down. It was the Umbralox. They took it, but we fought them back. The house... it's gone, but you and Monica are here, and that's what matters."

Tears welled up in Lorinda's eyes, but she nodded, her voice steady despite the tremor in her lips. "Thank you for telling me the truth."

Celia smiled softly, brushing a stray hair from Lorinda's face. "You're stronger than you know, Lorinda. Take your time. We'll rebuild, one step at a time. And remember, you're not alone in this."

Lorinda nodded again, her resolve hardening as she wiped her tears. "I know. Thank you, Celia."

Celia stood, giving her one last reassuring smile before heading out of the room, leaving Lorinda to gather her strength. Though the pain of loss was still fresh, Lorinda felt the warmth of the family around her—and the determination to face whatever came next.

19

The roar of Looking Glass Falls filled the air as Ridge, Lincoln, and Lynx stood at the edge of the viewing deck, keeping an eye on their surroundings while Bronte Sutton worked diligently at the crevice entrance to the portal. The man had barely spoken since arriving, and the Beaumonts had quickly learned that Sutton wasn't one for idle chatter.

From down at the base of the falls, Sutton's gruff voice echoed up to them. "Hey! I need one of you down here. Now."

Lincoln glanced at Ridge and Lynx, then stepped forward. "I'll go," he said, heading toward the narrow trail leading down to where Sutton stood. He ducked through the spray, his boots slipping slightly on the slick rocks as he made his way to Sutton.

When Lincoln got to him, Sutton was crouched near the crevice opening, tools scattered around him. He didn't look up as Lincoln approached, instead gesturing toward the swirling energy inside the cave with a wrench in hand.

"You got someone small who can fit back there?" Sutton asked, his voice gruff as always.

Lincoln frowned, crossing his arms. "Depends. Why?"

Sutton straightened, brushing his shaggy hair out of his eyes. "I've got the placements marked for the explosives, but some of them are in tight spots. Too tight for me. I'll need someone small to crawl back there and set them. I can guide them step by step, but they've got to be steady and not afraid of getting close to this thing."

Lincoln considered the tight crevice behind the portal, its jagged edges and uneven surfaces illuminated faintly by the portal's glow. "Lynx might be able to do it. He's small enough, and he's good under pressure."

Sutton grunted, his version of agreement. "If he can't do it, we'll need a robotic arm rig. I don't have one with me, but I know a guy. Problem is, that'll take time we probably don't have."

Lincoln nodded, then turned to call out, "Lynx! We need you down here!"

A moment later, Lynx appeared at the crevice opening, ducking through the veil of water in front of the narrow cave entrance. "What's up?" he asked, shaking droplets of water from his hair.

Sutton turned to him, his sharp blue eyes assessing. "Think you can squeeze back there and follow instructions without screwing it up?"

Lynx raised an eyebrow. "I can squeeze into pretty much anything. And I don't screw up."

"We'll see," Sutton muttered, gesturing toward the tight space of the portal. "You'll need to place charges here, here, and here." He pointed to the glowing markers he'd managed to somehow place on the walls and floor, the locations just barely visible in the cramped space. "I'll give you the charges and talk you through setting them."

Lynx nodded, crouching to get a better look at the space through the crevice opening. "Yeah, I can do it. Just hand me what I need."

Ridge's voice called from the bottom of the trail where he had followed Lynx down, cutting through the roar of the falls. "Is the water flow causing a problem? If it is, we can dam up the river upstream. Buy you some time."

Sutton straightened, turning toward Ridge with an incredulous look. "Why the hell would I want to stop the waterfall?" he asked, his voice dripping with disdain. "That's the dumbest damn idea I've ever heard. I can work around it."

Ridge's face twitched with suppressed irritation, but he managed to keep his tone calm. "I'm just trying to help. Figured it might make things easier."

Sutton shook his head, muttering something unintelligible under his breath. "Leave the river alone. I've worked in worse conditions."

Lynx smirked, glancing at Ridge. "Guess that settles that."

"Yeah, I guess it does," Ridge muttered, stepping back up the trail a few steps to keep watch.

Sutton turned back to Lynx. "Alright, if you're going to do this, let's get started. The longer we sit here, the more likely we'll have that company you talk about."

Lynx nodded, his expression serious as he crouched near the portal. Sutton handed him the first explosive charge, a compact device with a blinking light on top. "This one goes in the lower corner," Sutton said, pointing. "Press it flat against the rock and twist the base until it locks. Got it?"

"Got it," Lynx said, taking the charge and carefully maneuvering into the tight space.

Lincoln stood nearby, ready to assist if needed, while Sutton watched intently, his hands on his hips. "Don't rush it," he said gruffly. "We only get one shot at this."

As Lynx worked, Ridge's voice echoed faintly from outside. "Let's just hope the Umbralox doesn't decide to crash the party while we're down here."

Sutton snorted. "If it does, you boys better be ready to hold the line. I've got enough on my plate without dodging shadow monsters."

Lincoln chuckled dryly. "Don't worry, Bronte. We're used to handling the Umbralox. You just focus on imploding this thing in on itself."

With Lynx carefully placing the charges and Sutton directing him step by step, the group worked quickly, their collective focus on the task at hand. The roar of the falls and the faint hum of the portal filled the cave, a constant reminder of the ticking clock they were all racing against.

The kitchen of Sage Manor buzzed with quiet activity as Elara, Sanodia, and Waverly worked at the long wooden table, jars, herbs, and tincture bottles spread out before them. The air was fragrant with the earthy, healing scents of their concoctions, and the morning sunlight streamed through the windows, casting a warm glow on their work.

The sound of soft footsteps caught their attention, and they looked up to see Lorinda standing hesitantly in the doorway. She was dressed simply, her hair pulled back, and though she still looked tired, her color was better, and there was a strength in her posture that hadn't been there the day before.

"Lorinda!" Waverly exclaimed, a wide smile spreading across her face. She set down the mortar and pestle she had been using and hurried over. "You're up! And you look great!"

Elara and Sanodia both rose as well, their expressions lighting up with relief and joy.

"It's so good to see you," Elara said warmly. "How are you feeling?"

"Better," Lorinda replied, her voice a little shy but steady. "Still a little tired, but I couldn't stay in bed any longer. I needed to see everyone. And Monica..." Her voice softened. "She's alright, isn't she?"

"Monica's perfectly fine," Waverly reassured her, taking her by the arm and leading her toward the breakfast nook. "She's with Bethany, Francis, and the kids. Now, sit. You're not doing anything until I get you some food."

"I can—" Lorinda started, but Waverly cut her off with a mock stern glare.

"Sit," Waverly commanded, pointing to the cushioned bench at the nook. "You've had enough excitement. Let me handle this."

Lorinda chuckled softly and obeyed, sinking into the seat. Sanodia poured her a cup of tea and set it in front of her with a kind smile.

"We're so glad to see you up and about," Sanodia said as she placed a small jar of honey next to the cup. "Your recovery is a blessing."

Elara nodded. "We've been worried, but it seems your strength is returning."

Waverly returned a few moments later with a plate of eggs, toast, and fruit, setting it in front of Lorinda with a flourish. "Eat up. You need your energy."

Lorinda smiled, touched by their concern. "Thank you. All of you." She picked up her fork and took a bite, savoring the food as the three women took their seats around her.

As she ate, she glanced at each of them, her brow furrowing slightly. "So... can someone bring me up to speed? What's been happening since yesterday? After... after my house burned down?"

Waverly exchanged a glance with Elara and Sanodia, then let out a low whistle. "Wow, where do I even begin?"

She leaned back in her chair, folding her arms. "Alright, here's the short version—or as short as I can make it. After we got you back here, Sanodia worked her magic to help you heal. The sheriff showed up. He told us the General was planning to bring in his troops and turn Pisgah National Forest into a combat zone."

Sanodia picked up the story. "Fortunately, your President intervened and issued a stand-down order. The General has 72 hours to stay out of the forest. It's a temporary reprieve, but it gives us time to deal with the portal."

"The portal?" Lorinda asked, her brow furrowing, still obviously suffering from the trauma.

Elara leaned forward. "The Umbralox is tied to a portal hidden behind Looking Glass Falls. That's where its power is concentrated. If we can destroy the portal—implode it inward—we can trap the Umbralox and stop its spread."

Waverly nodded. "That's where Ridge, Lincoln, and Lynx are now. They went out early this morning to scout the area upstream from the falls to see if they could temporarily dam the river. It would help give access to the crevice where the portal is."

Lorinda tilted her head, concern flickering across her face. "And they haven't come back yet?"

"No, but—" Waverly started, then stopped, her expression shifting. "Actually, they have been gone for a while."

Elara raised a hand, her voice calm. "If anything had happened, the warriors with them would have alerted us. No news is good news."

Sanodia nodded. "The warriors are vigilant. If there was trouble, we'd know."

Waverly frowned but nodded reluctantly. "You're probably right. Still, I wish they'd check in. Oh, and Bronte Sutton finally showed up. He is quite the character, refuses to lodge in the house. He prefers sleeping in a tent he set up near the pond."

Lorinda glanced between them, her worry clear. "Is he with Lincoln, Ridge, and Lynx at the falls? Are they safe out there? With trying to implode the portal and everything else going on?"

"They'll be fine," Elara said firmly. "The warriors are prepared, and the Beaumont men are... resilient."

Waverly smirked. "That's one way to put it."

Lorinda managed a small laugh, her tension easing slightly. "Well, I guess I'll have to trust that they'll come back in one piece."

"You don't have to just trust," Waverly said. "You're part of this now, Lorinda. We're all in it together."

Elara and Sanodia both nodded in agreement, their expressions warm and encouraging. Lorinda looked at each of them, a flicker of determination rising in her eyes. For the first time since the ordeal began, she felt a spark of strength—fueled by the family and allies who surrounded her.

"Then let's finish this breakfast," Lorinda said, her voice steady. "Because it sounds like there's a lot of work to do."

Just as Lorinda finished her last bite, the kitchen door leading to the patio creaked open. Rykas stepped inside, his towering figure framed by the soft morning light spilling in from the garden. His face was tense, his normally calm demeanor tinged with urgency.

"Elara," he said, his voice low but commanding. "I need you outside. There's trouble at the falls."

Elara immediately rose to her feet, her expression shifting to one of focus. "What kind of trouble?"

Rykas gestured for her to follow. "The warriors just sent word through the communicator orb. The Umbralox is active again. It's attacking the area around the falls—stronger this time. Ridge, Lincoln, and Lynx are still there."

Waverly pushed back her chair, already on her feet. "I'm coming too."

Elara hesitated for a moment but then nodded. "Fine. We may need your power. Sanodia, stay with Lorinda. We'll call for you if healing is needed."

Sanodia inclined her head, her expression calm but resolute. "Be careful."

Lorinda, still seated, reached out and grabbed Waverly's hand before she could leave. "Bring them back," she said softly, her eyes full of worry. "All of them."

Waverly squeezed her hand reassuringly. "I will. Don't worry."

As Waverly, Elara, and Rykas stepped out onto the patio, the gravity of the situation pressed down on them. The air felt heavier, the wind carrying a faint, unnatural chill that sent a shiver down Waverly's spine.

"What are we walking into?" she asked Rykas as they hurried across the garden.

"More tendrils," he said grimly. "Larger and more aggressive than before. The portal's energy seems to be amplifying them. The warriors are holding the line, but they won't be able to for long."

"And Ridge, Lincoln, and Lynx?" Waverly pressed.

"They're fighting," Rykas replied. "But they're outnumbered."

Elara quickened her pace, her voice steady despite the urgency. "We'll do what we have to. The portal must not remain unchecked."

Waverly's jaw tightened as they reached the garage. "Then let's move. We don't have time to waste."

With that, the three of them piled into Lincoln's truck with Waverly at the wheel, their resolve unshaken as she raced toward the falls.

20

The roar of the waterfall was deafening, but Lynx was focused entirely on the intricate task in front of him. Inside the cramped crevice behind Looking Glass Falls, he carefully maneuvered the compact explosive charge, following Bronte Sutton's instructions to the letter. Sweat trickled down his temple as he placed the device against the portal's shimmering, swirling energy.

"That's the last one," Lynx said, securing it. But as he did, the brightness of the portal flared unexpectedly, and the low humming that had been a constant background noise grew louder, vibrating through the stone walls.

"Uh... guys?" Lynx called out, his voice trembling slightly. "The portal's doing something. It's getting brighter."

Sutton, crouched just behind him, scowled. "What are you talking about? I'm not done yet."

Lynx didn't turn to look at him, his eyes fixed on the now-pulsing portal. The humming grew louder, almost a rhythmic thrum that resonated in his chest. "Portal's active!" he shouted, panic rising in his voice.

He scrambled to back out of the crevice, but Sutton, oblivious to the danger, was blocking the narrow entrance. "Where do you think you're going?" Sutton barked.

"Move!" Lynx yelled, his urgency cutting through Sutton's gruff tone. "It's activating! We need to get out now!"

Ridge and Lincoln, standing guard with the Tanzloran warriors outside the falls, heard Lynx's shout. Without hesitation, they sprinted toward the crevice. Ridge shoved Sutton out of the way, his strength sending the man tumbling backward. Sutton lost his footing on the slick rocks, his body crashing into the rushing river below. The sharp sound of his impact against the rocks echoed over the roar of the falls.

Ridge and Lincoln each grabbed one of Lynx's arms, yanking him out of the crevice just as the first massive tendril lashed out from the portal. The shadowy appendage whipped through the air, striking the rock face with a force that shook the ground.

Callum, ever watchful, was on the tendril in an instant. His laser dagger flashed as he slashed through the thick, writhing mass, severing it cleanly. The tendril disintegrated into a swirling black mist, but more poured out of the portal, each larger and more aggressive than the last.

"Move!" Callum roared, turning to the other warriors. "Hold the line!"

Ridge, Lincoln, and Lynx scrambled up the slippery trail on all fours, their breaths ragged as they clawed their way to safety. Behind them, Callum and his warriors fought valiantly, their laser daggers cutting through the seemingly endless tide of tendrils and tentacles.

One of the warriors noticed Sutton lying motionless on the riverbank, blood staining the rocks and water around him. He reached down, pulling the man out of the current and laying him on the bank. "Callum! The earthling is badly injured!"

Callum glanced over but didn't falter in his defense. "Leave him! Fight! If we fall, no one survives this."

The warriors continued their desperate battle, but the Umbralox forces were overwhelming. Tendrils surged from the crevice in waves, larger and more coordinated than any they had faced before.

At the top of the trail, Ridge, Lincoln, and Lynx stopped to catch their breath, turning back to see the chaos unfolding below them. "This is worse than anything we've seen," Lincoln muttered, his voice filled with dread.

He called out instinctively. "Mistara, we need you now!"

"Ignissa!" Lynx shouted, his hands already glowing with fire.

"Terraveta!" Ridge roared, slamming his hand into the ground.

The elemental spirits appeared in bursts of energy, their ethereal forms glowing with power. Mistara's cool, flowing presence surged through the river, amplifying its currents and washing over the tendrils to push them back. Ignissa's flames erupted in brilliant arcs, searing the writhing masses and reducing them to ash. Terraveta's power rose from the earth, jagged crystals shooting up to pierce through the heart of the Umbralox forces.

The Beaumonts began their descent back down the trail, their powers cutting a path through the chaos. Each step forward was hard-fought, the air thick with the acrid smell of burning tendrils and the eerie sound of their hissing shrieks.

Ridge's eyes darted toward Sutton, still lying motionless on the riverbank. To his horror, a massive tentacle was snaking its way toward the man, coiling around his legs. "No!" Ridge shouted. "Terraveta, help me!"

A sharp crystal shot up from the ground beside Sutton, slicing through the tentacle and causing it to recoil with a deafening hiss. Ridge reached Sutton's side and tore away the remaining tendrils, his hands trembling with urgency.

He knelt beside the man, his fingers searching for a pulse. "Sutton? Can you hear me?"

Sutton's eyelids fluttered, and he mumbled something incoherent.

"What? Speak up!" Ridge urged, leaning closer.

Sutton's voice was barely audible. "Blow..."

Ridge froze, realization dawning on him like a cold wave. "Blow?" His eyes darted to the crevice, where the explosives Lynx had just placed were still active. "Oh no..."

He shot to his feet, his voice thundering over the noise. "Everyone get away from the falls! Now! It's going to blow!"

The warning came just in time. The small cave behind the falls erupted in a deafening explosion, the force of the blast sending shockwaves through the air. Ridge threw himself over Sutton, shielding him as debris rained down around them. The explosion scattered the warriors and the Beaumonts, tossing them onto the riverbank and into the water.

When the dust settled, Ridge pushed himself up, coughing and disoriented. The mist around the falls thickened, swirling unnaturally, as if the air itself were alive. The faint hum emanating from the cave behind the cascading water grew louder, its pitch climbing with every passing second. Everyone exchanged alarmed glances. "What's happening?" Ridge asked, his voice tense.

Before anyone could respond, the ground beneath their feet trembled, a low rumble echoing through the forest. The water from the falls seemed to recoil for a moment, then surged forward with unnatural force. He looked toward the crevice, his heart sinking at the sight.

The explosion had left a gaping hole in the rock face behind the falls, and from that hole emerged a massive, pulsating mass of writhing tendrils and tentacles. The Umbralox influence poured out of the portal. It shimmered with an otherworldly iridescence, its tendrils slithering upward like grotesque snakes seeking the sky. As the entity grew larger, its mass began to rise above the treeline, casting an ominous shadow over the forest.

The Umbralox had taken a new form—a horrifying, writhing ball of darkness that hovered above the ground, its shadowy appendages spreading out like a living storm. It pulsed with malevolent energy, its tendrils reaching skyward as if to claim the very heavens.

Ridge's voice was hoarse as he yelled, "What is that?"

Lincoln and Lynx staggered to their feet, their eyes wide with shock. Lynx's hands lit with fire again, but even he hesitated at the sheer size of the creature.

Lincoln's heart sank as he watched the monstrous form coalesce into a singular, horrifying mass. "It's heading for the Pink Beds," he murmured.

Callum immediately reached for the communicator at his side. His sharp, commanding voice cut through the rising chaos. "This is Callum. Warriors at the Pink Beds, be on full alert. The Umbralox influence is heading your way. Activate laser knives to full intensity—you'll need it."

The communicator crackled as a voice on the other end responded. "Understood, Callum. We're ready to engage."

Callum turned to his warriors. "One of you go find Rykas and tell him he needs to mobilize the Arcmyrin forces to the Pink Beds area. This thing is growing stronger and it could infect the entire area."

The Beaumonts stood frozen for a brief moment as the Umbralox began its slow, menacing march in the air toward the Pink Beds area, Ridge turned to Callum. "We need to stop it there if that's where it lands. We can't let it spread any further."

Callum nodded, gripping his laser knife tightly. "We'll hold it as long as we can. But you know this battle won't end until the core is destroyed."

"Then we'll destroy it," Lincoln said firmly. "Whatever it takes."

The ground quaked again as the massive entity surged forward, its tendrils reaching out toward the surrounding trees. The forest seemed to recoil from the malevolent force, the air growing colder and heavier with every inch it advanced. A few stray tendrils lashed out, snapping branches and leaving a trail of decay in their wake.

"Everyone, move!" Callum barked. "Defensive positions now!"

The warriors sprang into action, their laser knives humming to life with a bright, searing light. The Tanzlorans formed a defensive line, slashing at the tendrils with precision. Each cut produced a sickening shriek from the entity, the severed tendrils disintegrating into ash.

Lincoln, Ridge, and Lynx joined the fray, their elemental daggers blazing with energy. Ridge called upon Terraveta, summoning sharp crystals from the earth to slice through the writhing mass. Lynx, his dagger glowing with Ignissa's fiery essence, unleashed bursts of flame that burned through the tendrils. Lincoln, with Mistara's guidance, sent torrents of water crashing against the advancing tendrils, forcing them back momentarily.

Despite their efforts, the entity continued to grow, its pulsating core visible through the dense mass of black. It was a bright red orb, veined with dark, throbbing tendrils that seemed to feed its power. The sight of it filled them all with dread.

At the Pink Beds, the warriors stationed there heard the faint rumble of the approaching Umbralox. Their communicator buzzed again, Callum's voice urgent. "It's moving fast. Prepare to engage. Do not let it breach the perimeter."

The lead warrior at the site responded, his voice steady but grim. "We're ready. We'll hold the line."

As the monstrous entity loomed closer, the warriors prepared for what would undoubtedly be the most critical battle yet. The fate of the forest—and perhaps the world—hung in the balance.

Callum and the remaining warriors regrouped, their weapons ready but their expressions grim. "It's not over," Callum growled. "This is just the beginning."

As the Beaumonts and their allies prepared for the fight of their lives, the Umbralox let out a deafening roar, shaking the ground beneath them all.

21

The truck skidded to a sudden stop in the middle of the road, gravel flying as Waverly slammed the brakes. Her heart pounded as she stared out the windshield, her mouth agape in shock. Above the tree line, a massive, pulsating ball of Umbralox influence loomed in the sky. Its shadowy tendrils writhed outward, their malevolent energy stretching ominously toward the Pink Beds area of Pisgah National Forest.

"What is that?" Waverly breathed, gripping the steering wheel so tightly her knuckles turned white.

Beside her, Elara leaned forward, her usually calm demeanor shaken. "It's worse than we thought. It's migrating—spreading."

In the passenger seat, Rykas was already unbuckling his seatbelt. "Stop the truck!" he barked.

"It's already stopped!" Waverly snapped, but Rykas was already halfway out the door. He jumped to the ground and took off running, his long strides carrying him swiftly toward the distant warriors. Waverly squinted and saw what had drawn him—Arcmyrin warriors emerging from the forest, racing toward the Pink Beds to confront the massive evil force.

"Rykas!" Elara called after him, but he didn't slow down.

Waverly shook her head in disbelief, her gaze flicking between the retreating figure of Rykas and the sinister ball of tendrils in the distance. "I can't just sit here," she muttered, slamming the truck back into gear. The tires screeched as she accelerated toward Looking Glass Falls, the tension in the air palpable.

As Waverly and Elara reached the parking area near the falls, the sight of Ridge's Jeep brought a flicker of hope. Waverly parked behind it and jumped out, Elara right on her heels. The sound of distant fighting echoed through the forest, mingling with the rush of the waterfall and the occasional shout of warriors.

They sprinted toward the viewing deck, their shoes pounding against the gravel trail. Just as they reached the clearing, they saw a group of figures ascending the trail from below. Callum and another Tanzloran warrior were carrying Bronte Sutton between them, the demolition expert's limp body a grim sight. Blood stained the side of Sutton's head, and his face was pale.

Behind them came Ridge, Lynx, and Lincoln, their clothes torn and faces streaked with soot and sweat. Two more Tanzloran warriors followed, one of them hobbling with the aid of his comrade, his leg clearly injured.

"What happened?" Waverly shouted, her voice breaking with urgency as she rushed to Ridge's side.

"It's gone," Ridge said, his voice rough with exhaustion. He gestured toward the falls behind them, where the shattered remnants of the portal's crevice were barely visible through the spray. "The portal's destroyed. But when it blew..." He trailed off, his eyes darkening and he pointed up in the air. "That thing came out of it."

"That thing is headed for the Pink Beds," Elara said, her voice sharp as she pointed toward the horizon. "Do you realize what's happening over there?"

"We know," Lincoln said grimly. "We can hear the fighting from here."

Waverly glanced at Bronte Sutton as Callum and the other warrior laid him down gently on the flat part of the trail. "Is he alive?"

"Barely," Callum said, his voice tight. "He hit his head on the rocks. He needs a healer, and fast."

Elara knelt beside Sutton, her hands glowing faintly as she placed them over his wound. "I'll stabilize him, but we need Sanodia to finish the job."

Waverly turned to Ridge and Lynx, her mind racing. "What about the other injured warrior?"

Callum motioned to the hobbling Tanzloran warrior being supported by his comrade. "He's hurt, but he'll live. The portal's destruction didn't come without a cost."

"We need to focus on the Pink Beds," Ridge said, his voice cutting through the noise. "If that thing keeps spreading, it won't stop there. It'll take the whole forest—and then the towns."

"And we don't have another portal to blame," Lynx added. "It's out in the open now."

Waverly felt a cold chill run down her spine. "We need to get the injured back to Sage Manor, regroup, and figure out a plan. We can't fight that thing head-on without backup."

"We don't have time to regroup," Ridge said, his tone sharper than usual. "The longer we wait, the stronger it gets."

Elara stood, her hands now stained with blood but her expression determined. "You're right. But we need the councils to weigh in. The forces we're facing are no longer isolated to one portal. This is an escalation we can't handle alone."

Callum nodded in agreement, his warrior instincts tempered by strategic thinking. "We'll send word to the warriors already positioned in the Pink Beds to hold the line. But we can't afford to lose more ground."

Waverly looked to Lincoln, her voice trembling. "What do we do?"

Lincoln's jaw tightened. "We fight. But we fight smart. Let's get Sutton and the injured warrior back to Sage Manor. Then we split forces—one group to defend the Pink Beds, the other to protect the manor."

"And the elemental spirits?" Elara asked.

"They're with us," Ridge said firmly. "They've already helped us this far. They'll help us again."

The group began their slow ascent back toward the parking area, the weight of their losses and the looming threat pressing down on them. Callum and his warriors carried Bronte Sutton and the injured Tanzloran with care, while Waverly walked beside Ridge, her heart heavy with worry.

When they reached the vehicles, the distant sound of fighting was louder now, the faint glow of the Umbralox influence visible over the treetops. Waverly clenched her fists, her frustration bubbling over. "We can't let this thing win. Not after everything we've already lost."

"We won't," Ridge said, his voice steady. "But we need to be ready for the worst. Whatever it takes, we stop it here."

As they loaded the injured into the vehicles and prepared to head back to Sage Manor, a sense of grim determination settled over the group. The battle was far from over, but they knew one thing for certain: they were the last line of defense, and they wouldn't let the forest—and their world—fall without a fight.

The convoy arrived at Sage Manor in a blur of motion and urgency. Gran Celia was already standing on the porch, her sharp eyes scanning the approaching vehicles with a mix of concern and determination. As soon as the doors opened, Callum and the other Tanzloran warriors carefully carried Bronte Sutton and their injured comrade up the steps. The latter was groaning softly, his leg wrapped in makeshift bandages, while Sutton remained eerily silent, his head lolling to one side.

"Bring them in," Celia commanded, her voice firm but warm. "We'll set up in the media room. It's the largest space."

Inside the manor, Lorinda stood near the staircase, a hesitant but resolute look on her face. Her color had returned, and she looked steadier than she had in days. "Celia, let me help. I'm a nurse. I can assist with whatever they need."

Celia nodded, a small smile breaking through her stern expression. "Good. We'll need every set of hands we can get."

Callum, still carrying the injured Tanzloran, turned to Celia. "I'll send two of my warriors to assist you with setting up. Just tell them what you need."

"Perfect," Celia replied. "Follow me."

Celia led Callum and two of his warriors to the media room, a spacious area typically reserved for family gatherings and movie nights. Now, it was to become a hospital ward. The warriors gently laid the injured Tanzloran and Sutton on the long sectional couch while Celia surveyed the room with a critical eye.

"We'll need to clear this out and make space for at least eight," she said. "We'll use the attic cots and extra bedding. The bathroom across the hall will be Sanodia's healing station."

"Understood," Callum replied. He motioned to his warriors. "Go with her. Get whatever is needed."

Lorinda rolled up her sleeves, her gaze shifting to the injured warrior. "I'll stay here and start assessing their conditions. Where's Sanodia?"

"She's on her way," Celia said over her shoulder as she hurried to the attic with the warriors.

Meanwhile, Bethany and Francis had already started bringing in baskets filled with herbal mixtures and tinctures from the chamber's stores, setting them up in the bathroom to create a functional healing station. Sanodia arrived moments later, her calm presence steadying the room. She immediately began examining Sutton, her glowing hands hovering over his injuries as she murmured a healing incantation.

Elara arrived shortly afterward, carrying more supplies from the chamber. "Sanodia, let me assist," she said, setting the bundles on the counter.

Together, the two healers worked seamlessly, their combined knowledge and energy directed toward stabilizing the injured. Lorinda moved between them, checking vitals and administering basic care where necessary. The team's coordination turned the chaos into a quiet hum of activity.

Meanwhile, Lincoln, Keelee, Ridge, Lynx, and Waverly sped through the forest in Lincoln's truck, the urgency in the cab thick as the distant sounds of battle grew louder. The closer they got to the Pink Beds, the more oppressive the atmosphere became. The massive ball of Umbralox influence loomed over the treetops, its pulsating tendrils casting eerie shadows across the landscape.

As they reached the edge of the battlefield, Lincoln slammed the truck into park, and they jumped out, weapons and powers ready. The Tanzloran and Arcmyrian warriors were already in the thick of the fight, their blades and energy weapons cutting through tendrils as fast as they appeared. But for every one they destroyed, two more seemed to grow in its place.

"This is insane," Waverly said, her voice barely audible over the cacophony of battle. "How do we even fight this thing?"

"We don't have a choice," Ridge growled, summoning Terraveta as he slammed his hands into the ground. Sharp crystals erupted upward, piercing through a cluster of tendrils and momentarily pushing them back. "We take it out, or it takes us out."

Keelee's calm but commanding voice cut through the chaos. "Stay focused. Aim for the tendrils closest to the base. We weaken it from the foundation."

Lincoln called on Mistara, using her power to amplify a wave of water that surged toward the heart of the Umbralox mass. The water struck with force, but instead of disintegrating the tendrils, it was absorbed, the energy fueling the monstrous form.

"It's feeding on the elements!" Lynx shouted, his flames faltering for a moment as he realized his attacks were only making the creature grow larger.

"We're fueling it," Waverly said, panic creeping into her voice. "Everything we throw at it, it just gets stronger!"

Keelee's blade flashed as he struck at a cluster of tendrils trying to encircle a Tanzloran warrior. "Then we need a new strategy. This isn't just a battle—it's an infestation."

Ridge, his breathing labored, called out, "We can't hold this position much longer! We need reinforcements!"

Waverly spun, creating a vortex of wind to push back a wave of tendrils threatening to overtake them. "I don't think reinforcements will make a difference unless we figure out how to cut off its source of power."

Keelee nodded grimly. "We need to isolate it. Cut it off from everything it's using to grow."

"That includes us," Lincoln said, his tone sharp. "We're only making it worse."

Lynx, his flames flickering, glared at the massive form. "If we can't attack it, how do we stop it?"

Keelee's eyes narrowed as he studied the creature, its writhing mass pulsating with a sickening rhythm. "We need the councils. This thing is beyond anything we've faced. It's not just feeding—it's evolving."

The group retreated slightly, regrouping near the edge of the forest as the warriors continued to hold the line. Waverly looked at the others, her face pale but determined. "We need serious help."

Lincoln nodded, "If we don't figure this out fast, there might not be anything left to save."

Ridge stared at the monstrosity, his jaw clenched. "We'll figure it out. We have to."

As the battle raged on in the distance, the group prepared for what felt like an impossible task—facing an enemy that seemed to thrive on their every effort. The Pink Beds burned, their beauty overshadowed by the relentless march of the Umbralox. And though the battle seemed hopeless, the Beaumonts and their allies knew one thing for certain: the fight wasn't over.

22

The distant wail of sirens signaled the arrival of reinforcements as the district ranger's truck, followed by two deputy vehicles and the sheriff's SUV, roared into the Pink Beds parking lot. Dust and gravel sprayed as the convoy came to a screeching halt, their headlights cutting through the haze of smoke and shadow that hung over the battlefield.

Sheriff Marshall Bowen stepped out first, adjusting his hat as his sharp eyes scanned the chaos before him. Beside him, District Ranger Seth Dixon and his deputies exited their vehicles, their faces grim as they took in the sight that stretched beyond the tree line.

The massive ball of Umbralox influence loomed in the open field beyond the picnic shed, a pulsating, writhing nightmare of black, snake-like tendrils and tentacles. The air was thick with the stench of decay, and the ground trembled faintly beneath the sheer weight of the creature's presence. Tendrils lashed out in all directions, striking at anything that moved too close, while Tanzloran and Arcmyrian warriors fought to hold their positions.

"What is that?" Sheriff Bowen muttered, his voice low and filled with disbelief.

"Hell on Earth," Dixon replied grimly, his hand instinctively going to the radio on his belt.

One of the deputies, wide-eyed and pale, whispered, "It's like something out of a horror movie..."

Before anyone could respond, Keelee, Ridge, and Lincoln approached the group, their clothes torn and streaked with dirt and ash. Behind them, Lynx and Waverly stood close, their exhaustion evident but their resolve unbroken.

The Tanzloran and Arcmyrian warriors were no longer keeping to the shadows or trying to conceal their identities. The enormity of the situation had stripped away any need for subterfuge. At this point, people from other planets were the least of anyone's concerns—it was the massive, malevolent ball of evil towering in the field that demanded all their focus.

The sheriff's gaze lingered for a moment on Keelee and the warriors, his expression unreadable, but he quickly returned his attention to the Beaumonts. "Lincoln, what am I looking at?"

"This," Lincoln said, gesturing toward the monstrosity, "is the Umbralox—a force of pure malevolence from another world. It's consolidated here, which is both good and bad. Good because it's no longer spreading across the forest. Bad because it's concentrated all its power in one place."

"And the warriors?" Dixon asked, glancing at Keelee and the others, whose alien features and weapons now stood out starkly under the artificial lights of the parking lot.

"They're our allies," Ridge said firmly. "Without them, we wouldn't have gotten this far."

"They're from Tanzlora and Arcmyrin, sister planets to Earth," Waverly explained quickly, her voice calm but firm. "They're here to help us stop this thing."

Dixon raised an eyebrow but nodded slowly. "At this point, I don't care where they're from as long as they can fight that... whatever it is."

Keelee stepped forward, his expression resolute. "The only thing that matters now is defeating this enemy. If we fail, Earth, Tanzlora, and Arcmyrin—all of our worlds—are at risk."

Dixon nodded, the weight of the situation pressing heavily on his shoulders. "Then let's focus on what needs to be done."

As the deputies set up their posts and the warriors regrouped, the Beaumonts huddled together with Keelee and the other leaders. The massive ball of Umbralox influence continued to pulsate in the distance, its tendrils reaching for the sky like a living storm.

"We're going to need everything we have," Keelee said, his tone grim. "The elemental spirits, the warriors, and the daggers."

Waverly nodded, gripping her dagger tightly. "And precision. If we don't time our strikes right, it'll just keep regenerating."

"Callum's warriors are ready," Keelee added. "And Rykas is already leading the Arcmyrians in an effort to weaken its base."

Lincoln glanced at Ridge. "Ready for round two?"

Ridge gave a humorless chuckle. "I was born ready."

The group turned back toward the battlefield, the enormity of the task ahead weighing heavily on them. But as they prepared to face the Umbralox once more, their resolve was clear. This was their forest, their world—and they would fight to their last breath to protect it.

The air in the parking lot of the Pink Beds was heavy with tension as the battle raged in the field beyond. The massive ball of writhing Umbralox tendrils loomed like a dark storm, its pulsating energy casting an eerie glow against the treetops. Warriors stood ready, their blades and energy weapons gleaming under the faint light of the moon, while the Beaumont family, the sheriff, and the district ranger waited for their next move.

Keelee, standing at the edge of the group, closed his eyes and took a deep breath. He didn't use his telepathic abilities often—it required an immense amount of focus and energy. But now, with time running out and the stakes higher than ever, he knew he had no choice. He needed the Tanzloran council.

Turning to Callum and another warrior, Drexel, Keelee gestured for them to step closer. "I need your help to amplify my frequency. The council must know what's happening here, and I can't reach them alone."

Callum nodded immediately, stepping forward without hesitation. "Of course. Whatever you need."

Drexel joined them, his face calm but focused. "We're with you."

Keelee glanced briefly at the others. Lincoln, Waverly, Ridge, and Lynx stood nearby, their expressions a mix of curiosity and concern. Behind them, Sheriff Bowen, Ranger Dixon, and their deputies watched with wide eyes, their unease evident.

"What are they doing?" Bowen asked, his voice low.

"They're reaching out to their council," Lincoln explained, his tone steady despite the strange circumstances. "The Tanzloran elders are their planet's leaders—wise, ancient beings with a connection to the spiritual and elemental forces of their world."

Dixon frowned, his eyes darting between Keelee and the warriors. "And they can just... talk to them from here?"

"It's telepathy," Waverly added. "Keelee doesn't use it often, but when he does, it's powerful. You're about to see something incredible."

The law enforcement officers exchanged skeptical glances but remained silent, their attention fixed on Keelee and the warriors.

Keelee, Callum, and Drexel formed a tight circle, their hands extended but not touching, their palms facing inward. Keelee closed his eyes again, his breathing slowing as he began to focus his energy. Callum and Drexel followed suit, their faces relaxing as they tuned their frequencies to match Keelee's.

The air around them seemed to shift, growing still and charged with an unseen energy. A faint hum began to resonate, soft at first but gradually building, as if the atmosphere itself were vibrating in response to their efforts.

Lincoln spoke quietly to the sheriff and ranger. "What you're feeling right now—that's them harmonizing their frequencies. It's how they reach across the distance between worlds."

"I'll be damned," Bowen muttered, his voice laced with awe.

A faint blue glow began to emanate from the center of the circle, spreading outward like ripples on a still pond. The hum intensified, and the glow grew brighter, flickering as though struggling to maintain its form.

"It's working," Waverly whispered, her eyes wide.

Keelee's voice rang out, low and resonant, though his lips didn't move. "Council of Tanzlora, this is Keelee. I reach out to you with urgency and the gravest of news."

The glow wavered, then solidified, forming the faint but unmistakable shapes of the Tanzloran council. Though their holographic forms were flickering and translucent, their presence was undeniable. The council elders, draped in flowing robes that shimmered with an ethereal light, stood in a half-circle, their expressions calm but alert.

"Keelee," Elder Brakar said, her voice rich and layered with wisdom. "We feel your distress. Speak, and we will listen."

Keelee opened his eyes, his voice steady as he began to explain. "The portal at Looking Glass Falls has been destroyed, but the explosion released the Umbralox's energy in a new form—a massive, pulsating entity that has consolidated all its strength into a single point in this forest. It is stronger than anything we've faced before."

Callum stepped forward, his voice firm. "Our warriors are holding the line, but it regenerates faster than we can destroy it. It absorbs elemental energy, which only makes it grow stronger."

Lincoln chimed in, addressing the council directly. "This thing is no longer a hidden threat. It's out in the open. If we can't stop it here, it won't just destroy the forest—it'll spread, and Earth won't be able to contain it."

The sheriff, who had been silent up to this point, stepped closer, his hat in his hands. "I don't know who you are or what this thing is, but we need answers. How do we kill it?"

Elder Brakar closed her eyes briefly, as if searching for the right response. When she opened them again, her gaze was grave. "The Umbralox has become a singular entity. Its strength lies in its unity. To defeat it, you must shatter that unity—divide its essence so that it cannot regenerate."

Waverly frowned. "Divide it? How? Every time we strike it, it just grows back."

"You must weaken its core,"Elder Lumorith said. "Its heart is hidden within its mass. Locate it, sever its connection to the rest of the entity, and it will collapse."

Drexel spoke up, his tone measured. "Do we have the tools to do that? Or the time?"

Lumorith hesitated. "You have allies and the power of the elemental spirits. Use them wisely. But be warned—once the core is exposed, the Umbralox will lash out with all its remaining strength. You must strike quickly and decisively."

Keelee nodded, his resolve firm. "Thank you, elders. We will act immediately."

The holographic forms began to fade, their light dimming. "May the strength of Tanzlora be with you," Elder Brakar said as the connection broke.

As the glow faded, the sheriff and ranger stood in stunned silence, their skepticism replaced by awe.

"Well," Bowen said finally, his voice gruff. "I didn't expect to see anything like that today."

Dixon ran a hand through his hair, shaking his head. "You and me both. But if what they're saying is true, we've got a shot at stopping this thing."

Keelee turned to the group, his expression grim but determined. "We have our orders. The warriors will draw its focus while we search for the core."

"And once we find it?" Waverly asked.

"We destroy it," Lincoln said simply, his jaw set. "No matter what it takes. Does everyone have their dagger?"

"Yes!" Waverly confirmed with Ridge and Lynx echoing her answer.

The group moved quickly, rallying the warriors and organizing their next steps. As the battle loomed ahead, their resolve hardened. The endgame was clear—find the heart of the Umbralox and destroy it before it destroyed them.

23

The media room at Sage Manor buzzed with subdued urgency, transformed into a makeshift healing ward. The air was filled with the sharp scent of herbs and tinctures as Sanodia worked tirelessly over Bronte Sutton. The demolition expert lay pale and motionless on one of the cots, his breathing shallow. Across the room, the injured Tanzloran warrior rested on another cot, his color already returning thanks to Sanodia's expert care and the medicinal herbs brought from Tanzlora.

Lorinda hovered nearby, her brow furrowed with concern. She had seen plenty of injuries in her time as a nurse, but the sight of Sutton's pallor and the sluggish rise and fall of his chest unsettled her deeply. "He's lost too much blood," she said softly, her voice edged with frustration. "I can't stop thinking that what he really needs is a hospital. He needs a transfusion."

Sanodia looked up briefly, her hands glowing faintly as she pressed healing energy into the laceration on Sutton's head. The bleeding had stopped, but the wound was deep, and the herbs she packed into it weren't enough to undo the damage completely. "I have done what I can," she said, her tone calm but tinged with regret. "Our remedies are powerful, but they were not designed for Earthlings. His body is not responding as it should."

Elara, seated nearby and watching intently, folded her hands in her lap. "This is beyond what we prepared for. I defer to those with knowledge of Earthling healing."

Celia, who had been quietly observing, stepped closer to Lorinda. "What do you think, dear? Can he recover here, or should we send him to the hospital?"

Lorinda hesitated, her eyes darting to Sutton's ashen face. "If this were a Tanzloran or Arcmyrin warrior, I'd say let Sanodia finish her work. But Bronte's body needs something we can't provide—blood. The herbs and hands are helping, but they're not enough."

Sanodia nodded solemnly, stepping back from Sutton and wiping her hands on a cloth. "If you believe his best chance is at your hospital, then I will not oppose you. My work here has reached its limit."

Francis entered the room, her presence immediately softening the tension. "Bethany and I have the kids settled in the playroom," she announced before noticing the serious expressions around her. "What's going on?"

"We're deciding what to do about Bronte Sutton," Celia explained. "Sanodia's done all she can, but Lorinda thinks he might need a hospital."

Francis's gaze shifted to Sutton, her brow furrowing as she took in his pale complexion. "If he's lost blood, it would be foolish not to send him. We can't risk his life just to keep him here."

Celia nodded slowly, her lips pressed into a thin line. "I agree. He's a human, and he needs human care."

Lorinda stepped forward, determination in her eyes. "I'll go call for an ambulance."

Francis gave her an encouraging nod. "Good. We need to act fast."

Lorinda turned and left the room, heading toward the office with quick, purposeful steps. The sound of her footsteps echoed faintly through the hallway as the others exchanged concerned glances. None of them could have foreseen the chain reaction that would follow her call.

In the quiet of the office, Lorinda picked up the rotary phone and dialed 911. Her hands trembled slightly as she spoke to the dispatcher, giving Sutton's condition and the address of Sage Manor. She didn't think twice about the information going out over the scanner—it was standard procedure. But what she didn't know was who else was listening.

In a mobile command center parked near the WNC Agricultural Center, General Adamson sat with his team, poring over maps of the Pisgah National Forest. The 72-hour stand-down order grated on him, but he had reluctantly complied, awaiting further instructions from higher up. He was, however, monitoring every piece of information that came through local and emergency channels.

The moment the call came across the scanner—"Male, mid-50s, severe blood loss, head injury, en route from Sage Manor"—Adamson's head snapped up. His mind raced, piecing together the implications. Sage Manor was at the heart of the forest, near where the suspected activity had been reported.

He slammed his hand on the table, causing his aides to jump. "I don't care about that damn 72-hour stand-down. We're rolling out. Destination: Pisgah National Forest."

An aide hesitated. "But, sir, the President's—"

Adamson cut him off with a glare. "If the President wants to court disaster, that's his choice. I'm not waiting around while something dangerous festers in my jurisdiction. Move out."

In the media room, Lorinda returned, her expression both relieved and anxious. "The ambulance is on its way. They'll be here soon."

Celia gave her a reassuring smile, though her own unease was evident. "You did the right thing."

Sanodia stood beside Sutton's cot, her hands still faintly glowing as she continued to channel what energy she could into him. "I hope their methods will succeed where mine have not."

Francis placed a comforting hand on Lorinda's shoulder. "We'll get him the help he needs."

As they waited for the ambulance, the group turned their focus back to the Tanzloran warrior, who was sitting up and already looking much better. His recovery was a stark contrast to Sutton's, a testament to the effectiveness of Sanodia's treatments on her own kind.

"It's incredible how quickly he's healing," Francis remarked, glancing at the warrior. "I wish it could be the same for Bronte."

"The human body is different," Elara said softly. "It does not respond to our methods as naturally."

The sound of distant sirens cut through their conversation, growing louder as the ambulance approached. They all turned toward the door, relief mingling with apprehension.

What none of them realized was that their decision to save one man's life would draw the attention of a far greater force—a force they weren't yet ready to confront. As the ambulance neared Sage Manor, so too did the convoy of military vehicles that General Adamson had ordered into action.

The battle for Pisgah was far from over.

The hum of the ambulance siren grew louder as the vehicle approached Sage Manor, cutting through the stillness of the estate. Lorinda and Gran Celia stood on the porch, arms crossed, waiting anxiously as the flashing lights illuminated the gravel driveway.

Sanodia and Elara had decided to assist the Tanzloran warrior who had been injured into the kitchen to prepare a meal for him and to keep all of them out of sight of the paramedics so as not to alarm them.

The ambulance came to a halt, and two paramedics jumped out, pulling a stretcher from the back. Lorinda stepped forward, meeting them halfway.

"Where is the patient?" one of the paramedics asked, her voice brisk and professional.

"Inside," Lorinda said, gesturing toward the manor. "Follow me."

The group quickly made their way into the media room, where Bronte Sutton lay motionless on the cot. His breathing was shallow, and his complexion had taken on an alarming pallor. One of the paramedics knelt beside him, checking his pulse and vitals while the other began setting up an IV.

Lorinda leaned in, her voice calm but firm. "He has a large laceration on his scalp, and he's lost a lot of blood. The bleeding has stopped thanks to our care, but I'm worried about how much he's already lost. He hit his head on a rock during a small demolition job that went wrong."

She deliberately kept her explanation vague, omitting any mention of portals or otherworldly evil. The truth was too complex—and too dangerous—for outsiders to understand. "You might want to x-ray him for skull fractures and check for internal bleeding. His pallor is concerning."

The paramedics nodded, taking in the information as they worked efficiently to stabilize Sutton. One of them glanced up at Lorinda. "What about next of kin? Does he have any family we should contact?"

Lorinda hesitated for a moment before replying. "You can list Celia Beaumont as his emergency contact for now," she said, gesturing toward Celia, who stood nearby with a reassuring smile. "She's the closest thing he has right now."

Celia stepped forward and handed the paramedics a note with her contact information. "Please keep us updated," she said warmly. "We want to make sure he gets the best care possible."

The paramedics exchanged a quick glance before nodding. "Of course. We'll take good care of him."

With Sutton secured on the stretcher, the paramedics began to wheel him toward the ambulance. Lorinda followed close behind, her heart heavy with worry. As they reached the porch, she paused, placing a hand on the stretcher. "Thank you," she said softly. "For taking care of him."

The paramedics gave her a brief nod before loading Sutton into the ambulance. As the back doors closed, Lorinda stepped back, wrapping her arms around herself as she watched them prepare to leave.

The ambulance pulled away from Sage Manor, its sirens wailing as it sped down the driveway. As the vehicle neared the forest entrance, a sight they hadn't anticipated came into view.

A military convoy was stationed at the edge of the forest, a line of vehicles stretching across the entrance. Soldiers moved with purpose, their faces grim as they prepared for deployment. General Adamson stood at the front, his stance rigid and commanding as he barked orders to his men.

The paramedics exchanged uneasy glances as they slowed the ambulance slightly, their eyes widening at the sight of the massive military presence. The soldiers barely paid attention to the ambulance as it passed, their focus entirely on their preparations.

"What's going on here?" one of the paramedics muttered.

"No idea," the other replied, gripping the steering wheel tightly. "But it looks serious."

As the ambulance disappeared down the road, the military convoy remained a looming presence, a stark reminder of the mounting tension in the Pisgah National Forest.

The Pink Beds were a frenzy of tension as the helicopters' distant thrum filled the air, growing louder with each passing second. Tanzloran and Arcmyrian warriors exchanged uneasy glances, their focus momentarily shifting from the writhing mass of the Umbralox to the approaching military force. Ridge, Lincoln, Waverly, and Lynx stood among them, their expressions grim as the impending clash between Earth's forces and the supernatural threat loomed.

A deputy's voice crackled over Sheriff Bowen's radio, cutting through the oppressive air. "Sheriff, the military convoy is on the move. ETA to Pink Beds is fifteen minutes, and they've got helicopters in the air heading straight toward you."

The words hit Bowen like a jolt of electricity. "Dammit," he muttered, his jaw tightening. "They're going to make this worse."

Waverly turned to him, alarm clear in her voice. "What do we do? If those helicopters get too close—"

"They'll be destroyed," Keelee said bluntly, stepping up beside her. "The Umbralox doesn't distinguish between enemies. It will lash out at anything that threatens it."

"I'm not letting that happen," Bowen said firmly. He turned to his deputies. "Stay here and keep everyone updated. I'm going to stop that convoy."

Without waiting for a response, he climbed into his patrol car, his radio blaring with updates from his team. The tires screeched as he pulled onto the main road, heading straight for the convoy's route.

24

General Adamson's convoy rolled through the forest with precision and purpose, a line of military vehicles bristling with firepower and personnel. The general sat in the lead vehicle, his expression set in stone as he reviewed the latest updates. The Umbralox's presence, coupled with the reports of alien warriors and inexplicable phenomena, had him on edge. He didn't like mysteries, and he didn't like being told to wait.

As the convoy rounded a bend, Adamson's expression darkened. A sheriff's patrol car was parked sideways across the narrow road, its lights flashing defiantly. Sheriff Bowen stood in front of it, arms crossed, his posture a clear message: You're not going anywhere.

Adamson's lead vehicle screeched to a halt, followed by the others in the convoy. Soldiers spilled out of their vehicles, their weapons at the ready. Adamson stepped out, his face red with fury.

"What the hell is this?" he barked, marching toward Bowen. "Sheriff, get that car out of my way, or I'll have it towed out by force."

Bowen stood his ground, his voice steady but firm. "General, you can't go any further."

"Excuse me?" Adamson's voice rose, his eyes narrowing dangerously. "This is a federal operation. I'm here to secure this forest and neutralize whatever threat is inside it. You have no jurisdiction to stop me."

"With all due respect, General," Bowen shot back, "this isn't a threat you can neutralize with firepower. If you charge in with helicopters and troops, you're going to lose people. I'm trying to save lives, not get in your way."

"Save lives?" Adamson sneered. "You've got a monster running wild in your backyard, and you're worried about my troops? Stand down, Sheriff, or I'll have you arrested."

Before Bowen could respond, the sound of another vehicle approached. Lincoln's truck skidded to a stop behind the patrol car, sending a cloud of dust into the air. Lincoln and Ridge jumped out, hurrying toward the escalating confrontation.

"General," Lincoln called, raising his hands in a placating gesture. "We need to talk."

Adamson rounded on him. "Haven't you done enough? Obviously this is over you and your family's heads. Time to quit playing little boy alien games and let the men handle it."

"I refuse to let you goad me," Lincoln said, keeping his voice steady. "This forest is my family's backyard. We have protected it for decades. I know what you're up against, and I'm telling you—Sheriff Bowen's right. You can't just roll in there with firepower and expect to win."

Adamson's glare shifted to Ridge, who stood beside Lincoln with a similarly grim expression. "And you are?"

"Ridge Beaumont," he replied. "We've been dealing with this thing longer than you have, and I can tell you, bullets and missiles aren't going to do a damn thing except make it stronger."

"Stronger?" Adamson's voice dripped with skepticism. "Are you seriously telling me this thing feeds on firepower?"

Lincoln nodded. "Yes. It absorbs energy—physical, elemental, it doesn't matter. You need to understand what you're dealing with before you send your men in."

Adamson folded his arms, his glare unwavering. "Why should I believe any of this? You expect me to stand down based on the word of some locals and... what? Your alien friends?"

Ridge's temper flared, but Lincoln placed a calming hand on his shoulder. "Look, we get it," Lincoln said. "You don't trust us. But you've seen the damage this thing is doing. You've seen what's out there. You need to come and see it for yourself before you send those helicopters any closer."

Adamson looked unconvinced. "And what's to stop this thing from lashing out at me if I get close?"

"It won't," Lincoln assured him. "Not if you don't provoke it. Call off your helicopters and hold your troops back. Come with us to see what we're up against."

Adamson hesitated, his expression conflicted. Bowen seized the moment. "General, you're a smart man. You wouldn't send your troops into a battle blind. This is no different. Take the time to see what you're dealing with before you make a decision you can't take back."

The general's jaw tightened, his gaze flicking between the sheriff, the Beaumonts, and the soldiers waiting behind him. Finally, he exhaled sharply. "Fine. I'll take a look. But if this is some kind of ploy to waste my time..."

"It's not," Lincoln said firmly. "You'll see."

Adamson turned to his radio. "Ground the helicopters and hold the convoy here. I'm going with them."

The soldiers exchanged uneasy glances but followed their orders. The helicopters, whose distant thrum had grown ominously close, began to veer away, the sound receding into the distance.

Arriving at the Pink Beds, the scene that greeted Adamson was unlike anything he had imagined. The massive ball of Umbralox influence writhed and pulsed in the field, its tendrils lashing out like living nightmares. Warriors and deputies worked together to hold the perimeter, their weapons and elemental powers barely keeping the entity at bay.

Adamson stepped out of the truck, his face pale but composed. "What the hell is that?"

"The enemy," Ridge said grimly. "Now do you see why we're telling you firepower isn't the answer?"

Adamson stared at the monstrosity, his disbelief warring with the evidence before him. Finally, he nodded, his voice tight. "I see. Now tell me how the hell we're supposed to fight it."

The makeshift command center in the Pink Beds parking lot buzzed with activity. Tents had been hastily erected, military personnel shuffled between vehicles, and monitors flickered with surveillance footage of the massive Umbralox writhing in the distance. The faint hum of generators underscored the tension in the air. Despite the layers of preparation, the enormity of the threat in the field loomed heavily over everyone.

The Beaumonts—Lincoln, Ridge, Lynx, and Waverly—arrived together, their faces set with grim determination. Keelee and Elara walked closely behind, their dignified presence contrasting with the hustle of Earth's forces. Callum and Rykas had remained on the frontlines, directing their warriors as they hacked away at any tendrils or tentacles that dared slither beyond the perimeter.

General Adamson stood near the largest tent, his posture rigid as he observed a group of soldiers monitoring the Umbralox's activity through high-powered scopes. When he spotted the Beaumonts approaching, he turned, his expression unreadable but clearly skeptical.

"Let's hear it," Adamson said curtly as they neared. "You've got one chance to convince me not to bomb that thing into oblivion."

Lincoln stepped forward, his calm yet commanding voice cutting through the tension. "General, I understand your instinct to use brute force. But this isn't something you can just blow up. The Umbralox feeds on energy—whether it's elemental, physical, or even emotional. If you attack it head-on with missiles or gunfire, you'll only make it stronger."

Adamson's eyes narrowed. "And how exactly do you know that?"

"Because we've seen it happen," Ridge interjected, his tone sharper than his brother's. "We've fought this thing before on Tanzlora. Every time we attacked without a plan, it grew stronger, adapted, and fought back harder."

"Tanzlora?" Adamson repeated, his disbelief clear. "You're telling me this thing came from another planet?"

"Yes," Keelee said, stepping forward. His calm demeanor seemed to radiate authority. "The Umbralox is not of Earth. It is a malevolent force that seeks to consume and destroy. It has already devastated parts of my planet and that of my allies. We came here to stop it from doing the same to yours."

The general's gaze flicked to Keelee, his skepticism not entirely gone. "And you're... what? An alien warrior?"

Keelee inclined his head slightly. "I am the envoy of Tanzlora, and these are my warriors. We have dedicated our lives to eradicating the Umbralox. But we cannot do it alone."

Adamson crossed his arms, his eyes scanning the group. "So what exactly are you proposing?"

Lincoln exchanged a glance with Waverly, who nodded. Together, they laid out the plan.

"The Umbralox's strength lies in its unity," Waverly began. "Right now, it's consolidated in that massive form because it knows it's safest that way. If we can divide it—force parts of it to break away from the main mass—it becomes vulnerable."

"Divide and conquer," Ridge added. "Once it's fragmented, it can't regenerate as easily. That's when we can strike."

Adamson frowned. "And how do you propose to divide it?"

"Through coordinated strikes," Keelee explained. "Your troops and our warriors can work together to isolate segments of the Umbralox while the Beaumonts and the elemental spirits focus on locating its core. The core is its heart—its lifeline. Destroy that, and the entire entity will collapse."

Adamson's expression remained doubtful. "You're asking me to risk my men on a plan based on... what? Magic?"

"It's not magic," Keelee said firmly. "It's strategy. And it's the only way to save your planet."

The sheriff, Marshall Bowen, and District Ranger Seth Dixon stepped up to join the conversation, their presence adding a layer of weight to the discussion. Bowen's voice was steady but forceful as he addressed Adamson.

"General, I've seen what this thing can do. If we go in guns blazing, we're all dead. These people"—he gestured to the Beaumonts and their allies—"they know what they're talking about. You've already seen the devastation. Are you really willing to ignore their experience and risk making this thing unstoppable?"

Dixon chimed in. "And let's not forget—this is a national forest. If this thing spreads, it's not just the forest we're losing. It's the towns, the people, everything. We need to work together on this."

Adamson's jaw tightened, his gaze flicking between the group and the monstrous mass of the Umbralox in the distance. After a long, tense silence, he exhaled sharply.

"All right," he said grudgingly. "We'll try it your way—for now. But if this thing gets out of hand, I'm pulling the plug on your plan and taking over."

Lincoln nodded, extending a hand. "That's all we ask. Let's work together."

Adamson stared at the hand for a moment before shaking it briefly. "Don't make me regret this."

25

With the truce in place, the group began strategizing. Callum and Rykas were called over to discuss how the warriors and soldiers could collaborate. Maps were spread out on a table, marking the areas where the Umbralox's tendrils had been sighted.

"We'll keep slashing at the tendrils to prevent them from spreading," Callum said. "But we'll need your troops to hold the perimeter and provide cover."

Adamson nodded. "My men can handle that. What about the core?"

"That's where we come in," Waverly said. "Once we've weakened its defenses, we will go in with the daggers. The elemental spirits will help amplify our power to strike at the heart."

Adamson raised an eyebrow. "Daggers? Spirits? You're really leaning into the whole alien warrior thing, huh?"

"They work," Ridge said bluntly. "And you'll see for yourself soon enough."

As the meeting continued, the tension began to ease slightly. Soldiers and warriors exchanged cautious but respectful nods as they moved to their assigned positions. The sheriff and his deputies worked alongside the district ranger to ensure that curious civilians were kept far from the area.

As the sun dipped lower on the horizon, casting long shadows across the forest, the command center settled into a tense but focused rhythm. The Beaumonts stood together near the edge of the parking lot, watching the distant Umbralox as its tendrils writhed and pulsed.

"This is it," Lincoln said quietly. "Everyone's finally on the same page."

"For now," Waverly said, her voice tinged with caution. "Let's just hope it holds."

Ridge glanced at the warriors patrolling the perimeter. "It'll hold. It has to. We don't have another choice."

As the group turned back toward the command center, the massive shadow of the Umbralox loomed behind them—a dark reminder of the battle that lay ahead.

Lorinda sat at the desk in the office of Sage Manor, her fingers tapping nervously against the old rotary phone. The warm aroma of coffee lingered in the air, but she was too anxious to drink the cup Bethany had placed in front of her. Finally, the line connected, and a familiar voice answered.

"Robin! It's Lorinda," she said, relief flooding her tone.

"Lorinda, hey!" Robin replied, her voice bright but tinged with curiosity. "We've been wondering about you. The ER's been buzzing about your friend. What's going on out there?"

Lorinda exhaled, relieved to hear a friendly voice. "It's... a long story. But I need to check on Bronte Sutton. How's he doing?"

Robin chuckled softly. "You're lucky I'm on shift, or you'd probably still be waiting for someone to track down his chart. Give me a second."

There was a pause as Robin shuffled through some paperwork, then returned to the phone. "Okay, here we go. First, the good news: no skull fractures, which is honestly a surprise given the size of that laceration."

Lorinda smiled faintly. "That is good news."

"They did thorough x-rays and scans, and everything looks clear. The laceration itself was nasty but has been cleaned out and stitched. It's quite the topic of conversation around here. Everyone's curious about the mix of herbs and plants that stopped the bleeding. It's not something we see every day in the ER."

Lorinda laughed softly, though her nerves still fluttered. "I'll have to explain that later. What else?"

"No internal bleeding, thankfully," Robin continued. "But he did need a transfusion. He was severely dehydrated too, so we've got him on fluids. His color looks much better now, though, and he's stable. The doctors are optimistic he'll make a full recovery."

A weight lifted from Lorinda's chest. "That's such a relief. Thank you, Robin."

"Of course," Robin replied warmly. Then her tone shifted, taking on a curious edge. "But I have to tell you, Lorinda, Bronte's been... well, a little strange."

"Strange?" Lorinda's brow furrowed. "What do you mean?"

"Well, since he's been semi-conscious, he's been making these odd beeping noises. At first, we thought it might be a breathing irregularity or something. But one of the older nurses swore up and down it sounded like Morse code. We even checked to see if he might have some kind of military record, but so far, nothing's come up."

"Morse code?" Lorinda echoed, trying to make sense of it. "That's... unusual."

"Unusual is putting it lightly," Robin said with a laugh. "Oh, and one more thing—you might want to warn him when he wakes up fully. We had to cut off and shave his hair and beard to properly clean and stitch him up. He looked like a mountain man when he came in. Hopefully, he won't be too irate about the change."

Lorinda chuckled, imagining Bronte's reaction. "I'll make sure to soften the blow when I see him."

"You might want to do it sooner rather than later," Robin added. "The doctors expect him to regain full consciousness in the next day or so."

"Thanks, Robin. I really appreciate you keeping me in the loop."

"Anytime, Lorinda. And hey, if you get a chance, drop by and explain those herbs. They've got half the ER talking."

"I'll do that," Lorinda promised. "Take care."

"You too," Robin said, and the line went silent as Lorinda hung up.

Lorinda sat back in her chair, her mind racing. Relief washed over her at the news of Bronte's recovery, but the mention of beeping and Morse code left her puzzled. It was just one more mystery in an already overwhelming situation. Taking a deep breath, she resolved to bring the update to the rest of the family and, when the time came, figure out what secrets Bronte Sutton might still be hiding.

The playroom at Sage Manor was alive with the cheerful chaos of children. Maya and Maddox were constructing an elaborate tower of blocks, their giggles ringing out as Monica provided enthusiastic advice on how to make it taller. Bethany and Francis sat on the plush rug, occasionally offering assistance while Gran Celia observed from a cozy chair by the window, knitting something intricate and colorful.

The door creaked open, and Lorinda stepped in, her face carrying a mix of relief and curiosity. Gran Celia looked up, immediately noting her expression. "Well, dear, what's the news?"

"I just got off the phone with Robin," Lorinda began as she moved to sit on the edge of the couch. The chatter of the children briefly faded as the adults turned their attention to her. "Bronte's stable. No skull fractures, no internal bleeding. They've stitched the laceration and given him a transfusion. He's severely dehydrated, but they're confident he'll make a full recovery."

"That's wonderful news!" Francis exclaimed, her hands clasping together.

Maddox looked up from the tower they were building. "Who's Bronte?"

"A friend," Lorinda said with a small smile, ruffling his hair. "He's at the hospital getting better."

Monica tilted her head, curious. "Is he coming here?"

"Maybe," Lorinda replied. "Once he's better."

Gran Celia nodded approvingly. "Sounds like Robin and her team are taking good care of him. Anything else we should know?"

Lorinda hesitated, then added, "Robin did mention something... unusual. Bronte's been making these strange beeping noises while he's semi-conscious. One of the older nurses thinks it sounds like Morse code."

Bethany and Francis exchanged a look, their eyebrows raising in unison. "Beeping noises?" Bethany repeated. "Like actual Morse code?"

"That's what they said," Lorinda confirmed. "They don't know what to make of it. And, oh, they had to shave his hair and beard to treat him properly. Robin said he looked like a mountain man before." She chuckled softly, imagining Bronte's reaction when he wakes up.

Bethany leaned forward, her eyes alight with intrigue. "That might not just be some weird unconscious habit. It could be connected to him being a Starseed."

Francis nodded eagerly. "Exactly. If he really is a Starseed, it's possible that whatever entity or higher frequency he's aligned with is trying to communicate with him—or even help him heal."

Gran Celia raised an eyebrow, pausing her knitting. "Help him heal? From where? Across the galaxy?" There was a teasing note in her voice, but the skepticism was evident.

"Why not?" Francis replied, her tone serious. "We've already seen so much we once thought impossible. Tanzlorans and Arcmyrins are real. They've shown us there's more out there. Why is it so hard to believe that other entities might exist, too?"

Bethany chimed in, "Think about it. Most people on Earth don't even believe in life beyond our planet. But we've seen firsthand that it's real, and not just the destructive kind like the Umbralox. Good beings exist too. If Bronte is a Starseed, he might be connected to something—someone—that we can't even comprehend."

Lorinda looked doubtful, folding her arms. "You're saying something out there could be... what? Talking to him? Healing him?"

"Exactly," Francis said, her voice rising with excitement. "Maybe whatever entity he's connected to senses his injury and is intervening in some way. That beeping could be their version of communication."

Gran Celia put down her knitting, a sly smile tugging at her lips. "I'm not saying it's impossible. But you're making quite the leap."

Bethany crossed her arms, narrowing her eyes playfully at Celia. "Oh, come on, Celia. Of all people, I'd think you'd be open to the idea. After everything this family has seen and done, you can't possibly think the three sister planets are all there is."

"Exactly!" Francis added. "We've already shattered the illusion that Earth is alone in the universe. Who's to say there aren't more beings out there, ones we haven't met yet?"

Gran Celia's smile widened as she leaned back in her chair. "I didn't say I don't believe it. I just enjoy watching you two try to convince me. You're very passionate."

Bethany and Francis exchanged a glance, both slightly exasperated and amused. "You're impossible, Celia," Bethany said with a laugh.

"Not impossible, dear," Celia replied with a twinkle in her eye. "Just pragmatic."

The room grew quiet for a moment as the adults considered the possibility. The children resumed their game, their laughter a gentle backdrop to the conversation.

Finally, Lorinda broke the silence. "I suppose it doesn't really matter what's causing it, as long as Bronte recovers. But it's a lot to think about."

Bethany smiled warmly. "Exactly. And maybe one day, we'll know for sure. Until then, we can only keep an open mind."

Gran Celia nodded, her smile softening. "And keep doing what we do best—protecting what's important."

The room returned to its comfortable rhythm, but the conversation lingered in the air, leaving each of them with a sense of wonder about the possibilities that lay beyond their understanding.

Gran Celia picked up her knitting again, the clicking of her needles adding a rhythmic backdrop to the playful sounds of the children. Bethany and Lorinda exchanged glances, a silent agreement passing between them.

Finally, Bethany broke the silence. "I can't just sit here wondering what's happening. We know Lincoln, Ridge, Waverly and Lynx are out there, but we have no idea what's going on. What if they need something, or worse, if something's gone wrong?"

Lorinda nodded. "I've been thinking the same thing. The last update we got was when they retrieved Elara and headed out to meet the general. We should try to get closer to the command center at Pink Beds and see if we can get any information—or at least talk to one of the warriors guarding the perimeter."

Gran Celia paused her knitting, her sharp eyes narrowing. "And how exactly do you plan on doing that, dear?"

Bethany grinned. "Simple. We'll take your car."

Celia sighed but didn't object. "Just promise me you won't do anything reckless. If the warriors tell you to stay back, you listen to them. They're there for a reason."

"Of course," Lorinda assured her. "We just want to get a sense of what's happening and make sure they're okay."

Francis looked up from where she was helping Maya rebuild the block tower. "Do you think it's safe to go out there? With the Umbralox so close?"

Bethany shrugged. "Safe? Not entirely. But the command center is far enough from the main mass, and the warriors are keeping the perimeter secure. We'll stay cautious."

Gran Celia sighed. "Well, if you're determined to go, take the car, the keys are hanging just inside the garage door and be careful. Bring us back some real answers."

Bethany gave Celia a grateful smile. "Thank you. We'll be quick."

As Bethany and Lorinda stood to leave, Francis gave them a pointed look. "Don't get yourselves caught in the middle of something. The last thing we need is for both of you to end up on one of those makeshift cots with Sanodia trying to put you back together."

Bethany chuckled. "We'll be fine, Francis. Keep the fort down while we're gone."

With a final nod from Celia and a hug to the children, Bethany and Lorinda left the playroom. A few minutes later, the low rumble of Celia's car echoed through the driveway as the two women set off toward Pink Beds, determination fueling their every mile.

26

The drive toward Pink Beds was tense, the atmosphere inside Gran Celia's car charged with apprehension. Bethany gripped the steering wheel tightly, her knuckles white, while Lorinda stared out the window, her hands fidgeting in her lap.

"How far do you think we'll get before they stop us?" Lorinda asked, breaking the silence.

Bethany sighed, her eyes fixed on the winding road ahead. "Not far, I'm guessing. They'll have the whole area locked down by now. But we've got to try."

The car rounded a curve, and both women gasped as the roadblock came into view. A sheriff's patrol car and two military Humvees were parked across the road, cutting off access. Several figures stood nearby—one in a sheriff's deputy uniform, the others in military fatigues. As Bethany slowed the car to a stop, they approached, their expressions grim.

The deputy reached the driver's side first, motioning for Bethany to roll down her window. She complied, trying to keep her expression calm. "Good evening, ma'am," the deputy said. "I'm going to have to ask you to turn around. This area is off-limits."

"Wait," Bethany said, her voice trembling slightly but firm. "Please, you need to contact Sheriff Bowen. I'm Bethany Beaumont, and I need to get in touch with my husband, Lincoln Beaumont. He's here."

The deputy's eyes flickered with recognition at the names, but before he could respond, one of the soldiers on Lorinda's side of the car spoke up. "I don't care who you are," the soldier barked. "Turn the car around and leave. Now."

Lorinda leaned forward, her tone sharp. "We're not leaving. The sheriff knows us, and we're here to check on our family. Let him decide."

The soldier's face darkened, his posture stiffening. "Ma'am, I'm giving you a direct order. Turn this vehicle around."

The deputy held up a hand, his tone calm but authoritative. "Stand down, soldier. I'll handle this."

"Sir, we've got orders," the soldier snapped. "No civilians past this point."

"And I've got a job to do," the deputy replied, his voice firm as he reached for his handheld radio. "Now back off."

The soldiers exchanged a tense glance but reluctantly stepped away, their glares fixed on the car. The deputy turned back to Bethany and Lorinda, his expression softening slightly. "Give me a second to reach Sheriff Bowen."

He stepped aside, raising the radio to his mouth and murmuring into it. Bethany and Lorinda exchanged a worried glance, the tension in the air palpable. The soldiers continued to hover nearby, muttering amongst themselves but keeping their distance.

Finally, the deputy turned back to them, his radio still in hand. "The sheriff's tied up right now, but I'll take you two into my vehicle and figure out how to get you in touch with him."

The soldiers bristled, one of them stepping forward. "Sir, they're not authorized to be here—"

"Stand down!" the deputy barked, his patience snapping. "I said I've got it handled. Go back to your post."

The soldier hesitated, his jaw tightening, but he finally stepped back. "We're just following orders," he muttered.

The deputy ignored him and opened the door to his patrol car. "You two, get out of this car and into mine. I'll take you away from this mess and get you some answers."

Bethany and Lorinda climbed out of Celia's car, both casting wary glances at the soldiers as they walked toward the patrol car. The deputy held the door open for them, his demeanor professional but understanding.

"Let's get moving," he said, shutting the door behind them and climbing into the driver's seat. "I'll get you close enough to talk to someone who can help. Just sit tight."

As the patrol car pulled away, Bethany and Lorinda exchanged a silent look of relief mixed with trepidation. They weren't sure what awaited them at the command center, but at least they were one step closer to finding out.

The deputy's patrol car pulled into the makeshift command center near the Pink Beds. Floodlights illuminated the area, casting harsh shadows on the tents, vehicles, and people bustling around. The thrum of activity was overshadowed by the distant sight of the massive Umbralox pulsating like a living nightmare, its tendrils writhing against the efforts of the warriors and soldiers stationed around its perimeter.

As the car came to a stop, Waverly, who had been talking with Lincoln and Ridge near one of the tents, turned toward the vehicle. Her face lit up in surprise as she saw her mother and Lorinda step out, escorted by the deputy.

"Mom? Lorinda?" she exclaimed, hurrying over.

Bethany and Lorinda barely had time to react before Waverly wrapped them both in a tight embrace. "What are you doing here? Is everything okay?" she asked, stepping back to study their faces.

"We couldn't just sit at the manor not knowing what was happening," Bethany said, her voice thick with emotion. "We needed to see you all, make sure you were safe."

Lorinda nodded, her gaze moving beyond Waverly to the chaos of the command center. "But... what is this? What's going on here?"

Before Waverly could answer, their attention was pulled toward the horizon. Both women gasped audibly as they finally noticed the massive Umbralox in the distance, its grotesque form writhing ominously.

"What... what is that?" Lorinda whispered, her voice trembling.

Bethany's hand flew to her mouth, her eyes wide with disbelief. "That's the thing you've been fighting? How is this even possible?"

Waverly gently placed a hand on her mother's shoulder, her expression grave. "That's the Umbralox now. And it's getting stronger. But we're working on a plan."

She led them to the edge of the command center, away from the rush of activity but close enough to give them a clear view of the monstrous threat. "Right now, there's a fragile truce between the military, the sheriff's department, the district ranger, and our planetary allies. We're trying to come up with a coordinated way to destroy it."

Bethany's brow furrowed as she processed what Waverly was saying. "But I thought you said energy makes it stronger? Isn't that what you've been fighting against?"

Waverly nodded. "It does. The more energy it absorbs, the harder it is to destroy."

Bethany frowned, something clicking in her mind. "That doesn't make sense. When we fought it before, the Triadorne destroyed it—and the Triadorne was pure energy."

Waverly froze, her eyes narrowing in thought. "What did you just say?"

"The Triadorne," Bethany repeated. "It was made of pure energy, wasn't it? And it worked. It destroyed the Umbralox completely."

Lorinda added, "She's right. Why would energy destroy it then but make it stronger now?"

Waverly's mind raced, her heart pounding with a sudden urgency. "That's... that's a really good point. There's something we're missing."

Without another word, she turned and hurried toward the main tent, her focus now entirely on finding Keelee and Elara. "I need to talk to them. I need to know more about the Triadorne and how it was created. There might be something in its design that can help us now."

As Waverly disappeared into the command center, Bethany and Lorinda exchanged a glance, their concern for her mingling with a new-found hope. Whatever revelation Waverly was chasing, they could only trust that it would bring them one step closer to ending the nightmare looming in the distance. Meanwhile, they turned their attention back to the Umbralox, its massive, pulsating form a stark reminder of the stakes they all faced.

As the deputy walked toward his patrol car to return to his post, Lorinda hurried after him, her heart heavy with gratitude. She caught up to him just as he opened the car door.

"Wait," she called softly.

The deputy turned, his expression calm but curious. "Something else I can do for you?"

"I just wanted to thank you," Lorinda said, her voice earnest. "I know this was probably way out of protocol for you to bring us here, especially with everything going on. You didn't have to do this, and it means more than I can say."

The deputy's lips quirked into a faint smile, and he shook his head. "No thanks needed, ma'am. I was just doing what felt right."

Lorinda studied him for a moment, a flicker of recognition stirring in the back of her mind. "You seem familiar," she said tentatively. "Have we met before?"

The deputy nodded slowly. "You might not remember me, but I remember you. A few months ago, you were the nurse in the ER when my son came in. He was really sick—bad fever, trouble breathing. We were terrified we were going to lose him."

Lorinda's eyes widened as the memory clicked into place. "I do remember. Your son—Josh, right? He had a severe respiratory infection."

"That's right," the deputy said, his voice thick with emotion. "You stayed with him the entire time, explaining everything to us, calming him down. You even stayed past your shift to make sure he was stable before you went home. The doctors said he pulled through because of how quickly you acted."

Lorinda's cheeks flushed. "I was just doing my job."

He shook his head firmly. "No, you went above and beyond. My wife and I, we've talked about you a lot since then. We consider you the reason he's still alive."

She blinked, overwhelmed by his words. "I... I didn't know."

"Well, now you do," he said with a warm smile. "So, no thanks needed tonight. This is the least I can do for you and your family after what you did for mine."

Lorinda felt tears prick her eyes as she managed a small, grateful smile. "Thank you. That means a lot."

The deputy gave her a respectful nod. "Take care of yourselves out here. And if you need anything, don't hesitate to call."

With that, he climbed into his patrol car and drove off, leaving Lorinda standing there, her heart lighter despite the chaos around her. As she turned back toward Bethany and the others, she silently resolved to do whatever it took to protect this family and the people she cared about—just as she had once protected the deputy's son.

27

Waverly found Keelee and Elara standing near the command tent, deep in discussion with a group of Tanzloran warriors. The glow from the floodlights reflected off Keelee's armor, and Elara's ethereal presence seemed to calm the warriors gathered around them. Waverly approached quickly, her urgency evident.

"Keelee, Elara," she called out, and they turned toward her, immediately sensing her determination.

"What is it, Waverly?" Keelee asked, his tone steady.

Waverly wasted no time. "Do either of you know how the Triadorne was created? I've been thinking about it, and it doesn't make sense. If energy amplifies the Umbralox, how did the Triadorne's pure energy destroy it?"

Keelee exchanged a glance with Elara before shaking his head. "I know of the Triadorne, but its creation was a mystery even to us. The Tanzloran elders revealed its existence only a short time before your family arrived on Tanzlora to fight the Umbralox. Until then, it was an ancient legend."

Elara nodded. "The Arcmyrin council was just as surprised. None of us knew it was more than a myth."

Waverly frowned, her mind racing. "So, there's no one who knows how it was made?"

Keelee tilted his head thoughtfully. "The elders would know. They were the ones who revealed it and guided its activation. If we want to learn more, they are our best resource."

"Can we contact them?" Waverly asked. "I know you used telepathy earlier, but would that be enough for a detailed conversation?"

Keelee shook his head. "No, the telepathy is limited. For something like this, we would need to return to the chamber at Sage Manor and use the communicator orb. It is the only way to establish a proper connection for such a conference."

Elara nodded in agreement. "The orb allows for a stronger, longer-lasting connection. If there's any information to be gained about the Triadorne and its energy, we must pursue it."

Waverly hesitated only a moment before nodding. "Then let's go. If there's even a chance we can learn something that will help, we have to take it."

Elara's gaze swept over the command center. "Take Keelee and Ridge with you. The rest of us will stay here to hold the perimeter."

Keelee turned to Waverly, his tone firm. "We will need to act quickly. The Umbralox is growing stronger by the hour."

Waverly glanced around and spotted Ridge standing near the edge of the command center, talking to one of the deputies. "I'll get Ridge. Let's take Lincoln's truck."

Elara added, "Make sure Bethany and Lorinda return with you. They need to update Gran Celia and the others about what is happening here."

Waverly nodded and headed off to gather everyone.

In short order, Waverly, Keelee, Ridge, Bethany, and Lorinda piled into Lincoln's truck. The drive back toward Sage Manor was tense but determined. As they neared the roadblock, Ridge slowed the vehicle, pulling up to the checkpoint where the deputy and two soldiers stood.

Bethany rolled down her window to speak with the deputy. "We need to pick up Gran Celia's car and drive it back to the manor."

The deputy nodded, recognizing her from earlier. "Understood. Be careful out there."

One of the soldiers stepped forward, his expression stern. "What's going on?"

Ridge leaned across from the driver's seat, his voice calm but firm. "We'll be coming back through in about an hour in this truck, just so you're aware. Make sure no one gives us trouble."

The soldier opened his mouth to argue, but the deputy raised a hand to cut him off. "They're good. Let them through."

With a nod, Ridge drove past the checkpoint and stopped where Gran Celia's car was parked. Bethany and Lorinda hopped out, exchanging quick goodbyes before climbing into Celia's vehicle.

"We'll meet you back at the manor," Lorinda said as she started the car.

"Be careful," Waverly called, watching them drive off before Ridge turned the truck back onto the main road.

The group continued their journey to Sage Manor, the tension palpable in the confined space of the truck. Waverly stared out the window, her mind racing with questions about the Triadorne and its creation.

Keelee, sitting in the back seat, spoke up. "If the elders have the answers we need, this may be our best chance to turn the tide against the Umbralox."

Ridge nodded grimly. "Let's hope they're willing to share everything they know. We don't have time for half-truths or riddles."

Waverly clenched her fists, her determination growing with every mile. "We'll get the answers we need. We have to."

As the familiar outline of Sage Manor came into view, the group steeled themselves for what could be the most crucial conversation of their fight against the Umbralox.

The chamber beneath Sage Manor hummed with energy as Keelee, Waverly, and Ridge entered. The faint glow of the crystal gate illuminated the room, casting soft light over the walls and the large oval table at its center. Waverly and Ridge moved to take their seats at the table, their eyes immediately drawn to the four screens, each displaying one of the elemental spirits: Terraveta, Ignissa, Ambreela, and Mistara.

Ridge furrowed his brow, leaning forward slightly. "I didn't expect them to be here," he said, his tone laced with curiosity. "Terraveta, why are you waiting for us?"

The earth elemental, her form a serene blend of emerald greens and deep browns, gazed at him with an unblinking intensity. Her voice resonated deeply, like the rumble of distant thunder. "We are waiting for the Beaumonts to unite."

Ridge glanced at Waverly, his confusion mirrored in her expression. "What do you mean? We've been working together this whole time," he said.

Terraveta's expression remained calm, but her words carried a weight that made Ridge sit straighter. "You have been together, Ridge Beaumont, but you are not yet of one accord."

Waverly frowned. "I don't understand. We've been fighting side by side against the Umbralox. How are we not unified?"

Ambreela's voice, a soft, whispering breeze, answered from her screen. "Your family's intent is not fully aligned. Though you work as one in action, your hearts and minds do not yet share the same pure purpose. There are doubts, fears, and unresolved tensions that keep you from true unity."

The words hit Waverly and Ridge like a splash of cold water. Ridge leaned back in his chair, crossing his arms. "That doesn't make sense. We've been doing everything we can to stop the Umbralox."

"It is not enough to act together," Mistara said, her voice flowing like a gentle stream. "You must believe together. You must trust in one another without hesitation and seek the same goal with singular purpose."

Waverly exchanged an uneasy glance with Ridge. "How do we fix that? How do we become unified the way you're describing?"

Before the spirits could answer, the sound of approaching footsteps echoed through the chamber. Keelee entered, his expression focused and calm. "The elders should be appearing momentarily," he said, moving toward the communicator orb.

As Keelee approached the table, he paused, his sharp gaze flickering between Waverly and Ridge. He could sense the tension in the room, the weight of whatever conversation had taken place before his arrival. But he chose not to comment, instead turning his attention to the orb as it began to glow.

The chamber darkened slightly as the orb's light intensified, casting shimmering patterns across the walls. Moments later, the holographic forms of the Tanzloran elders materialized above the orb. Their presence was regal and commanding, their translucent forms radiating wisdom and power.

Waverly and Ridge sat up straighter, their unease momentarily pushed aside as the elders surveyed the room. The visionary elder, Sylvaris, spoke first, his deep voice resonating through the chamber. "You have summoned us. What do you seek?"

Keelee stepped forward, bowing his head respectfully. "Elders, we need guidance. The Beaumonts and their allies are fighting the Umbralox here on Earth, but its strength grows. We believe the knowledge of the Triadorne's creation may hold the key to its destruction."

Sylvaris exchanged a glance with the other elders before nodding slowly. "The Triadorne is a weapon of pure energy, forged from the unity of elemental power and unwavering intent. It is not a tool to be wielded lightly."

Waverly leaned forward, her voice steady but urgent. "How was it created? We need to know if we can make something like it again."

The elders regarded her in silence for a moment before another elder, Draven, spoke. "The Triadorne required more than the elemental spirits and the daggers. It required the hearts and minds of those who wielded it to be completely aligned. Their intent had to be pure and their trust in one another absolute."

The words hung heavily in the air. Ridge and Waverly exchanged another glance, each recalling the elemental spirits' earlier observations.

Waverly hesitated before asking, "If we can't achieve that kind of unity, does that mean we can't create something powerful enough to stop the Umbralox?"

Sylvaris's expression softened slightly. "Unity is not an impossible goal, Waverly Beaumont. But it requires effort, understanding, and trust. Without those, the power you seek cannot be harnessed."

The chamber fell silent as the weight of the elders' words settled over them. Keelee, sensing the tension, addressed the elders. "We will strive for that unity. But time is not on our side. The Umbralox grows stronger every moment."

Draven nodded. "Then you must act swiftly. The Triadorne was forged in desperation, and its creation exacted a great cost. Be certain that you are prepared to pay that price if you choose to pursue its path."

As the elders began to fade, their final words lingered in the chamber like an echo. "Trust one another. Only then can you hope to prevail."

When the room returned to its dim glow, Keelee turned back to Waverly and Ridge. "What did the spirits say before I arrived?"

Ridge hesitated, his voice low. "They said we're not unified. That we're together but not really one."

Waverly added, "And now the elders are saying the same thing. If we're not on the same page, we'll fail."

Keelee regarded them both for a long moment. "Then perhaps it's time to put everything on the table. No more doubts, no more secrets. You must truly trust one another."

Ridge exhaled sharply, running a hand through his hair. "That's easier said than done."

Waverly nodded slowly. "But it's the only way we're going to win."

Waverly sat silently, her gaze fixed on the table, the weight of the conversation pulling her deeper into thought. The elemental spirits' words, the elders' warnings, and the mounting pressure of the fight against the Umbralox swirled in her mind. Suddenly, a new thought struck her with such clarity that she couldn't help but voice it aloud.

28

"Maybe it's not just about the Beaumonts being unified," she said, her voice steady but thoughtful. Ridge and Keelee both turned to her, curious. "Maybe it's a bigger picture. We do have somewhat of a truce right now with the military, the sheriff's department, and the sister planets warriors. But there's no real trust. No unity among all of us fighting the Umbralox."

Keelee tilted his head, considering her words. Ridge frowned. "What are you getting at?"

Waverly leaned forward, her hands pressed firmly against the table. "Think about it. We're all fighting the same enemy, but we're still at odds with each other. Everyone's clinging to their own methods, their own authority, their own jurisdiction. There's no true united front."

She turned to Ridge, her expression intense. "Do you remember what you were told on Tanzlora about why a weapon like the Triadorne couldn't be allowed on Earth?"

Ridge's eyes widened slightly as the memory surfaced. "Yeah… something about how humans aren't ready for that kind of power. How it would tear us apart because we'd turn it against each other."

Waverly nodded. "Exactly. And we're seeing it now. Even though we have a common enemy, egos and power struggles are still getting in the way. The military doesn't trust the sheriff. The sheriff is skeptical of the warriors. And the warriors are cautious around the Earthlings. Everyone's fighting the same battle, but no one is truly working together."

Keelee's brows furrowed, his expression thoughtful. "You're saying that without true unity—not just among your family, but among everyone here—we cannot hope to defeat the Umbralox."

"Yes," Waverly said, her voice filled with conviction. "If we could somehow get everyone to set aside their egos, their power trips, their fears, their need to be in control—then we could achieve the kind of unity the elders and the elementals are talking about. Only then would we have a chance at true victory."

As she finished speaking, a soft breeze swept through the chamber, caressing her face and tousling her hair. Waverly gasped softly, recognizing the gentle touch of Ambreela. The breeze carried a sense of peace and encouragement, as if affirming her words.

All four elemental spirits on the screens brightened and flickered in unison, their forms glowing with a new intensity. Their collective presence seemed to radiate agreement, as though they were giving their blessing to her revelation.

Ridge sat back in his chair, stunned. "The elementals... they're agreeing with you."

Waverly turned to the screens, her eyes wide with wonder. "They've been trying to tell us all along. It's not just about us—it's about everyone."

Keelee crossed his arms, his expression resolute. "Then we must make it happen. If unity is the key to victory, we must find a way to unite all factions in this fight."

The glow from the elementals dimmed slightly, but their presence lingered as a steady reassurance. Waverly looked between Ridge and Keelee, her determination renewed. "We can't afford to waste any more time. We need to bring everyone together—the military, the sheriff, the rangers, the warriors—everyone. We need to show them that working together is the only way to win."

Ridge nodded, though his expression was cautious. "It won't be easy. There's a lot of bad blood between some of these groups."

"It doesn't have to be easy," Keelee said firmly. "It just has to be done."

Waverly stood, her resolve clear. "Then let's start. We have to find a way to make them see what's at stake. We have to get them to trust each other—even if it means forcing them into the same room until they do."

Ridge smirked slightly, rising to his feet. "A little Beaumont stubbornness might just do the trick."

Keelee gave a rare, faint smile as he stood alongside them. "Let us hope your determination is contagious."

With the elementals still flickering on the screens behind them, the three left the chamber, ready to take the first steps toward forging a true united front against the Umbralox.

Lorinda and Bethany pulled Gran Celia's car into the garage and quickly shut off the engine, the tension from their eventful trip still lingering. They climbed out, glancing at each other with wide eyes, and then hurried back into the manor. The sound of laughter and chatter guided them upstairs to the playroom, where Gran Celia and Francis sat supervising the children.

Maddox and Maya were busy constructing a fort out of cushions, while Monica stood nearby holding a stuffed animal, her attention divided between the fort and Celia. Gran Celia looked up as Bethany and Lorinda entered, her eyebrows raising at their slightly disheveled appearances.

"Well, you two look like you've been up to something," she said, her tone wry. "I trust you made it back in one piece."

Francis smirked, glancing at the duo. "And judging by those expressions, it sounds like you've got a story to tell."

Bethany opened her mouth to speak, but Gran Celia held up a hand. "Before you get started, you might want to take the children outside for some fresh air and playtime before dinner. They've been cooped up in here all afternoon."

Bethany hesitated, then nodded. "Good idea. They could use a break."

"I agree," Lorinda added. "Let's give them some time to run around."

In no time, the group had gathered the children and headed downstairs to the play area just outside the kitchen patio. The late afternoon sunlight bathed the yard in a warm glow, and the gentle breeze carried the scent of flowers from Gran Celia's garden.

Maddox, Maya, and Monica immediately ran off to play on the grassy lawn, their laughter filling the air as they chased each other and tried to catch fireflies beginning to emerge. On the patio, Gran Celia, Francis, Lorinda, and Bethany settled into the outdoor furniture, the tension from earlier now eased by the tranquil setting.

Gran Celia leaned back in her chair, her sharp eyes fixed on Bethany and Lorinda. "All right, ladies. Now that the children are happily entertained, tell us what happened on your little road trip."

Bethany leaned forward, her hands resting on her knees. "We made it to the Pink Beds command center, but not without some excitement. We ran into a roadblock just a few miles out. The deputy and the military were there, and let me tell you, they weren't happy to see us."

Lorinda nodded, picking up the story. "The soldiers were downright rude, yelling at us to turn around. But the deputy recognized Bethany's name and tried to contact Sheriff Bowen. He even had to yell at the soldiers to stand down."

Francis tilted her head, intrigued. "So the deputy took your side?"

Lorinda smiled faintly. "Yes. And it turns out, he had a personal reason for helping. His son was one of my patients in the ER a few months ago. He said they think I saved his life."

Gran Celia's expression softened. "That's wonderful, dear. Sometimes, kindness has a way of coming back to us when we need it most."

Bethany nodded. "He put us in his car and took us straight to the command center. That's when things got... intense."

Bethany continued, her tone serious. "We saw the Umbralox. That massive, writhing ball of evil—it's like nothing I've ever seen before, not even on Tanzlora. It's horrible. You can feel the malice radiating off it."

Lorinda shuddered. "And the warriors and the military—they're all trying to fight it, but it's relentless. Everyone is there working to come up with a plan. It's clear they're doing everything they can, but it's not enough."

Francis frowned, her hands clasped tightly in her lap. "Did they say anything about what's next?"

Bethany nodded. "The only way to destroy it is to divide and conquer. They're trying to come up with a way to break it apart so it can't regenerate."

For a moment, the four women sat in silence, watching the children play. Maya and Monica were trying to climb the low branches of a nearby tree while Maddox shouted instructions from the ground. The simplicity of their joy was a stark contrast to the heavy burdens weighing on the adults.

Finally, Gran Celia broke the silence. "You did well to go and see for yourselves. Now that you've seen what's at stake, you'll understand why the family—and our allies—must work together, no matter the obstacles."

Lorinda nodded, her resolve hardening. "We're going to win this, Celia. We have to. For the children. For everyone."

Bethany reached over, squeezing Lorinda's hand. "We're all in this together."

Bethany was about to take a sip of her iced tea when the unmistakable shrill ring of the old rotary phone echoed from the office just off the kitchen. Her head snapped up, and she jumped to her feet, setting her glass down hastily. "I'll get it!" she called to the others as she dashed inside.

The phone rang again as she reached the office, her breath coming in quick bursts from the sudden sprint. She grabbed the receiver and pressed it to her ear. "Hello, this is Bethany Beaumont."

"Bethany, it's Marshall Stern," came a familiar voice on the other end. "Madre and I are at the airport, but we're hearing on the news that the area is shut down and under military control. Is there even a way for us to get to Sage Manor?"

Bethany's heart raced, and she quickly composed herself. "Dr. Stern! I'm so glad you called. Yes, you can get to the manor. The road to us is clear, but the military roadblock isn't far past the turn-off. You'll need to be cautious and watch out for onlookers. The road's been busy with curious people trying to get closer to the Pink Beds, but most of them are being turned away."

"That's a relief," Dr. Walsh chimed in, her calm and reassuring voice coming through the line. "We weren't sure if it was worth attempting the trip, but we're eager to help however we can so we had to try."

Bethany smiled, her nerves easing at their willingness to come. "We'll be ready for you when you arrive. Just take it slow and stay alert. I'll let everyone here know to expect you."

"Understood," Dr. Stern replied. "We're about 30 minutes out. See you soon."

"Safe travels," Bethany said before hanging up the phone. She stood there for a moment, catching her breath and gathering her thoughts, then headed back to the patio to share the news.

As Bethany stepped outside, her expression caught everyone's attention. "That was Dr. Stern and Dr. Walsh," she announced. "They're on their way here and should arrive in about 30 minutes. They called to make sure the roads were safe and passable with everything going on."

Gran Celia set her glass of iced tea down, her sharp eyes narrowing thoughtfully. "Well, we'd best get ready for them. I'll freshen up a bedroom suite. We need to make sure everything is comfortable for our guests."

Lorinda stood, brushing off her hands. "Bethany and I can start dinner. By the time they get here, it'll be just about ready."

Francis nodded, her gaze still on the children as they played. "I'll stay here and keep an eye on the little ones. They're enjoying themselves too much to bring them in just yet."

Gran Celia rose with her usual grace, nodding approvingly. "Good plan. Let's get to it."

The house buzzed with activity as everyone took on their tasks. Gran Celia went upstairs, selecting a guest bedroom with a view of the garden. She worked quickly, fluffing pillows, laying out fresh linens, and placing a small vase of flowers from her greenhouse on the nightstand. Satisfied with her work, she moved on to freshen up the adjoining bathroom.

Meanwhile, Bethany and Lorinda worked side by side in the kitchen. The comforting aroma of roasted chicken, garlic, and fresh herbs began to fill the air as they prepared a hearty meal for the family and their visitors.

"I'm glad they're coming," Lorinda said as she chopped vegetables for a salad. "I have heard wonderful things about them from Francis and it'll be good to have their help, especially with everything happening."

Bethany nodded, her hands busy stirring a pot on the stove. "Dr. Stern's a brilliant mind, and Dr. Walsh is as sharp as they come. If anyone can help us figure out how to deal with the Umbralox—or Bronte Sutton's strange condition—it's them."

The clatter of pots and pans mingled with the soft sound of laughter from outside, creating a rare moment of normalcy amid the chaos. Francis occasionally peeked through the open patio doors to give them updates on the children, who were still running around the yard, their energy seemingly endless.

As the preparations neared completion, the sun dipped lower on the horizon, casting a golden glow over Sage Manor. Bethany glanced at the clock, wiping her hands on a towel. "They should be here any minute."

Gran Celia returned to the kitchen, her presence as calm and steady as always. "Everything's ready upstairs. How's dinner coming along?"

"Just finishing up," Lorinda said with a smile.

Bethany nodded toward the patio. "Francis has the kids in sight, so we're all set."

Gran Celia looked around the kitchen, her sharp gaze softening. "Good. Let's welcome our guests properly when they arrive. We could all use some fresh energy and wisdom."

As the anticipation grew, everyone found themselves quietly hoping that the arrival of Dr. Stern and Dr. Walsh would bring more than just expertise—they hoped it would bring a much-needed sense of direction in the fight ahead.

The Pink Beds command center buzzed with activity, the tension palpable as the military, law enforcement, and interplanetary warriors worked side by side under the uneasy truce. General Adamson stood in the center of the chaos, his posture rigid as he barked orders to his subordinates.

The shrill ring of his secure phone cut through the noise, and he frowned, pulling it from his pocket. A glance at the caller ID made his face pale slightly, but he quickly answered, his tone brisk. "General Adamson."

The voice on the other end was unmistakable. The President of the United States, calm but with an edge that promised no patience for excuses. "General, I just received word of your blatant disregard for my direct order. I told you to stand down for 72 hours, yet here you are, mobilizing troops and escalating the situation."

The general stiffened, his jaw tightening. "Mr. President, with all due respect, this situation required immediate action. We're dealing with an unprecedented threat, and sitting on our hands was not an option."

The President's voice sharpened. "Do not lecture me on options, General. This is a direct violation of my command, and—"

Before he could finish, Lincoln Beaumont, who had been standing nearby and overhearing the exchange, stepped forward. Without hesitation, he reached out and plucked the phone from the general's hand.

The general blinked in shock, his mouth opening to protest, but Lincoln was already walking away, the phone pressed to his ear.

"Hello, Mr. President," Lincoln said, his voice calm but firm. "I apologize for interrupting your call with the general, but we don't have time for this."

There was a pause on the other end before the President spoke, his tone icy. "Who is this? And who do you think you are interfering in a conversation between the commander-in-chief and a general of the United States Army?"

Lincoln's voice didn't waver. "My name is Lincoln Beaumont, Mr. President. I'm one of the people standing between this planet and a threat unlike anything you've ever seen. And I'm telling you right now, this isn't the time to worry about who broke an order."

The President's anger was evident. "Mr. Beaumont, I don't know who you think you are—"

"Who I think I am?" Lincoln interrupted, his voice rising slightly. "I'm a citizen of this planet who respects your office and the general's position. But with all due respect, sir, you're out of your depth. This isn't just a military operation or a political issue. This is an existential threat to Earth—and the galaxy. So maybe it's time for all of us, myself included, to eat a slice of humble pie and start working together."

The line was silent for a moment, and Lincoln took the opportunity to continue. "You need to see what we're dealing with, Mr. President.

This isn't something you can fight with guns, bombs, or helicopters. Your general has troops and technology that could get wiped out in seconds if they approach the Umbralox unprepared. And that's the reality we're facing."

Lincoln walked back to the general, who was still too stunned to react. "General, does this phone have a camera on it?" Lincoln asked, holding the device up.

The general blinked, then nodded. "It does."

Lincoln pressed the phone back into the general's hand. "Good. Mr. President, I think it's time you saw the enemy. General, show him."

The President's voice came through, skeptical but intrigued. "The enemy? You're telling me it's something you can record on a phone?"

Lincoln nodded toward the general, urging him to move. "Trust me, Mr. President. A picture—or video—will speak louder than any explanation I can give."

The general hesitated but then turned toward one of the command center's vantage points where the massive, writhing ball of Umbralox tendrils loomed in the distance. He switched the phone to video mode and began recording, zooming in on the horrifying sight.

As the general filmed, Lincoln continued speaking. "You're the President, sir. You've got the authority to bring people together like no one else can. Right now, we need unity—not just between your forces but with the interplanetary allies here as well. This isn't about jurisdiction or rank anymore. It's about survival."

The general handed the phone back to Lincoln, who brought it back to his ear. "Did you get the video, Mr. President?"

The President was quiet for a moment, then his voice came through, softer but still cautious. "I've got it. And I see what you mean. That... thing... it's unlike anything I've ever seen."

"That's because it's not from this world," Lincoln said. "But it's here now, and it's not going away unless we work together. Are you willing to help us do that?"

The President sighed audibly. "I'll need time to review this and speak with my advisors."

Lincoln's tone sharpened. "Mr. President, we don't have time. That thing out there is growing stronger every second. If we don't act now, it won't just be Pink Beds or Pisgah National Forest—it'll be every city, every town, every home. Including yours."

The weight of Lincoln's words hung in the air. Finally, the President spoke, his tone resigned but determined. "All right. I'll make some calls. But I want regular updates. You remind the general he is to report directly to me."

Lincoln smirked faintly. "He's standing right here. You can tell him yourself." He handed the phone back to the general, who took it with a look that was equal parts irritation and grudging respect.

As the general began speaking with the President again, Lincoln stepped back, crossing his arms and letting out a long breath. Sheriff Marshall Bowen, who had been watching the entire exchange, clapped a hand on his shoulder. "You've got guts, Lincoln. I'll give you that."

Lincoln shook his head, a weary smile on his face.

"Guts or stupidity. We'll find out soon enough."

Keelee, Waverly, and Ridge returned to the bustling Pink Beds command center. The tension in the air was palpable, with soldiers, deputies, and warriors alike moving with a sense of urgency. Floodlights illuminated the area, casting long shadows across the tents and equipment as the sun was starting to set.

Elara was the first to notice them, her sharp eyes catching their approach. She stepped forward, her brow furrowed. "You're back. What did the elders say?"

Keelee nodded in greeting, his expression thoughtful. "We have much to share. The elders confirmed the importance of unity—not just among the Beaumonts, but across all factions fighting the Umbralox. Without it, we cannot win."

Waverly stepped forward, her voice steady despite the gravity of her words. "It's bigger than us. The Triadorne worked because it harnessed pure energy created from complete unity. If we can't achieve that—if we don't unite every group here, from the military to the warriors, to the sheriff's department—this fight is already lost."

Elara's expression darkened, her gaze shifting toward the distant glow of the Umbralox. "A tall order, considering the egos and mistrust we've been battling here."

Before anyone could respond, Sheriff Bowen, who had been leaning against a nearby vehicle, overheard the conversation and approached.

His face was lined with weariness, but his eyes gleamed with a mix of frustration and admiration. "You're talking about unity? Funny you mention that," he looked over at Waverly, "your dad, Lincoln, just gave the President of the United States a lesson in humility."

Keelee tilted his head, intrigued. "The President?"

The sheriff nodded, crossing his arms. "Yep. General Adamson got a call from the President chewing him out for breaking the 72-hour stand-down. Before the general could get a word in, Lincoln snatched the phone and gave the President an earful about how this fight is way beyond military protocol. Told him to stop worrying about who's in charge and focus on saving the planet."

Waverly's eyes widened. "He did what?"

Sheriff Bowen smirked. "You heard me. Lincoln told the President to eat humble pie and get on board with a plan that actually works."

Lynx appeared from a nearby tent, his face a mix of amazement and regret. "I can't believe I missed that. I've been talking with Rykas and Callum about strategies for keeping the Umbralox from spreading."

Ridge chuckled, clapping his nephew on the back. "You missed a classic Lincoln moment. You'll hear about it for years."

As the group shared a brief laugh, Elara's expression turned serious. "Speaking of Callum and Rykas, the warriors are reaching their limit. They've been fighting without rest, and it's starting to show. If they don't get some relief soon, their strength will falter."

Keelee frowned. "We need Sanodia's herbal mixtures. They're the only thing that can replenish their energy and keep them attuned to Earth's environment."

Waverly's face fell. "I feel terrible. We could've brought a basket of vials from Sanodia when we left the manor, but it didn't even cross my mind."

Keelee sighed. "I didn't think of it either. We were so focused on the elders' message."

Lynx stepped forward, his determination clear. "Dad and I can go back to Sage Manor and get them. He could use a break from all this action anyway, and I need to hear more about that phone call firsthand."

Elara nodded thoughtfully. "It's a good idea. Lincoln has been going non-stop. A quick trip with you might do him some good."

Waverly turned to Keelee. "What do you think?"

Keelee nodded. "It's a sound plan. The herbal mixtures are vital, and Lincoln needs the chance to step away from the battlefield, even if only briefly."

The group quickly found Lincoln near the command tent, still radiating the aftershocks of his bold conversation with the President. When Lynx explained the plan, Lincoln hesitated for a moment, glancing toward the chaos of the command center.

"You sure you don't need me here?" he asked, his voice tinged with concern.

Waverly placed a hand on his arm. "We'll manage, Dad. You need to recharge, and the warriors need those mixtures. This is something only you and Lynx can do right now."

Lincoln nodded slowly, his resolve firming. "All right. Let's go."

As father and son climbed into Lincoln's truck and started the engine, the others watched them drive off into the night. Waverly turned to the group, her expression filled with determination.

"Now let's make sure we're ready for when they get back," she said as she looked at the looming doom of Umbralox in the distance. "Because the fight isn't stopping anytime soon."

30

Lincoln leaned back in one of the sturdy wooden chairs on Sage Manor's front porch, the cool air carrying the faint scent of pine from the surrounding forest. Lynx sat cross-legged on the porch railing, his eyes scanning the forest beyond the yard, his mind restless.

"Why do you think that huge ball of Umbralox isn't breaking apart and spreading out more than it is?" Lynx asked, breaking the silence.

Lincoln folded his arms, his brow furrowing as he considered the question. "I've been thinking about that too. It's throwing out plenty of tendrils and tentacles, trying to infect and destroy, but for the most part, it's staying intact."

Lynx nodded, watching his father closely. "So what's your theory?"

Lincoln sat forward, his elbows resting on his knees. "I think it has to stay intact to keep its power concentrated. Like the elders said, its strength comes from unity—its own twisted form of unity. If it spreads out too much, it might lose the cohesion that makes it dangerous."

He paused, his gaze distant as memories of Tanzlora surfaced. "Think about what we saw at the Inbula Dustria. The mass coming out of the planet's core was massive, destructive—but it never fully formed like this thing. It kept spreading out and destroying everything in its path, never consolidating."

Lynx tilted his head. "Why didn't it consolidate there? What's different here?"

Lincoln shrugged, leaning back in his chair again. "Maybe it didn't have enough time. Or maybe it hadn't learned how. Whatever was left of it after Tanzlora—it evolved. It learned. And it used the portal here to grow, to gain a foothold on Earth. Now it's stronger and smarter."

Lynx let out a low whistle. "So it's like the Umbralox figured out how to make itself nearly unstoppable."

"Exactly," Lincoln said grimly. "But it still has a weakness. It's staying intact because it has to. If we can find a way to break it apart, to divide it, we can weaken it."

Lynx opened his mouth to respond, but his words were interrupted by the faint glow of headlights at the end of the driveway.

"Who's that?" Lynx asked, hopping off the railing as the vehicle approached.

Lincoln stood, narrowing his eyes as the car came to a stop in front of the manor. The headlights dimmed, and two familiar figures stepped out.

"Well, I'll be," Lincoln said, a faint smile tugging at the corner of his mouth. "Dr. Stern and Dr. Walsh."

The two doctors looked around as they closed the car doors, their faces lighting up when they saw Lincoln and Lynx standing on the porch.

"Evening, Beaumonts!" Dr. Stern called out, his voice warm and friendly despite the long journey.

"What brings you two here?" Lincoln asked as he descended the steps to greet them.

Dr. Walsh gave a small laugh. "Oh, you know, just a little curiosity about the end of the world as we know it. Figured we'd stop by and lend a hand."

Lincoln chuckled, shaking their hands in turn. "Well, you came to the right place. Welcome back to Sage Manor."

Lynx stepped forward, grinning. "Hope you're ready for the wildest experience of your lives."

Dr. Stern's eyes twinkled with curiosity. "Considering what I have been hearing and seeing on the news about what's happening, I'd say it's going to be quite an adventure."

As they all moved toward the porch, Sanodia emerged from the front door, her arms full of a basket laden with vials. She stopped short, her gaze landing on the new arrivals. "Ah..."

Dr. Walsh raised an eyebrow.

Sanodia gave her a faint smile and handed the basket to Lincoln. "Here. These will replenish the warriors' strength. Be swift in delivering them."

Lincoln nodded as he watched Sanodia scurry back inside, he then turned to the doctors. "You're just in time. Come into the parlor. We've got a lot to discuss."

The parlor at Sage Manor was dimly lit, the soft glow of a few lamps casting warm light over the room. Lincoln and Lynx had just settled into armchairs, Dr. Stern and Dr. Walsh perched on the edge of the couch, listening intently as Lincoln recounted the events leading up to the current crisis. The air was heavy with tension, but the room carried an undercurrent of determination.

Gran Celia and Bethany entered the parlor, their expressions a mix of curiosity and relief at seeing the new arrivals. Gran Celia stepped forward, her usual calm demeanor guiding her words.

"Dr. Stern, Dr. Walsh, welcome back to Sage Manor," she said, her voice warm but firm. "I wish it were under better circumstances."

Dr. Stern stood and extended a hand. "Celia, good to see you again. We could not just sit at home and watch the news about what is happening here if we could help in any way."

Gran Celia took his hand with a small smile. "And we are glad you're here, I am confident both of your expertise will be welcomed."

Bethany sat on the loveseat near the window, "We were just about to bring everyone up to speed. There's been a lot happening."

Over the next twenty minutes, Lincoln and Lynx, with occasional interjections from Gran Celia and Bethany, filled the doctors in on everything: the emergence of the massive Umbralox, the fragile alliance at the command center, the failed demolition attempt at the portal, and Bronte Sutton's injury.

When they described Sutton's injury and subsequent hospitalization, Madre Walsh leaned forward, her concern evident. "Wait a moment—are you telling me Bronte was badly injured during the demolition attempt? And he's in the hospital right now?"

Bethany nodded, her tone apologetic. "Yes. He took a nasty fall into the riverbed after the explosion. Lorinda called an ambulance, and they took him to the hospital. She got an update earlier today that he's stable, but..."

"But?" Madre pressed, her eyes narrowing.

Gran Celia stepped in, her tone calm but deliberate. "He lost a significant amount of blood before the paramedics arrived. Sanodia was able to stop the bleeding and pack his wounds with herbs, but the laceration on his skull required stitches, and he was severely dehydrated. They also mentioned something peculiar."

Bethany nodded, taking over. "One of the nurses told Lorinda that Bronte has been making strange beeping noises while unconscious. Some of the older staff thought it sounded like Morse code. It's odd, to say the least."

Madre exchanged a sharp look with her husband. "Marshall, that doesn't sound like just a simple injury to me. Bronte is... well, you know how connected he is to things most people wouldn't understand. What if this is more than a physical reaction?"

Dr. Stern tilted his head thoughtfully. "You're saying it could be something... supernatural?"

"Yes," Madre said firmly. "We need to go to him, determine what is happening."

Dr. Stern stood, his expression resolute. "Madre and I will go to the hospital and figure out what's going on with Bronte. If there's anything important, we'll let you know immediately."

Bethany glanced at Gran Celia. "Maybe we should call ahead and let the hospital staff know they're coming. One of the nurses Lorinda worked with, Robin, is assigned to Bronte's case. She'll make sure they can get in to see him."

"Good," Gran Celia said, nodding her approval. "Make the call. And Marshall—Madre—be careful."

As Bethany left the parlor to find Lorinda and make the call, Madre turned back to the group. "Is there anything else we need to know before we head out? Anything more about Bronte?"

Everyone looked around at each other but everyone was nodding their heads, most of them had not been around Bronte Sutton long enough when he was conscious to gain any knowledge about him.

Bethany returned. "Robin said she'll be expecting you. She's as curious as we are about the beeping noises. Bronte's stable, but she said he hasn't regained full consciousness yet."

"Thank you, Bethany," Madre said, giving her a reassuring smile. "We'll leave right away."

The rental car hummed softly as Madre Walsh drove along the winding roads leading to the hospital. The dashboard lights cast a faint glow across the interior, illuminating the thoughtful expression on her face.

Beside her, Dr. Marshall Stern sat with his arms crossed, his brow furrowed as he mulled over the information they'd received about Bronte Sutton.

"I still don't understand," Marshall began, breaking the silence. "How could Bronte be making those sounds? Morse code, of all things? Is it his subconscious? Something medical? Or something... more?"

Madre kept her eyes on the road, but her lips curved into a small, knowing smile. "Marshall, you've always been so practical. It's one of the things I love about you, but you know as well as I do that Bronte isn't like most people. This isn't just medical. It's communication."

"Communication with what?" he asked, leaning forward slightly. "Or who?"

"The Pluboria," Madre said softly, her voice carrying a mix of reverence and certainty.

Marshall shook his head, glancing at her. "The Pluboria. That's what you and Bronte have been talking about all this time? You really believe it's real?"

Madre glanced at him briefly, her expression resolute. "I don't just believe it. I know it's real."

Marshall sighed, running a hand through his graying hair. "Okay, then. Help me understand this. Explain it to me again—how does this work? How are you so sure?"

Madre's grip on the steering wheel tightened as she gathered her thoughts. "It started almost a year ago," she began. "I'd been having these... visions. Dreams. Over and over, the same entity appeared to me.

It wasn't a person, not in the way we think of people. It was a being of light, an entity that felt so familiar, it was almost like visiting myself."

Marshall frowned. "Yourself?"

Madre nodded, her gaze fixed on the road ahead. "Yes. It was as if this entity was connected to me in ways I can't fully explain. But it wasn't just familiar—it knew things. Things about the future. It would guide me, show me what decisions to make in situations I hadn't even encountered yet. And then, days or weeks later, those situations would happen, exactly as I'd seen them."

Marshall let out a low whistle, his skepticism giving way to intrigue. "And you think this... entity... is the Pluboria?"

Madre exhaled slowly. "Yes. Bronte and I both believe the Pluboria is where we originated. It's not a place, not in the traditional sense. It's more like a state of being—a collective consciousness. It's where Starseeds like us come from, and it's what connects us."

"Starseeds," Marshall repeated, leaning back in his seat. "I still have trouble wrapping my head around that concept."

Madre glanced at him again, her expression softening. "I know it's a lot to take in. I felt the same way at first. But over time, the dreams, the guidance, the sense of purpose—it became undeniable. And now, with Bronte making those sounds while unconscious, I can't help but think he's communicating with them. With the Pluboria."

The hospital's lights came into view as they rounded a bend, the parking lot sparsely populated in the late evening hours. Madre pulled into a spot near the entrance, turned off the engine, and turned to Marshall.

"I know you're still processing all of this," she said gently. "But I promise you, once we see Bronte, things will start to make more sense."

Marshall stared at her for a moment, then nodded. "You've never steered me wrong before, Madre. Let's go see what's happening with him."

Madre smiled faintly and opened her door. "Thank you for trusting me, Marshall. I'll explain more after we visit Bronte. But for now, let's focus on him."

The two of them stepped out of the car and made their way toward the hospital entrance, the weight of Madre's revelations lingering in the air between them. Inside, answers—and perhaps more questions—awaited.

31

Lynx and Lincoln pulled into the Pink Beds command center with the back of Lincoln's truck loaded with baskets of herbal vials carefully prepared by Sanodia, their potent mixtures vital for the Arcmyrian and Tanzloran warriors' energy for battling the Umbralox.

The parking lot was a flurry of activity. Warriors who had been stationed at Sliding Rock, Davidson River Campground, and Sycamore Flats were arriving, summoned by Keelee, Elara, Ridge, and Waverly to consolidate their forces at the Pink Beds. The warriors moved with disciplined precision, their expressions a mix of weariness and determination.

As Lynx jumped out of the truck and began unloading the baskets, Lincoln waved to the gathered group. "We've got your herbal mixtures, and not a moment too soon!"

Elara and Keelee stepped forward, their faces lighting up with relief. "Thank you, Lincoln," Keelee said. "These are needed more than you know."

Elara turned to Callum and Rykas, who were standing nearby with a group of warriors. "We need to organize shifts. The warriors cannot sustain this pace without rest, even with the herbal mixtures. Half of them will come here to recover and take their vials while the other half continues containing the Umbralox."

Callum nodded sharply. "Understood. We'll rotate them in and out to ensure no one is overwhelmed."

Rykas crossed his arms, his gaze sweeping over the warriors. "I'll see to it that the lines move quickly. The sooner they're replenished, the better."

As the first group of warriors began lining up for their vials, Lincoln and Lynx worked alongside Ridge and Waverly to distribute the mixtures. Waverly moved among the warriors, offering encouragement and checking on their well-being, while Ridge kept a watchful eye on the perimeter.

General Adamson, who had been observing the warriors with a mix of curiosity and respect, stepped forward and addressed Elara and Keelee directly. "I've been watching your people—your warriors—fight tirelessly without complaint. I can see they're exhausted, even with their discipline. Would it benefit them to bring all of your forces here for a much-needed break? My troops are ready to step in and contain the enemy."

The command center went silent. Sheriff Bowen, District Ranger Dixon, and the Beaumonts exchanged surprised glances, unable to hide their astonishment at the general's unexpected offer.

Keelee tilted his head, studying the general. "That is a very noble gesture," he said carefully. "And it is much appreciated. However, there is a concern."

Elara stepped forward, her tone both gracious and firm. "Your soldiers may not be able to wield the weapons required to fight the Umbralox effectively. The laser knives our warriors use are not just tools—they are extensions of the warriors themselves."

The general frowned slightly. "Extensions? What does that mean?"

Keelee explained, his voice calm and precise. "Our weaponry is controlled by the mind of the warrior wielding it. The intensity of the laser can be increased as needed based on the strength of the enemy. The warriors' frequency, consciousness, and focus are integral to the knives' effectiveness."

Elara added, "This isn't something that can be learned quickly. It requires years of training and a deep connection to one's own energy and the energy of the weapon. Without that connection, the knives would be ineffective."

The general's eyes widened as he took in their words. "So you're telling me that these weapons—these laser knives—are essentially alive? Controlled and amplified by the user's mind?"

"Yes," Keelee confirmed. "And because the Umbralox is growing stronger, our warriors must continually increase the intensity of their weapons to cut through and destroy its tendrils. This is why the herbal mixtures are so vital—they help replenish the warriors' energy and maintain their focus."

The general crossed his arms, a look of amazement on his face. "I had no idea your technology was so advanced—or so dependent on the individual using it. It's... remarkable."

The sheriff, who had been listening intently, stepped forward and clapped the general on the back. "See, General? This isn't just about brute force. These folks are fighting a battle unlike anything we've ever seen. We've got to trust them to do their part, just like they're trusting us to do ours."

The general nodded slowly, his respect for the warriors—and the allies who stood with them—evident. "I see that now. And I appreciate the explanation. If there's anything my troops can do to support your efforts, you let me know."

Elara inclined her head, a small smile softening her usual seriousness. "Your willingness to work together is already a great help, General. Unity is what will win this fight."

As the warriors continued to receive their vials and the rotation of fighters began, the mood at the command center shifted. The fragile truce was growing stronger, forged not just by necessity but by a burgeoning sense of mutual respect and understanding.

And in the distance, the pulsating mass of the Umbralox loomed, waiting for the next move in the battle that would decide the fate of them all.

The warriors moved through the forest with measured haste, each carrying vials of the herbal mixtures carefully cradled in their hands. The dim light filtering through the canopy cast eerie shadows on the ground, and the air was thick with tension. The tendrils of the Umbralox writhed ominously in the distance, a constant reminder of the malevolent force they faced.

Several warriors whispered quietly as they approached a small clearing where some of their comrades lay sprawled on the forest floor, too weak to make the journey back to the command center. Their breaths were shallow, their eyes half-closed from sheer exhaustion. One warrior knelt beside a fallen comrade and held up a vial. "Here, drink this. It'll help."

As the warriors carefully distributed the vials, a sudden movement from the underbrush caused them to freeze. A massive tendril lashed out from the shadows, its oily, black surface glinting in the dim light. The warriors scrambled to avoid it, but in the chaos, several vials slipped from their hands and shattered on the ground.

The mixture spilled across the earth and splattered onto the tendril. Immediately, the Umbralox shrieked, a horrible, high-pitched sound that echoed through the forest. The tendril writhed violently before dis-integrating into ash, the remains scattering in the light breeze.

The warriors stared in stunned silence.

One of the warriors, recovering from the shock, stepped forward, holding a vial tightly in his hand. His voice was low but steady. "What if it's the mixture? What if it can destroy them?"

He uncorked the vial and poured its contents directly onto a large tendril that had begun to creep toward them. The liquid sizzled on contact, and the Umbralox let out another terrible screech. The tendril twisted and flailed before crumbling into ash, leaving a gaping void where it had been.

The warriors exchanged wide-eyed glances. "Did you see that?" one of them whispered.

From a distance, Callum and Rykas had been observing the group. The sound of the Umbralox's shrieks and the warriors' sudden move-ments caught their attention. They exchanged a quick glance before sprinting toward the scene.

"What happened?" Callum demanded as they reached the warriors.

One of the warriors stepped forward, his voice filled with a mix of disbelief and excitement. "The vials. The mixture. It... it destroys them. Look."

He pointed to the patches of ash where the tendrils had once been. "They attacked us, and when the vials accidentally spilled, the mixture landed on the tendrils. They disintegrated. So we tried it again on purpose—and it worked."

Callum and Rykas crouched down to examine the ash. Their expressions shifted from surprise to amazement as they processed what the warriors were saying.

"This changes everything," Rykas murmured. "Callum, we need to tell Keelee and Elara."

Callum nodded, his face grim but resolute. "Agreed. Stay here with the warriors. Make sure they're safe. I'll get Keelee and Elara."

Callum quickly returned to the command center, his urgency evident. As he explained what had happened, Keelee and Elara listened intently, their expressions shifting from disbelief to determination.

"You're certain this happened?" Keelee asked, his voice low but steady.

"Yes," Callum replied firmly. "Rykas and I saw it with our own eyes. The mixture doesn't just replenish our strength—it can destroy the Umbralox."

Elara stepped forward, her sharp gaze fixed on the horizon. "We need to test this ourselves. If this is true, it could be the breakthrough we've been waiting for."

Keelee nodded. "Let's go."

Keelee and Elara each took a vial from the remaining stash at the command center and headed out with Callum to the edge of the forest. The warriors stood at a safe distance from the tendrils, their eyes fixed on the leaders as they prepared to test the mixture.

Keelee uncorked his vial and approached cautiously. He held out his hand, allowing a few drops of the mixture to fall onto a small tendril creeping across the ground. The reaction was immediate. The tendril recoiled violently, shrieking before disintegrating into ash.

Elara followed suit, pouring a small amount of her vial onto a larger tendril that was coiling nearby. The same result occurred—the Umbralox dissolved into nothing, leaving behind a faint, acrid smell.

The warriors murmured among themselves, their disbelief giving way to hope.

"It works," Keelee said, his voice filled with wonder. "The mixture works."

Elara turned to the gathered group, her eyes blazing with determination. "We have a weapon. A way to fight back. But we need to act quickly. The Umbralox is gaining strength, and we can't afford to waste time."

Callum nodded, his jaw set. "We'll need Sanodia to prepare more of the mixture and we will need to determine a method of distribution.

Don't know how this will work," he said as he looked at the large mass in the distance.

Keelee looked at Elara. "And we'll need to let the Beaumonts know. They'll want to see this for themselves and hopefully have an idea of how to administer it in large capacity."

As the group returned to the command center, a newfound sense of hope filled the air. For the first time since the battle began, they had a tangible way to fight back against the growing darkness—and they were determined to use it.

32

The parlor at Sage Manor was quiet except for the soft crackle of the fire in the hearth. Gran Celia, Lorinda, Bethany, and Francis sat in the plush chairs and couches, sipping tea and unwinding after the chaotic day. The children were finally asleep, and the house seemed to exhale in collective relief.

Bethany leaned back in her chair, her eyes reflecting the firelight. "It's hard to believe everything that's happened in just one day. It feels like we've been living a month's worth of events."

Francis nodded, setting her teacup down. "It's a lot to process, but at least we've made some progress. And now that we've got everyone working together, maybe we'll start to see a real shift."

The sound of the front door opening interrupted their conversation. A moment later, the voices of Dr. Marshall Stern and Dr. Madre Walsh echoed in the hallway. The group exchanged curious glances as the two doctors entered the parlor, their faces alight with conversation.

"Good evening!" Gran Celia said, rising to greet them. "You're back. How is Bronte?"

Marshall smiled faintly. "Stable, thankfully. He's still unconscious, but his condition is improving. The hospital staff was... curious about the herbs Sanodia used, to say the least."

Madre nodded. "They've never seen anything like it. But that's not surprising."

Francis gestured to the couch. "Please, sit. Have some tea and tell us about your visit."

The doctors exchanged a glance before taking seats near the group. Gran Celia noticed the thoughtful expression on Marshall's face and tilted her head. "You two seemed deep in conversation when you came in. What were you discussing?"

Marshall hesitated, glancing at Madre. "We were talking about... well, it's a little unconventional."

Gran Celia raised an eyebrow, intrigued. "You forget who you're talking to. Nothing is too unconventional in this house. Go on."

Madre chuckled softly. "She's right, Marshall. I think it's time we share this."

Madre leaned forward, her hands resting on her knees. "I was explaining to Marshall earlier about the visions and dreams I've been having for the past year. It's always the same—a light form, a figure that feels so familiar, like I'm looking at a part of myself. This being guides me, shows me things about the future, and helps me make decisions."

Gran Celia nodded, her interest piqued. "Go on."

Madre took a breath. "One day, about a year ago, the light form spoke to me directly. It told me to reach out to Bronte Sutton. I didn't know him at the time—we'd never met. But I was told that we were siblings, not here on Earth, but on Pluboria."

"Pluboria?" Lorinda asked, leaning forward. "What's that?"

"It feels like a collective consciousness, another realm of existence," Madre explained. "I don't think it's an actual planet, not a place you can point to on a map. It's more like a state of being. The light form told me that Bronte and I chose to leave Pluboria to have an Earth experience. We wanted to understand this world."

Bethany blinked. "So, you're saying you and Bronte are... aliens?"

Madre shook her head with a smile. "Not aliens, not in the way most people think. Starseeds. Fragments of a consciousness that exist in multiple places. We're part of something larger. We always have been."

Francis leaned back, her eyes narrowing thoughtfully. "And you said the light form told you that you and Bronte are siblings? But neither of you has a sibling here on Earth?"

Madre smiled wistfully. "Exactly. I've always felt like something was missing in my life, like I was meant to have an older brother. And Bronte—he's always wanted a younger sister. When we started talking, it was like finding a piece of ourselves we didn't even know was lost."

Marshall chimed in, his voice measured but curious. "What's even more fascinating is that they've only spoken on the phone. Madre has never seen Bronte in person until today, yet their connection is undeniable."

Gran Celia sat back in her chair, her sharp gaze fixed on Madre. "So, all this time, you've been communicating with Bronte about these visions and dreams, and tonight was the first time you met face-to-face?"

"Yes," Madre said, her voice soft. "We've spent countless hours on the phone, sharing our experiences, piecing together what we've learned. It's eerie how aligned our dreams and visions have been. And now, seeing him in the hospital... it's like I've known him my whole life."

Bethany shook her head in amazement. "This is... incredible. I mean, we've all come to accept that the universe is a lot bigger and stranger than we thought, but this—this is something else."

Gran Celia smiled faintly, her eyes glinting with curiosity. "I think it's beautiful. To find someone you're connected to so deeply, across realms and realities—it's a gift."

Madre's expression grew serious. "But there's more to it than just our connection. I believe the Pluboria is reaching out to us through Bronte. The beeping sounds, the possibility of it being Morse code of some kind—it's not random. It's a message. We need to figure out what he's trying to say."

Marshall nodded. "And if he is communicating with the Pluboria while unconscious, it could mean they're trying to help us in this fight against the Umbralox."

Gran Celia leaned forward, her eyes intent. "Then we need to help Bronte recover. Whatever he knows, whatever he's trying to tell us, could be the key to saving us all."

Madre met her gaze, her determination clear. "We'll do everything we can. Bronte's story isn't finished yet—and neither is ours."

The group gathered at the Pink Beds command center under the waning light of the day. The energy was tense but hopeful as Keelee and Elara stood at the center of the group, their presence commanding attention. The Beaumonts—Lincoln, Ridge, Lynx, and Waverly—were flanked by General Adamson, Sheriff Marshall Bowen, and District Ranger Seth Dixon. Arcmyrian and Tanzloran warriors stood guard nearby, their vigilant eyes scanning the perimeter.

Keelee took a deep breath and began. "We've just returned from observing an unexpected development. During a skirmish in the forest, a vial of the herbal mixture spilled onto a tendril of the Umbralox. To everyone's shock, the mixture destroyed the tendril, reducing it to ash."

A ripple of surprise ran through the group, followed by murmurs of intrigue.

"Destroyed it?" Sheriff Bowen asked, leaning forward. "Just like that?"

Elara nodded. "Yes, but we're not certain of its limitations. It worked on small, stray tendrils, but we don't know if it would have the same effect on the larger masses or the central core."

Keelee folded his arms, his brow furrowed. "We also have a major concern. The herbs and plants used to make the mixture are limited. They're essential not only for this possible weapon but also for sustaining the Arcmyrian and Tanzloran warriors who are on Earth to help in this fight. Without them, the warriors will weaken."

General Adamson crossed his arms, his expression skeptical but intrigued. "You're saying this mixture is your secret weapon against these things, but you're not sure it'll work on the big one? Why not give it a try?"

Ridge raised a hand to interject. "General, this isn't a standard enemy. The Umbralox is supernatural, otherworldly. It's unpredictable. Just because something worked on a small scale doesn't mean it'll scale up."

Lynx nodded in agreement. "If we waste the herbs and it doesn't work, we'll lose a critical resource for our allies to keep them sustained."

Sheriff Bowen rubbed his chin thoughtfully. "But if it does work, we could be looking at a real chance to end this thing."

Elara sighed. "That's true, but we also have to consider the logistics. Creating a large enough batch of the mixture to even attempt something on this scale would take time—and it would deplete our supply of herbs and plants."

It was District Ranger Seth Dixon who finally spoke up, his tone practical. "Why not test it first? Make a big enough batch for a single pass over the monstrosity. We could use the same process we do in fighting forest fires—airdrop it from above. One pass. See what happens."

The group fell silent, staring at him as his words sank in. Lincoln, standing at the edge of the gathering, broke the silence with a low whistle. "That... might actually work."

Waverly's face lit up. "It's brilliant. We wouldn't have to waste the entire supply at once. Just enough for one attempt."

The General nodded slowly. "We'd need to coordinate with the military helicopter pilots already stationed nearby. I have the best and bravest pilots that would have no problem getting that close to those massive tentacles to kill that monster. This plan—this might just be the best idea I've heard since this nightmare started."

Sheriff Bowen clapped Dixon on the back. "Ranger, you might've just cracked this wide open."

Ridge, who had been quietly observing, finally spoke. "If we're going to do this, we need to act quickly. The Umbralox is growing stronger with every passing hour. And if this plan works, we need to be ready to follow through immediately with whatever comes next."

Elara and Keelee exchanged glances before nodding. "We'll begin preparing the mixture right away," Keelee said. "But we'll need help. Sanodia and the others at Sage Manor will need to increase their efforts."

Ridge stepped forward. "I'll head back to the manor to help them. Lynx, you coming?"

Lynx grinned. "Always."

Elara turned to the General. "We'll also need your pilots briefed and ready. Can you ensure they're prepared for this operation?"

The General gave a curt nod. "Consider it done."

As the group began to disperse, their determined steps echoing the urgency of their mission, Waverly lingered at the edge of the gathering. The weight of the battle ahead pressed on her shoulders, but for the first time, she felt a glimmer of hope. They had a good plan—one that united them in purpose and action.

The faint sound of rustling leaves caught her attention, though the air was still. A soft, cool breeze brushed against her skin, and she turned to see a faint shimmer in the air before her. Slowly, the swirling form of Ambreela, the elemental spirit of air, materialized in a gentle, ethereal glow.

Waverly's breath caught in her throat as the spirit circled her, its presence comforting and affirming. The shimmering figure seemed to radiate approval, its light flickering softly as though it was nodding in agreement with the plan they had just solidified.

As the spirit completed its gentle orbit around Waverly, a faint whisper echoed in her mind.

"The winds of change are near. The end is within reach. Stay united, and victory will come."

Waverly closed her eyes briefly, letting the message settle into her heart. When she opened them again, Ambreela was gone, her soft glow fading into the twilight. But the reassurance she left behind was palpable.

She turned to find her family and allies scattered, each heading off to fulfill their roles in the plan. A small smile tugged at the corners of her mouth. The war wasn't over, but they were moving in the right direction. They were one step closer to ending this nightmare and eradicating the Umbralox forever.

The breeze around her grew still once more, but Waverly felt lighter. She took a deep breath. The end of the battle felt closer than ever.

33

The dim light of the seed vault flickered as Ridge and Lynx descended the stone stairs, their boots echoing on the steps. Sanodia was already inside, her hands flying over shelves lined with jars, bundles, and dried plants. The air was thick with the earthy aroma of herbs, intensified by the urgency of their task.

As they approached, Sanodia turned, her expression a mix of disbelief and determination. "I still can't believe what you're telling me. The herbal mixture reduced the Umbralox tendrils to ash?"

Lynx nodded, his voice steady but urgent. "It did. We saw it with our own eyes. But we need to make a much larger batch if we're going to test it on the main mass."

Sanodia shook her head in amazement but wasted no time. "We'll need everything we have. Start pulling down jars of Thymazincus, Elaris root, and those dried Ashtora petals over there," she instructed, pointing to various shelves. "I'll find the Arkenwood sap and the powdered herbs."

Ridge and Lynx quickly got to work, their hands moving swiftly but carefully to avoid damaging the precious ingredients. "How much do we need of each?" Ridge asked, his voice strained as he reached for a high shelf.

"As much as you can carry," Sanodia replied. "We're making the largest batch we've ever attempted, and I don't know if it will even be enough."

Meanwhile, up near the house, Gran Celia and Francis were combing through the greenhouses. The evening air was cool, but sweat dotted their brows as they moved from one planter to the next. Celia carried a handwritten inventory, her finger running down the list as she muttered to herself.

"Here it is—Arkenwood seedlings," Celia said, pointing to a small row of plants. "They're not mature, but we can use the sap."

Francis nodded, carefully clipping the stems and placing them in a basket. "Do we have enough Thymazincus? Sanodia mentioned it was critical."

"Not much, but there's some," Celia replied, moving toward another section. "Let's hope it's enough to make a difference."

Back in the kitchen, Bethany and Lorinda scoured the cabinets and storage rooms for oversized pans, buckets, and anything else that could hold large quantities of liquid. "This one will do," Bethany said, lugging out a massive stockpot.

Lorinda chuckled despite the tension. "I don't think this was meant for saving the world, but it'll work."

As the ingredients began to come together, Lynx ran up to the manor from the chamber to check on progress. He found Gran Celia and Francis returning from the greenhouse, their arms full of plants, while Bethany and Lorinda were arranging the pots and pans on the kitchen counters.

"We're getting there," Lynx said, his voice edged with urgency. "The helicopter's on its way. It'll land on the front lawn by the gazebo any minute now."

Celia straightened, her expression firm. "We'll have enough ready by the time it arrives. Tell Sanodia to prepare the mixture as quickly as she can."

Lynx nodded and dashed back to the seed vault. By the time he returned, Sanodia and Ridge had assembled all the ingredients. Sanodia worked furiously, her hands a blur as she measured, mixed, and crushed herbs into a thick paste before diluting it with water.

"We need to be precise," she said, her voice calm despite the chaos. "If it's too diluted, it might lose its potency."

Ridge glanced at the large kettle they had filled halfway. "This is all we've got?"

Sanodia nodded grimly. "It'll have to do."

Outside, the sound of rotors filled the air as a military helicopter descended onto the front lawn. The pilot carefully maneuvered the massive helicopter bucket into position near the gazebo, where the team was ready to load the mixture. Soldiers stepped out, ready to assist with the transfer.

Bethany and Lorinda emerged from the house, carrying pots of the mixture they had prepared in the kitchen. Lynx and Ridge followed, hauling the larger kettle with Sanodia guiding them.

"We're not going to be able to fill the bucket completely," Lynx said, his voice tense. "It'll be a little under halfway."

The pilot climbed down from the helicopter, his face grim. "It's better than nothing. We'll have to make it count."

As the mixture was carefully poured into the helicopter bucket, Ridge watched, his face flushed with urgency. "The warriors at the command center are holding their ground, but the Umbralox is growing more aggressive. This has to work."

Once the bucket was loaded, the pilot climbed back into the helicopter. The team stepped back, shielding their faces as the rotors kicked up a whirlwind of dust and debris. The helicopter lifted off, carrying its precious cargo toward the Pink Beds.

Gran Celia placed a reassuring hand on Sanodia's shoulder. "You've done everything you can. Now it's in their hands."

Sanodia nodded, her usual calm exterior giving way to a flicker of hope. "Let's hope it's enough."

As the helicopter disappeared over the treeline, the group stood together, watching it fade into the distance. The mixture was a gamble, a desperate attempt to turn the tide of the battle. But in that moment, united in purpose, they felt a spark of optimism.

The warm glow of the kitchen lights contrasted with the tension still lingering in the air. Gran Celia leaned against the counter, her hands clasped before her as she addressed the group. "Ridge, Lynx, you two need to get back to the Pink Beds. Whatever happens when that mixture is dropped on the Umbralox, they're going to need strong, capable hands there to deal with the fallout."

Ridge exchanged a glance with Lynx, both nodding in agreement. "You're right, mom," Ridge said. "We'll head out now and be ready."

Celia turned her attention to the others. "Bethany, Lorinda, can you two help me tidy up in here? We made quite the mess mixing part of the herbal batch in the kitchen, and I'd like to get it back in order."

"Of course," Bethany said, grabbing a dishcloth.

Lorinda nodded in agreement, though her gaze briefly flicked to Ridge.

Sanodia cleared her throat gently. "Francis, could you assist me in the seed vault? I need to clean up and take inventory of what herbs and plants we have left after this massive batch."

"On it," Francis said, already heading toward the door.

The group began to scatter, each moving toward their assigned tasks. Ridge hesitated for a moment, then reached out to grab Lorinda's hand as she started to follow Bethany toward the counter.

"Lorinda," Ridge said softly, his grip on her hand firm but gentle. She turned to him, her eyes wide with curiosity and a hint of surprise. He pulled her a few steps away into the office, out of sight and earshot of the others.

"What is it?" she asked, tilting her head.

Ridge's voice dropped, a rare tenderness coloring his tone. "I'm so glad you're feeling better. Seeing you up and about again—it's the best thing that's happened in days."

Her lips parted as if to respond, but she couldn't find the words. He stepped closer, his eyes locking with hers. "When this is all over, I think we need to have a long talk."

"A long talk?" Lorinda asked, her brow furrowing slightly in confusion.

Before she could say more, Ridge leaned down and kissed her. It wasn't hurried or impulsive; it was deliberate, filled with unspoken words and emotions that had been building between them. For a moment, the chaos of the world outside faded, leaving only the two of them in their shared space.

When the kiss ended, Ridge straightened, his expression both serious and soft. "That," he said with a faint grin, "is what we need to talk about."

Lorinda blinked, her cheeks flushed, her heart racing. Before she could muster a response, Ridge squeezed her hand one last time and released it. "I'll see you soon."

And with that, he turned and joined Lynx back in the kitchen, the two of them heading out the door and back toward the Pink Beds. Lorinda stood rooted to the spot, her fingers brushing her lips as she replayed the moment in her mind.

Bethany glanced over her shoulder and smirked as Lorinda walked back into the kitchen from the office. "You okay, Lorinda? You look a little... distracted."

Lorinda blinked and quickly busied herself with gathering the dishes. "I'm fine. Just a lot on my mind."

Gran Celia's sharp eyes flicked to Lorinda but said nothing, a knowing smile tugging at her lips. "Well, let's get this kitchen back in order. We've got plenty to do before the next storm hits."

As Lorinda worked alongside Bethany and Celia, her thoughts drifted back to Ridge's words—and the kiss. A small, hopeful smile played on her lips, a bright spot in the midst of the uncertainty and danger surrounding them.

Meanwhile, as Ridge and Lynx drove through the darkened forest toward the Pink Beds, Ridge stared out at the passing trees, his mind replaying the same moment. For the first time in days, he felt a glimmer of something beyond the battle—a future worth fighting for.

The hum of activity at the Pink Beds command center was almost deafening. Ridge and Lynx pulled up in the truck just as the low, rhythmic thrum of helicopter blades echoed through the air. The sound grew louder as they stepped out, the rotors creating a steady, pulsing rhythm in the otherwise tense stillness. The helicopter hovered in the distance, waiting for the green light to drop its precious cargo of the herbal mixture onto the massive, writhing form of the Umbralox.

They made their way through the crowd of warriors, military personnel, and local law enforcement, heading toward Lincoln and Waverly, who stood near a large tactical table under a hastily erected tent. The table was covered in maps, diagrams, and scribbled notes outlining their plan.

Lincoln looked up as Ridge and Lynx approached. His face was lined with fatigue, but his eyes were sharp and focused. "Good, you're here. We're just about ready."

Waverly nodded, pointing to the tactical table. "We've devised a multi-pronged approach. It's the only way we have a shot at destroying this thing."

Elara and Keelee stood nearby, flanked by Callum and Rykas. Elara began explaining, her voice calm and steady. "The Arcmyrian and Tanzloran warriors will hold the front lines. Their job is to contain the tendrils, preventing further spread. They'll use their laser knives to cut through anything that tries to escape."

Callum added, "The military forces will act as our backup, using the remaining vials of Sanodia's herbal mixture to neutralize any tendrils that get past the warriors. Each team has been equipped with containers holding the mixture, and have been instructed on how to apply it effectively."

Lincoln leaned forward, tapping the map at the center of the table. "That leaves us—me, Waverly, Ridge, and Lynx. Our job is to locate the core of the Umbralox and destroy it. That's the only way to end this once and for all."

Waverly's eyes hardened with determination. "We'll use the daggers. Combined with the elemental spirits, their power should be enough to destroy the core."

Keelee's voice was quiet but firm. "You'll have to act quickly. The core will defend itself viciously. It knows that if it's destroyed, the Umbralox dies with it."

34

The tension in the air was palpable as the group finalized the plan. Warriors armed themselves with laser knives, their movements precise and disciplined. Military personnel loaded containers of the herbal mixture into transport packs, their faces a mixture of determination and apprehension. General Adamson, Sheriff Bowen and District Ranger Dixon moved among their teams, offering last-minute instructions and encouragement.

Ridge stood beside Lynx, checking the sharpness of his dagger. "You ready for this?"

Lynx smirked, though his eyes betrayed the weight of the moment. "Ready as I'll ever be. You?"

"Always," Ridge replied, gripping the hilt of his weapon tightly.

Lincoln approached them, his own dagger gleaming in the low light. "We've faced worse odds before. Stick together, and we'll come out of this."

A radio crackled nearby, and General Adamson stepped forward, addressing the group. "The helicopter is ready and waiting for the signal. We just need confirmation to proceed. Is everyone ready?"

Lincoln exchanged a glance with Waverly, then nodded to the general. "Let's do this."

General Adamson gave the command, and moments later, the helicopter began its approach. The sound of its blades grew louder, almost drowning out the murmurs of the gathered warriors and soldiers. All eyes turned toward the massive monstrosity of the Umbralox, its tendrils writhing and snapping as if sensing the impending attack.

As the helicopter hovered over the Umbralox, its bucket ready to release the herbal mixture, Waverly closed her eyes, reaching out mentally to Ambreela. A soft breeze swirled around her, carrying a whisper of encouragement. Ridge felt a faint tremor beneath his feet and knew Terraveta was with him. Lynx glanced at his dagger, its blade glowing faintly with Ignissa's fiery energy.

Lincoln stood at the forefront, Mistara's calming presence washing over him like a cool wave. "This is it," he said quietly, gripping his dagger. "We finish this here and now."

As the helicopter began its descent, the first drops of the herbal mixture spilling toward the monstrous Umbralox, the battle was about to reach its crescendo. Everyone held their breath, ready to fight with everything they had to end this ancient evil once and for all.

The helicopter hovered above the writhing mass of the Umbralox, its bucket swinging precariously. Everyone held their breath as the pilot adjusted his position and released the first load of herbal mixture onto the pulsating monstrosity below.

The effect was immediate and violent. The Umbralox shrieked—a high-pitched, guttural sound that echoed through the forest and made everyone flinch. Tendrils lashed out wildly, their movements erratic as parts of the mass began to disintegrate into thick, dark ash. The herbal mixture worked its way into the flesh-like surface, causing the writhing tentacles to recoil and crumble.

"It's working!" Lynx shouted, his voice cutting through the chaos.

But then the Umbralox began to shift, its movements becoming more purposeful. The massive entity thrashed, as if trying to adapt to the new attack. Tendrils extended farther and struck harder, lashing out in all directions. Yet, for all its attempts to defend itself, large portions of its mass began to peel away, revealing the bright red pulsating core at its center. Dark veins spiderwebbed across the core, pulsing with a malevolent rhythm.

Keelee and Elara, positioned near the command center, observed its movements with sharp focus. Elara pointed toward the exposed core. "Look at how it slows when the mixture hits close to the core. That's its weakness—it can't protect itself and attack simultaneously."

Keelee nodded. "That's where the Beaumonts need to strike. If we can keep it exposed, the core will be vulnerable."

Callum and Rykas barked commands to the warriors, rallying them into action. The Arcmyrian and Tanzloran warriors surged forward, their laser knives gleaming. Each swing of the glowing blades sliced through the massive tendrils, severing them with precision and skill. Military forces backed them up, pouring vials of the herbal mixture onto any tendrils that got too close, the combination of attacks preventing the Umbralox from regaining ground.

Ridge, Lincoln, Lynx, and Waverly moved closer to the core, daggers drawn. The elemental spirits responded to their determination, their presence palpable. Mistara's cool energy surrounded Lincoln, steadying his nerves. Ambreela's gentle breeze whipped into a fierce wind, pushing

Waverly forward with renewed strength. Terraveta's deep rumble vibrated through Ridge's feet, grounding him as the chaos swirled around them. Ignissa's fiery glow illuminated Lynx, his dagger blazing like a beacon.

"Stay close," Lincoln commanded, his voice firm but calm. "We're almost there."

As they reached the edge of the exposed core, the tendrils intensified their attacks, lashing out with desperate ferocity. One massive tendril wrapped around Ridge's leg, but a warrior slashed it free before it could drag him away. Another tendril reached for Waverly, only to be doused in herbal mixture by a nearby soldier, disintegrating into ash before it could make contact.

"Now!" Keelee shouted from the command center. "Unite the daggers and focus on the core!"

The Beaumonts formed a circle around the core, their daggers glowing brighter with each passing moment. The elemental spirits amplified their energy, the air crackling with power. The core pulsed violently, its dark veins throbbing as if aware of the impending attack.

"Together!" Lincoln yelled.

They thrust their daggers forward, the blades emitting a blinding light that merged into a single, unified beam. The energy struck the core directly, penetrating its pulsating surface and flooding it with pure, radiant energy.

The core convulsed, its veins expanding and bursting as the light consumed it. The Umbralox let out a final, deafening shriek that shook the ground beneath their feet. The massive entity began to collapse inward, its tendrils and tentacles disintegrating as the core imploded on itself.

The force of the implosion sent a shockwave through the field, knocking everyone off their feet. The warriors, military personnel, and the Beaumonts landed hard, dazed but unharmed. When the dust cleared, a massive crater remained where the Umbralox had once stood. The air was thick with the acrid smell of ash, causing everyone to cough and retch.

Ridge sat up slowly, his body aching but his heart pounding with relief. "Did we... did we do it?" he asked, his voice hoarse.

Lincoln coughed, nodding as he leaned on his dagger for support. "It's gone. The core's destroyed."

Waverly wiped ash from her face, her eyes scanning the battlefield. "We did it. It's over."

Lynx let out a shaky laugh, his exhaustion evident. "I can't believe it."

Keelee and Elara approached, their faces weary but triumphant. Keelee offered a hand to Ridge, helping him to his feet. "You did it. All of you."

The group exchanged tired smiles, the weight of the victory settling over them. Around them, the warriors and military forces began to regroup, their cheers mingling with the crackle of burning ash.

Gran Celia's words echoed in Waverly's mind as she looked at the crater, the acrid smoke rising into the sky. Unity is the key. And they had done it—together.

Though they were battered and weary, they had prevailed. The Umbralox was no more, and for the first time in what felt like an eternity, hope shone bright.

As the dust began to settle, General Adamson, Sheriff Bowen, and District Ranger Dixon emerged from the command center, their expressions a mix of relief and disbelief. The massive crater where the Umbralox had stood was a stark reminder of the battle they had just won.

The General approached the Beaumonts first, his usual stern demeanor softened. "I've seen my share of battles, but nothing like this," he admitted, his voice low. "You saved this forest—and likely the world. I owe you all my thanks."

Lincoln, still leaning on his dagger, extended a hand. "It wasn't just us. It was everyone here. Warriors, military, forest service rangers, law enforcement—we all came together."

The General clasped his hand firmly. "A true united front. Maybe there's hope for humanity after all."

Sheriff Bowen walked up next, tipping his hat as he surveyed the exhausted but triumphant group. "Well, I'll be. When you said this wasn't an ordinary fight, I didn't quite believe you. Now I see what you meant."

Waverly smiled, brushing ash from her face. "We had a little help from some extraordinary friends."

Bowen chuckled. "That's an understatement. I'll sleep a lot easier tonight knowing this thing is gone."

Ranger Dixon joined the conversation, his eyes still lingering on the crater. "I never thought I'd see anything like this in my lifetime. You didn't just save the forest—you saved everything that depends on it."

He turned to Keelee and Elara, offering a respectful nod. "I've been skeptical, but seeing what your people and ours can do together... well, let's just say I'm a believer now."

Around the crater, cheers and laughter began to break out as the warriors, soldiers, and law enforcement personnel let the victory sink in. Despite the acrid smell of ash and the exhaustion etched into every face, there was a palpable sense of camaraderie.

Callum and Rykas led the warriors in a chant of triumph, their voices echoing across the battlefield. Soldiers clapped them on the back, and some even attempted to mimic the chant, their efforts drawing laughs and smiles.

General Adamson raised his voice, addressing everyone gathered. "I don't care where you're from—Earth, Tanzlora, Arcmyrin, or anywhere else. Today, you've proven what can be accomplished when we stand together. You've all earned my respect."

Cheers erupted again, louder this time, as everyone felt the weight of the General's words. For once, titles and ranks didn't matter. They were all just individuals who had fought a common enemy and emerged victorious.

As the group began to disperse, the Beaumonts stood together near the edge of the crater, their daggers still glowing faintly with residual energy from the battle. Waverly looked at her family, then out at the warriors, soldiers, and allies who had stood with them.

"This isn't just about the Umbralox," she said softly. "This is about what we can accomplish when we stop fighting each other and start fighting together."

Lincoln placed a hand on her shoulder. "You're right. If this battle has taught us anything, it's that unity isn't just a strategy—it's the solution."

As the group stood together, a cool breeze swept through the clearing, carrying with it the faintest shimmer of Ambreela's presence. The elemental spirits, though unseen, were undoubtedly there, their approval felt by all.

In that moment, amidst the ash and the scars of battle, hope was born anew. They had faced the darkness and won—together. And the bonds they had forged in this fight would guide them toward whatever challenges lay ahead.

35

The kitchen was a flurry of activity as Bethany, Lorinda, and Francis worked to prepare breakfast. The tantalizing aroma of sizzling bacon and fresh coffee filled the air, mingling with the soft clatter of dishes and the hum of conversation.

Suddenly, the sharp ring of the old rotary phone in the office off the kitchen sliced through the morning bustle. Lorinda glanced up from the skillet she was tending, her brow furrowing. "I'll get it!" she said, setting the spatula down and wiping her hands on a dish towel as she rushed toward the phone.

She lifted the receiver, slightly breathless. "Hello?"

"Lorinda, it's Robin," came the voice of her colleague from the hospital. The urgency in Robin's tone was unmistakable. "Bronte Sutton is awake, and he's... well, let's just say he's not exactly cooperative. He's pulling at every plug and wire he's hooked up to and demanding we get him clothes so he can leave. We've tried reasoning with him, but he's not listening. If he doesn't calm down soon, we're going to have to sedate him."

Lorinda groaned, pinching the bridge of her nose. "Oh no. Just hold tight, Robin. Don't sedate him yet—I'll see what I can do."

Without another word, she set the receiver down and bolted out of the office, her heart racing. She hurried through the hallway and into the dining room, where Madre, Gran Celia, and Dr. Marshall Stern were seated at the table, deep in conversation.

"The news coverage is incredible," Gran Celia was saying, her voice tinged with awe. "This breakthrough in unity with the sister planets—it's going to change everything."

"Not just for us," Marshall added, his tone thoughtful. "For the entire galaxy. The fact that humans worked alongside the Tanzlorans and Arcmyrins to stop the Umbralox is going to redefine how we see ourselves and our place in the universe."

Madre sipped her tea, her expression a mix of pride and apprehension. "And the world is watching. Every news station is carrying live coverage. The exclusive interview with General Adamson, Sheriff Bowen, and Ranger Dixon is about to air. The President plans to use it as a segue to his address tonight, where he'll introduce Keelee and Elara and disclose the existence of Tanzlora and Arcmyrin."

Gran Celia nodded, her gaze steady. "It's a new era. But with new opportunities come new challenges."

Lorinda rushed into the room, her eyes wide with urgency. "Madre, I hate to interrupt, but we've got a problem."

Madre set her cup down, concern flashing across her face. "What's wrong?"

"It's Bronte Sutton," Lorinda said, gesturing for Madre to follow her. "Robin called from the hospital. He's awake, and he's—well, let's just say he's not taking his recovery well. He's pulling out plugs, demanding clothes, and trying to leave. If he doesn't calm down, they're going to sedate him."

Madre shot to her feet, her expression tightening. "Oh no. I need to speak to him."

Lorinda nodded and led the way back to the office, Madre close on her heels. Gran Celia and Marshall exchanged a glance, the weight of the new reality they were navigating momentarily set aside for the chaos of a stubborn and determined Bronte Sutton.

Madre took the phone from Lorinda, her voice calm but firm as she addressed Robin. "This is Dr. Madre Walsh. Can you put Bronte on the phone, please?"

There was a muffled shuffle on the other end before Bronte's voice came through, rough and agitated. "I'm not staying here another minute, Madre. I've got things to do, and I don't need anyone poking and prodding at me."

"Bronte, listen to me," Madre said, her tone authoritative but gentle. "You're not going anywhere until you're fully healed. I understand you feel fine, but you've just been through something traumatic, and your body needs rest."

"I don't have time for rest," Bronte snapped. "You, of all people, should understand that."

"I do understand," Madre replied, her voice softening. "But I also know that if you don't take care of yourself, you won't be able to help anyone. Let them finish what they need to do, and I promise I'll come see you as soon as I can. I am here in Galen Valley at Sage Manor. We'll figure out the next steps together."

There was a long pause on the other end of the line before Bronte sighed heavily. "Fine. But only because you asked."

Madre smiled in relief, glancing at Lorinda. "Good. Now promise me you'll cooperate with the nurses."

"Yeah, yeah," Bronte muttered, his gruffness barely masking his grudging compliance.

Madre hung up the phone and turned to Lorinda, shaking her head with a wry smile. "I swear, that man is the most stubborn person I've ever known."

Lorinda laughed softly, the tension easing from her shoulders. "Well, if anyone could talk sense into him, it's you."

As they walked back to the dining room, Madre's thoughts shifted to the monumental changes unfolding in the world. Bronte's recovery was just one small piece of a much larger puzzle, but she knew every piece mattered.

Just as Madre was recounting her call with Bronte Sutton, Waverly entered, her steps light but her face thoughtful.

"Good morning," Waverly greeted, her voice bright but tinged with curiosity. "Where is everyone else?"

Gran Celia motioned for her to take a seat as she poured another cup of tea. "Ridge and Lincoln are in the chamber with Keelee and Elara. They're conferring with the Tanzloran Elders and Arcmyrin Councils about tonight's presidential address."

Waverly paused, her eyebrows lifting. "Of course they are," she said with a small laugh, sliding into a chair next to Lorinda. "It's still hard to wrap my head around all of it. Keelee and Elara being introduced to the entire planet. The existence of Tanzlora and Arcmyrin being revealed. All the secrecy finally gone."

Her smile was warm and genuine, but the reaction around the table was immediate. Gran Celia, Madre, Lorinda, and Dr. Marshall Stern all exchanged knowing glances, and Madre let out a soft laugh.

"Oh, Waverly," Gran Celia said gently, shaking her head. "There are still secrets. And there always will be."

Waverly's brow furrowed, her gaze bouncing from one person to the next. "What do you mean? Isn't that the whole point of tonight's address? To let the world know the truth?"

Dr. Stern leaned forward, his voice calm but firm. "The truth, yes. But not the whole truth. Some things are too dangerous or complicated to be shared, especially all at once."

Madre nodded in agreement. "This is just the beginning, Waverly. People need time to process what they're being told tonight. Too much too fast, and it could cause more harm than good."

Gran Celia added, "And some truths aren't meant for everyone, not yet. Just as there are parts of Earth's history that remain classified, there are parts of the sister planets' histories and their roles in the galaxy that will remain undisclosed for now."

Waverly sat back in her chair, digesting their words. "I guess that makes sense," she admitted after a moment. "It's just... I don't know. I was hoping we were finally free of all the secrets and complications."

Lorinda reached over and gave her hand a reassuring squeeze. "We've come a long way, Waverly. And tonight is a huge step forward. But the world isn't ready for everything all at once. It's progress, though, and that's what matters."

A faint smile returned to Waverly's lips. "You're right. It is progress. And I suppose that's enough for now."

As the first dishes of breakfast were placed on the table, Bethany stood and stretched. "I'll go get the kids," she said, heading toward the stairs. "Monica, Maya, and Maddox will love hearing about what's going on—and, of course, they'll love the pancakes."

The group chuckled, and Waverly glanced toward the window, her expression softening as she watched the sunlight stream through the trees outside. "It's strange," she said quietly. "After everything we've been through, sitting here feels so normal. Almost like nothing has changed."

"Everything has changed," Gran Celia corrected gently, "but some things remain the same. Like family. Like breakfast at this table. Those are the constants that keep us grounded."

Waverly nodded, her heart swelling with gratitude. As Bethany returned with the children, their excited voices filling the room, the Beaumonts and their allies gathered together, ready to face the next chapter in their extraordinary journey.

# SECRETS OF SAGE MANOR BOOK 4

### *Journey to Pluboria*

When Bronte Sutton suffers a devastating head injury, neither the advanced healing arts of Arcmyrin, the mystical remedies of Tanzlora, nor Earth's medical science can help him fully recover. Desperate to save him, Lincoln, Ridge and the enigmatic Drs. Marshall Stern and Madre Walsh take Bronte on an unconventional journey to the mysterious Pluboria.

Meanwhile, Lynx travels to Tanzlora, Waverly to Arcmyrin, Gran Celia and Lorinda to Washington, D.C., each embarking on a daring mission to unite the sister planets. Their goal: establish a seamless interstellar alliance where resources, knowledge, and travel flow freely, paving the way for an unprecedented era of galactic oneness.

With the Umbralox and Abasimtrox vanquished, hope flickers on the horizon—but old rivalries and unspoken fears linger. As alliances are tested and the promise of harmony falters, will the sister planets rise above their differences to form a unified future? Will a newly discovered planet cause a rift? Will the dream of interstellar peace remain out of reach?

*Journey to Pluboria* is a heart-pounding tale of healing, unity, and the courage to embrace a shared destiny among the stars.

AVAILABLE NOVEMBER 2025

Thank you to all the readers who have journeyed with the Beaumont family - your presence made this story come alive. I appreciate you for taking the time to read this series.

Sincerely,

LG Rice

Visit my website: www.authorlgrice.com

Contact me: hello@authorlgrice.com